Chris Bunch is the author of the Sten Series, the Dragonmaster Series, the Seer King Series and many other acclaimed SF and fantasy novels. A notable journalist and bestselling writer for many years, he died in 2005.

Find out more about Chris Bunch and other Orbit authors by registering for the free monthly newsletter at www.orbitbooks.co.uk

DRAGONMASTER

BOOK THREE
The Last Battle

Chris Bunch

orbit

www.orbitbooks.co.uk

ORBIT

First published in Great Britain by Orbit 2004
This edition published by Orbit 2005
Reprinted 2005

A CIP catalogue record for this book
is available from the British Library.

ISBN-13: 978-1-84149-223-0
ISBN-10: 1-84149-223-X

Typeset in Sabon by M Rules
Printed and bound in Great Britain by
Clays Ltd, St Ives plc

Orbit
An imprint of
Time Warner Book Group UK
Brettenham House
Lancaster Place
London WC2E 7EN

For Monsieur Jack-Attaque Demong
(d.o.b. 23-12-02)

1

Dragonmaster Hal Kailas, Lord Kailas of Kalabas, Member, King's Household, Defender of the Throne, Hero of Deraine, and so on and so forth, banked his great dragon Storm out over the Eastern Sea, and looked back at the land.

Spring was about to arrive. Here fishing boats ran out their nets. There, just inland, along the cliffs, farmers were beginning to plow.

The trees of the orchards were budding, putting forth green shoots.

Villages and farms dotted the landscape, the chimneys of their houses curling smoke up into the sharp air.

All was prosperous, all was peaceful, all belonged to the Dragonmaster.

Big frigging deal, Hal thought.

It was as if there was a gray gauze veil between him, his mind, his thoughts, and this world of peace.

It was two years since the great victory, when Roche had been driven down to defeat and ruin.

Kailas at times almost wished for the fighting to come back.

He wasn't bored – at least he didn't think so – but nothing much mattered to him these days.

The armies had been paid off, and the men and women had made their way back to their homes, if they admitted to them any longer.

Others went to the cities, found jobs, and tried to settle down.

Still others just wandered.

They called themselves tramps, or beggars, but Hal, who'd been a tramp himself before the war, saw no sign of their wanting work beyond the moment, or even a full begging bowl.

They did not seem to want anything that was offered them, no matter what it was.

Whatever anyone had expected peace to bring, it seemingly hadn't brought anything for great numbers of soldiers – and civilians as well – too many of whom unconsciously missed the excitement of battles and victories.

Of the three great nations who'd battled, Deraine was in the best shape, having nothing worse than economic decline to worry about.

Sagene, once Deraine's ally, had had its eastern provinces torn and laid waste, the land lying fallow, unworked, too many farms abandoned.

Roche, as King Asir of Deraine had worried so long ago, was in chaos, barely a nation now, with barons fighting other barons for a meaningless throne, and little law on the land save what a warrior could carve out for him- or herself.

Hal Kailas, at least, didn't want for anything. The war had not only brought him fame, but land, honor and riches.

But happiness? Contentment?

Even his marriage to Lady Khiri Carstares now lay behind that gray veil.

Perhaps if they'd had children, it might have been different.

He wondered why his marriage seemed to have almost vanished, like one of the cloud wisps that drifted past Storm's soaring wings.

Maybe he and Khiri had wanted too much, expected too much, used their marriage to block off the war, to give them what comfort they'd been able to seize.

Perhaps there'd been too much blood shed. Blood of her family, blood of the enemy.

But now he went little to her estates on the west coast, nor she to his, here across the country on Deraine's eastern coast. Mostly, she spent her time in the capital, Rozen.

The little they were together, they still slept in the same bed, still made love. But Hal felt the coupling was almost mechanical.

He didn't know, was afraid to ask, what Khiri felt.

He banked Storm again, back toward land. Just on the edge of the horizon now was his great estate. He'd flown away from it just before noon, feeling its gray, its stone, its brooding.

Not that taking Storm up had improved matters any.

Realizing his mood was growing darker, he decided, since there was still time in the day, to travel north-north-east, to visit Bab, Lord Cantabri of Black Island.

He was certainly warmly clad, with a riding cloak covering him from stirrups to waist, and a hooded sheepskin coat. Hal could have flown for a week, loving the sharpness of the spring air against his face.

He felt the irony of his destination.

Cantabri, a yellow-eyed, scarred warrior, really had little in common with Kailas.

But he and Hal had soldiered long and well in the service of the king.

They had little else to unite them, though. Cantabri was frank about missing war's seductions of brotherhood, excitement, authority.

Hal missed none of that.

But he missed . . . something.

Like the wanderers, he didn't know what it was.

And, he realized, he and Bab seemed to be quickly turning into dotards, with not much to talk about besides their experiences in the war.

Storm honked a lazy challenge, seeing another dragon in the distance.

Hal hoped to see someone on its back, but the monster was wild.

He might have been a war dragon once.

But when the armies were cut back, the dragons were mostly set loose, abandoned, as the now-dead Danikel, Lord Trochu, Sagene's greatest killer, had gloomily predicted.

There'd been much discussion during the war of using dragons for quick transport.

But the beasts were deceptive – they might have been enormous, but their carrying capacity was slight. The Roche and, occasionally, the Derainians had used paired dragons to carry baskets full of infantry. But this was for very short distances, and was hardly a successful way of fighting.

There'd been some excitement about using them to carry people about, people who were in a hurry to get somewhere.

But weather and the natural intemperateness of dragons brought that to a quick halt, as did the loss of half a dozen or so adventurous rich men.

A few dragons became polished popinjays, their owners offering flights for the citizenry for a few silver coins. But the monsters' eyes seemed as dull as the fliers who took the villagers aloft.

At least Storm was fat, happy, and lazy, although when he saw another dragon he still bristled, his huge tail whipping behind him, challenging combat.

He was in the very prime of life, perhaps seven or eight years old, gray and black. He was about fifty feet long, twenty feet of that in his huge whip of a tail, and about twelve feet tall, on all four legs. His natural weapons were many: his head with cruel fangs and dual horns, and spikes on either side of his neck. All four legs had taloned "hands," and there were talons on the leading edges of his wings. They stretched more than a hundred feet from tip to tip.

Fat and happy . . . but there were too many dragons, once feared weapons of the king's forces, now cast aside as unneeded.

There'd been enclaves set up by the King's Master of Remounts, to take care of wounded, crippled dragons. But Kailas had heard that these hospitals had gone unfunded. He had visited a handful of them, finding them all empty, and desolate but for the lingering reek of the monsters.

He'd heard rumors that these dragons had been killed, or taken to a desolate island and just abandoned, but they were only rumors.

In any event, to see a dragon with a rider these days was a surprise, the handful Hal had encountered being wild.

He'd sent letters to Garadice, at the king's palace, about the hospitals, offering to pay for their costs as best he could, but never received an answer. He'd heard that Garadice had quit his post in disgust over the maltreatment of his monsters, gone off on an expedition to Black Island and on into the north, but was never able to confirm the story.

Hal's King's Own First Dragon Squadron still existed, as a ceremonial unit only the size of a flight. There were two other such "squadrons" in the Royal Army.

They'd regularly written Hal, requesting the pleasure of the Dragonmaster's presence at one or another ceremony.

Hal had declined them all, somehow realizing that witnessing these hollow shells would further depress him.

As for the handful of men and women who'd flown with him, and somehow lived, he'd been able to find out what had happened after the war to only a few.

Mynta Gart had, as she'd vowed, put together a shipping firm that grew and grew. She was now very rich, with more than twenty-five bottoms under her command, and, seemingly, very content.

Sir Loren Damian had retreated to his estates in the west, and busied himself in stock breeding. Hal got an occasional letter from him, always swearing that he didn't miss dragons or flying.

He wasn't the only ex-flier to firmly remain groundborne. Hal had wondered why people could walk away from the soaring joys of seeing dawn from the heights, long before the land-tied, or chasing a rainbow or just what lay on the other side of a mountain. Then he realized many ex-fliers remembered only the terror of being attacked by one of the Roche black dragons, or seeing a friend or lover torn from his or her saddle to fall screaming into death, and needed and wanted no reminders of those days.

Hal could understand what those fliers felt – the squadrons had taken a terrible toll during the war.

Farren Mariah, the city rogue, sometimes self-taught wizard, had simply vanished, and no one seemed to know of his whereabouts, although a few guessed prison or worse.

A flier he barely remembered from the squadron, a Calt Beoyard, who'd joined just before the war's end, still tried to keep some sort of squadron association alive, and circulated a round robin periodically. Hal read it, but without the interest he thought he should have felt.

Kailas, unlike his wife, went seldom to Deraine's capital, Rozen, or to the lavish apartment he and Khiri had across the Chicor Straits, in Sagene's city of Fovant.

Khiri, however, throve on travel.

Which made Hal's life on his estates more empty, but somehow the emptiness wasn't unwelcome.

Within an hour, Hal was overflying Lord Cantabri's land. When King Asir had decided to reward Hal with property, it had been Cantabri who'd pressured the king into making Hal his neighbor in the east, telling Kailas that he always felt more comfortable living near a man who'd been tested, and Cantabri felt the only real test of a man or woman was war.

Cantabri might have been a friend as well as a war leader, but Hal always had a bit of trouble using his first name, in spite of Cantabri's insistence.

The demarcation between the two lords' lands was clear – the farmhouses on one side were a little shabby, the lands not as well tended, the villages a bit on the rundown side.

Cantabri had been a fierce soldier, but he was, in Hal's eyes, far too indulgent to his farmers and workers, always ready to grant a boon, or an exemption from estate taxes.

But that was Bab.

Ahead was Cantabri's great castle, sitting solitary on an easily defensible promontory.

That showed another difference between the two – the manor that Hal used the most was nestled in a valley that stretched to the sea, all rich farmlands with small villages nearby, with sere moorlands above it, on the fells.

Hal sent Storm slanting downward, already half smiling in expectation of his welcome.

Cantabri would growl him out of his foul mood, as would Cantabri's wife.

He was only half a hundred feet from the ground, just level with the castle walls, when he saw that the great banner that normally flew from the battlements was gone, replaced by a somber black pennon.

Other black flags hung from the ramparts.

Hal felt a sudden clench in his guts.

He brought Storm in for a landing in the huge forecourt, and an equerry ran out to take his reins.

The man's face was flushed, and his eyes red.

"The Lord . . . the Lord Cantabri is dead," he managed, and burst into tears.

2

Hal slid from his saddle, grabbed the man by the shoulders.

"How? When?"

"It must've been his heart . . . or something," the man said, fighting for control. "He . . . it was just after the morning meal, and he was going to ride out to see the new piggery . . . and then . . . then . . . he didn't even say anything . . . just fell on his way to the stables . . . no one knows . . ."

That was about all he could get from the retainer.

Grimly, Hal went looking for Lord Bab's wife. No, widow, he corrected himself.

Two days later, he was airborne, headed back for his own home.

House, he corrected himself. Home is supposed to be welcoming, and those cleverly piled reddish rocks offered him no seductions.

The last two days had been just as painful as he could have expected.

Lady Cantabri was very brave, and very firm, except periodically, when the reality of the loss made her dissolve in sobs.

Part of Hal was unshocked. He'd had too many friends die around him in the war to not have an armored shell around his heart.

Part of him found it a bitter irony that Cantabri, having lived through a nightmare, should drop dead before looking at a collection of pigs.

And a very selfish, unacknowledged part led him to the realization of just how alone he now was.

He wished Khiri would be waiting for him.

Then he corrected his thought. He wanted the Khiri that was.

His mind made another wry correction.

Maybe the Khiri that was . . . waiting for the Hal that the war had killed . . . the Hal Kailas had never been? The Hal that had been part of a flying circus, in the days when dragons were creatures to marvel at, and cosset?

The sprawling castle, built when Deraine was still torn by civil war, was even emptier than he'd thought it would be.

But Hal didn't notice it for a time.

Waiting for him were two letters:

The longest was, finally, from Garadice. It ran:

Dear Lord Kailas,

My humblest apologies for not returning your posted inquiries, but I have just recently returned to Deraine, after a protracted expedition to the north countries.

I took the assignment, which came directly from His Royal Highness, feeling the bitter frustration after my attempt to provide shelter for our dragons, which I trained, and which fought for us so well, and wanted little to do with my country for a time.

I will be preparing a paper before the Royal Society of the Sciences, but that will be months in the offing, and you might be curious about what we found, since you were always the dragon-flier most interested in the beasts we tamed and rode.

There were almost 200 of us who sailed from the north of Deraine, aboard the venerable Bohol Adventurer, which I assume you remember full well from the war.

It has not improved any in its lack of seaworthiness nor victualing.

There was also a frigate with the Adventurer, since no one knew what to expect once we sailed beyond Black Island.

Twenty of us were scientists in one specialty or another, three diplomats, one magician, a certain Bodrugan that you'll remember, who sends his greetings. All of the rest sailors or soldiers, already in the king's service. His Majesty mounted the expedition to satisfy his curiosity about unknown lands, and chose these men, and I quote him, "because they're already eating me out of house and home."

At any rate, to continue.

We sailed north and east, seeing no other ships in our passage, not even fishermen.

Black Island was exactly as we left it in our raid — Roche did not bother to rebuild its dragon-breeding station after we destroyed it.

But there was a cheerful note — there was more than a plethora of black dragons, soaring, dipping around the island heights. Evidently they needed little encouragement to breed, and those we studied from a respectful distance were very healthy, and had little interest in man other than barely suppressed hostility.

We sailed on, this time due north, and wearisome were the days for me, since I had no interest in labeling the various fishes that we brought up.

There were dragons a-plenty, some flying overhead, others on the water, being blown along with their wings furled over their heads, in the peculiar rafting position you, I believe, were the first to describe.

These last were sometimes healing from wounds suffered some time ago, and were being driven east.

They behaved toward us like wild dragons who'd never let Man on their backs. Some of the ones in the air seemed to recognize Man, but did not care to come close.

After a week's sail, while storms howled around us, we came upon a solid wall of ice, with bergs breaking off at intervals.

It was impassable, and so we turned east, keeping the wall within sight, hoping to find either a breakdown in it so we could continue our northern quest, or something other that would be of interest to the king.

We were almost on the land before we saw it. The day before landing, we sighted sharp rises, which we thought were skerries in the middle of the ocean. They were not.

They were sharp pinnacles that rose from an almost flat land, what is called tundra, no more than slowly drying peat, from long-vanished forests.

And here we found dragons galore.

They flocked to every pinnacle as if they were rookeries, living off fish they brought up like great cormorants or, more plentifully, the shaggy wild oxen that grazed in the tundra.

And here, too, we found Man.

There are fairly primitive tribes occupying these lands. They were not particularly friendly.

Bodrugan devised a language spell, so we could communicate

with them. But mostly they seemed interested in procuring, either by trade or theft, our nets and fishhooks.

We found they were the remnants of other, more "civilized" tribes, which meant, as far as I could tell, tribes that had more sophisticated methods of killing.

These tribes had migrated south, and I'm told have been providing great pain to the poor damned Roche and other nations to the east.

The reason for the migration was simple — the coming of the dragons.

There were food supplies enough for only one race, these people thought, and fearing the dragons, sought other lands to vanquish.

The dragons, we were told, had but recently come to these lands, within the memory of a grandfather's grandfather's grandfather.

Once again, the question becomes, what has made the dragons migratory, since it appears their real home lies to the far west?

I do not know, and have not a clue even as to what line of questioning I should pursue.

I do wish that someone would commission an expedition west, to discover the nature of dragons in what might be termed its raw state.

One thing of extraordinary interest came about when we studied the dragons.

Each of the rookeries was crudely organized, so there would be dragon leaders, and herdsmen, who would chouse the shaggy bison into death traps. Other dragons . . . not parents . . . would guard the nurseries, changing shifts on a regular basis.

I do not mean to compare intelligence, but these dragons behaved like particularly well-trained packs of dogs, except being far, far brighter, of course.

This alone, to me, justified the expedition, although I'm afraid the diplomats and soldiers were bored silly.

I wish I could write more about this society of dragons, but I'd barely begun my studies when we were attacked by a coalition of savages, and driven back out to sea.

I shall, however, go back, to learn more.

I shall write more when I deduce more from my notes, and, of course, will invite you to be present when I present my paper.

Your Obedient Servant,

Garadice

Pondering what this might mean lessened Hal's mourning.

Again, the mystery of the dragons' flight from the west was evident.

The second letter contained shocking information. It was a clipping from a Sagene broadsheet:

Roche Dragon-
Criminal To Hang

Arch-criminal Bayle Yasin, once one of the evil Roche hierarchy, and commander of an infamous black dragon formation guilty of the most heinous war crimes, including murder, arson, and rapine, has finally been brought to the bar of justice in Frechin, accused of controlling a smuggling ring, bribing public officials and personally flying many loads of contraband, including arms, from Sagene back into his native land.

Yasin sneered at the courtroom proceedings, arguing that it was no crime to attempt to feed starving people, nor give them weapons to defend their lands and lives, and refusing to recognize the obvious right of Sagene to try him.

It took less than half a glass for the court judges, two of whom had served nobly under the colors, to find him guilty, and sentence him to suffer the maximum penalty.

The sentence will be carried out immediately after the new year, and after Yasin, in Sagene's infinite mercy, has exhausted all appeals.

"Son of a bitch!" Kailas swore in shock.

His wartime nemesis still lived.

Yasin had been, before the war, head of a dragon circus that had almost certainly hidden espionage as it traveled Sagene.

Hal had hated him from the first time he saw him, helping euchre Athelny of the Dragons out of his circus.

Later, he and Hal had jousted in the skies when Yasin led a black dragon formation, and, when Kailas became a prisoner of the Roche, Yasin tried to have him killed as a criminal.

But, in the end, in the final battle over the Roche capital of Carcaor, fighting the obscene sorcerous monster beyond the city, Hal had killed Yasin, sending a crossbow bolt into his chest, watching Yasin's dragon crash and vanish into a river.

Or, at any rate, he thought he had.

The bastard still lived.

At least he would, until the Sagene fitted him with a manila neck cloth.

But to hang a man for smuggling?

Smuggling food?

That was no way for a dragon-flier, no matter how big a shit he might be, to die.

The weapons might be another matter, but that was to be determined.

Hal packed carefully, as if he were intending to go to the field.

The next dawn, he flew south on Storm, toward the Deraine capital of Rozen, not sure, or at any rate unwilling to admit, just what he planned to do next.

3

Hal took his time flying south, considering what might be either a noble gesture or climactic stupidity. He laid over just outside Rozen at a country inn he remembered fondly from his days wooing Khiri.

He shouldn't have stopped. The chef he'd admired had run off with a scullery maid, and there were new owners, determined to extract the maximum amount of gold from their guests.

They recognized Hal, about the time he saw a plaque behind the front desk showing a dragon landing outside the inn, with a rider wearing full antique armor.

Of course they wanted him to sign the plaque, somehow endorse the inn and its now pedestrian fare.

Equally, of course, they charged him full rates.

It was almost funny.

Hal flew Storm into Rozen early the next morning, scratching at what he was fairly sure was a bedbug bite on his ankle.

It had been some months since he'd been in the capital.

Then, he'd found it depressing. Gray, wintry streets filled with gray, wintry people, jostling, wearing shabbiness.

There were old men and women, children, and a scattering of young women.

He didn't remember seeing any young men, and realized they were either working, or casualties of war.

This time, in spite of spring sunshine, Rozen was even less attractive.

He flew low over streets whose businesses were boarded up, or whose shops clamored liquidation sales.

There were more beggars out than before, even this early in the morning. Many of them were clustered around the still-occupied palaces of the wealthy.

He passed over Sir Thom Lowess's palace. It was darkened, with no sign of occupancy. Sir Thom was most likely off finding someone or something else to glorify.

Lowess was Deraine's most famous taleteller, who'd figured out, early on, that the path to fame and fortune was less being a superb writer than a Presence, particularly a Presence Who Discovered and Heralded Heroes.

Hal was one of his first, and he never forgot that, were it not for Lowess's mythmaking, which sometimes in his case was the truth, he'd likely have gone to an early grave as an unknown dragon-flier.

Lowess also was the one who'd introduced Hal and Khiri.

Beyond Lowess's house was a large stable that had seen profit in housing dragons belonging to transient fliers.

Hal landed there, and Storm was the only dragon about.

The owners were eager to house and feed Storm, especially seeing Kailas's red gold, and they rented Kailas a carriage.

He smiled wryly at that. At one time, he wouldn't have been happy with anything other than a spirited charger. But time wears, and the spring weather was showery and brisk.

He rode to the apartment he and Khiri had bought, located in an immaculate sector not far from the king's palace.

He'd only been there half a dozen times, but Khiri loved it, close to her city friends, shopping, and exclusive restaurants.

He left the carriage in front, and stood, taking deep breaths, determined not to spoil Khiri's mood with his current dark thoughts.

Forcing a smile, and making himself think it was real, he put his saddlebags over his shoulder and went up the steps to the apartment.

Hal realized he'd left the damned keys back at his castle, and knocked hard.

A thousand thousand times he would relive the next few moments.

Khiri's voice came from inside, wondering who that could be.

Then came a man's voice, clear, much closer to the door.

"Prob'ly the post, lover. I'll get it."

The door came open, and a handsome young man, about Khiri's age, stood there. He was barefoot, wore expensive dress trousers, and was stripped to the waist. His face was half-lathered, and he held a razor in one hand.

Hal's razor.

The world stopped.

Hal's first impulse was to grab the man by the throat and throw him to the ground. Or draw the old dragon-flier's dagger he still foolishly wore.

But he fought for, and found, control.

The man stared at him. Over his shoulder, Hal saw Khiri, quite lovely in a wispy green silk dressing gown, and nothing else.

He'd bought her that gown on her last birthday, and somehow that made it worse.

Hal tried to find something to say that wouldn't be utterly foolish:

How long has this been going on . . . How could you . . . Who is this man . . . and various obscenities.

All were stupid.

Khiri's mouth hung open, and there was a great roaring in Hal Kailas's ears.

But all he managed was:

"I'll have my representative contact you."

There came a blur, then he found himself untying the reins of the carriage, and he was moving through the city streets, trying to keep the horse from galloping, and sucking in great lungsful of air, as if he'd been in battle.

Hal probably should have gone back north until his head cleared.

But he didn't.

He thought of various friends he could stay with in Rozen, didn't call on any of them. They, no doubt, would provide a place for him to stay.

But he thought of how many people found a cuckold's plight humorous, and didn't feel like making himself into a laughing stock.

Or rather, more of a laughing stock than he already felt himself to be.

That might well push him over the edge, and make him bring out the dagger.

He found an anonymous suite in one of the large inns that had sprung up during the war, advised the stables he wished to keep the carriage for an indeterminate time, and asked them to continue caring for Storm.

He had no thirst, which was good. Kailas had never sought the bottle when times were hard. He also had no appetite, which was not good, and so he found a comfortable tavern where no one knew who he was, nor would they have cared if they did.

He was chewing a ham steak, which he found tasteless, when his ear was caught by a man at the table next to him, talking about a certain advocate he'd come against in his business. According to the man, the bastard had three rows of teeth, all facing inward like a shark.

The man didn't sound like he meant disparagement.

Hal took note of the advocate's name. He slept little that night, and the next day got directions to that advocate's office.

The man was Sir Jabish Attecoti. Hal thought the knighthood a good sign. He'd obviously helped, in one way or another, someone with influence, enough to have him named to the peerage.

Attecoti was of medium height, and rather rotund. His face fairly beamed goodwill, and was framed in carefully trimmed muttonchops.

Hal might have thought Sir Jabish an amiable philanthropist, until he noted the man's eyes. Steel blue, they were as hard and cold as any warrior Kailas had known.

Attecoti listened intently to Hal's story, and Hal realized

that while very few people actually heard every word, Attecoti could probably recite their conversation word by word a year later.

He finally finished, a little proud of himself that he hadn't burst into tears or raised his voice.

"Nasty," Attecoti murmured. "Very nasty indeed, Lord Kailas. There are many actions I might take in this matter. What is your preferment?"

"Why . . . to end my marriage, as I said."

"Since both you and Lady Khiri are known public figures, you might realize this will be a matter for the broadsheets. How do you wish it played?"

Hal thought of dragging Khiri's name through the mire. But what would that give? And his own would be equally tarred, no doubt.

"Just end it," he said. "She has great properties in her own right. Let her keep what was hers, and I mine. And I wish no mention, if possible, of the cause of the divorcements. Call it irreconcilable matters."

The words tore at his heart, but they were the truth.

"I shall open on that front," Attecoti said. "If it worsens, though . . ."

"Do what you must," Hal said.

"I have some instructions for you," Attecoti said. "First, stay away from the broadsheets. Do not go to any taletellers, even if you now think them friends."

Hal nodded, thinking of Sir Thom Lowess.

"It would be wise for you to absent yourself from the capital until the hearing is set," Attecoti continued. "Go back to your estates.

"If you have . . . shall we say lady friends . . . it would be wise to avoid their company for a time."

"I have none such," Hal said.

Attecoti nodded, didn't comment.

"This case could well be the biggest I have yet handled," he said.

"Name your price," Kailas said indifferently. "I can meet it."

"In time," Attecoti said. "Oh yes. One other thing. Try to avoid having contact with Lady Khiri. That will not make things easier for me."

"I have nothing to say to her," Hal said, and, surprisingly, found it to be the truth. He wondered how long it *had* been that.

"Be advised I shall be retaining a seeker," Attecoti said. "Less because I'm curious about either of your private lives, but because I like to know everything to do with a case I handle.

"Might I ask where you will be staying?"

Hal told him the name of the inn.

"But that will be for only a few days," he said. "I shall be abroad for a time."

This came, unbidden, from him, as he remembered the vague thoughts he had had while flying south.

"Have your seeker call on me," he said, "if you would. And retain a good one. I have another matter – matters – I would like his help with."

"I shall do that. Do keep me current as to your location," Attecoti said. "And . . . my sympathies, Lord Kailas."

He sounded as if he meant it.

Hal tried to force coherence on his jumbled brain, and looked up Calt Beoyard, who had a farm half a day's flight from Rozen.

Beoyard was delighted to see him, tried to insist on Kailas staying with him, "even though I know this place is far too simple for a lord."

Hal politely thanked him, said he had business in the capital. He wanted the addresses for Mynta Gart and Sir Loren Damian, and the last known place Farren Mariah had been seen at.

Tay Manus was slim, very calm, and very obviously an ex-warder specializing in crime investigation.

Hal told him he really wanted to find Farren Mariah . . . or, at least, if something had happened to him, what it was.

Then, cursing himself for being a romantic, he asked him to hunt up Aimard Quesney. Quesney had shared a tent with Hal when he'd been attached to another squadron, in the war's early days. He'd asked Quesney to join the First Dragon Squadron when it was being formed. Quesney, not for the first time, had called Hal a born killer and declined. Later, he had refused to kill any more, and been court-martialed.

Hal had sat on the board, and, realizing Quesney was facing execution for refusing battle, forced a verdict of insanity from the other board members, in spite of Lord Bab's rather explicit instructions that he wanted Quesney at least hanged as a traitor, if not tortured for being anti-war, whether or not the King's Regulations permitted such treatment.

The verdict may have been shameful and false, but it saved Quesney's life.

Now Hal wanted to see the man, and ask a few questions.

Manus said he didn't think either assignment would be difficult, and left.

Hal went to the shipping district, found Mynta Gart's rather imposing warehouses.

Gart was overwhelmed at Hal's emergence from the "northern bracken," as she called it.

She poured him a brandy, which he liberally watered, stared closely at him, and asked what the matter was.

Hal hesitated, then told her, without going into specifics, that his marriage had just crashed into the rocks.

"No hope of putting it back together?" Gart asked.

Hal shook his head.

Gart wryly poured herself a drink as well, closed the door to her glassed office, stuffed with ship models.

"Things like that happen," she said. "Remember Chincha? The flier Farren was sweet on?"

"I do," Hal said.

"Something like happened to them," Gart said. "I guess, when the fighting stopped, he and Chincha found out they didn't have much in common."

"So where is Farren?"

"I haven't a clue, sir," Gart said. "Which asks the question – what are you doing around here? Other than to renew old friendships, and all of that."

Hal told her, and she whistled.

"This nice suicidal idea didn't come to you after you and Lady Carstares came to a parting?"

"No," Hal said. "I was on my way down here, about half sure of what I was going to do . . . and then what happened, happened."

"I'll put the word out in Farren's district," Gart said. "But I don't know. Oh. One person I know of who might be interested in your idiocy is Cabet. He's doing nothing but running a dragon patrol for the king, chasing smugglers around the straits.

"He might be up to doing something stupid with you."

Cabet was the thin, detail-minded flier who'd commanded the 18th Flight of the First.

"Thanks for the compliments," Hal said.

Gart smiled a little.

"The war's over. I don't have to watch my words now.

"And, speaking personally, I've too much sense to involve myself in your scheme . . . outside of its launching, I mean."

"I didn't expect a stable young businesswoman like yourself to do something insane such as I propose," Hal said, letting just a bit of a sarcastic drawl into his voice. "And, since you said you'll help get things under way, pun not intended, I'd like to have you charter a transport for me, capable of carrying dragons around the capes to the Southern Ocean."

"I can do better than that," Gart said. "The old *Galgorm Adventurer*, which no one in his right mind would go near who doesn't want to lug dragons about, is set for the breakers' yard.

"I figure it ought to cost no more than a hundred pieces of silver, as she sits, just for the scrap metal in her hull. No one's ferrying dragons about these days, even for gold on the spot.

"I can have her in the shipyard tomorrow, being refitted."

"I may as well be hanged for a bull as a kit," Hal said. "Go ahead."

Cabet was the first to arrive, loudly proclaiming how little he liked peacetime bureaucracy, and that he spent more time filling out reports than he did chasing smugglers.

Hal hid a smile – Cabet was not only a good leader, but gloried in the fine details, never admitting that, somewhere inside, he had the soul of a bureaucrat.

Cabet had only one request – that if he was killed in this adventure, there would be an award for his widow.

He had been married less than a year.

Hal thought that a good idea, and had Attecoti find a bank willing to write such policies for anyone who would journey with him. He didn't tell anyone except Attecoti that it was in exchange for him agreeing to do part of his banking business with them.

Hal asked Cabet if he had a particular dragon he would like purchased for his mount.

Cabet said not – if he had time, he'd train any beast that came to hand.

Calt Beoyard also was an eager volunteer, having, to his surprise, found his excuses quite empty. Hal had him take a dragon up, and jousted with him in the skies over Rozen on Storm, refreshing his memory of how good Beoyard was.

Acceptable. Not a Danikel, not a Richia.

But, unlike the other two, still alive, which said something about his fighting ability.

The next recruit lounged into Gart's office, where Kailas was headquartering his expedition from.

"I heard," Bodrugan said, "you're planning something troublesome."

"Who's talking?" Hal asked sharply even before greeting the magician. If there was gossip about, his plan was probably doomed.

"No one," Bodrugan said. "But it's known that you've purchased a ship that happens to carry dragons. And I've heard you're not at your usual residence, nor staying with Sir Thom.

"I know nothing from nothing, but since the next expedition north won't set forth until next year at the soonest, I thought maybe you could use a wizard perhaps as demented as you are. I'm bored with civilization, I fear."

Hal grinned.

"Welcome aboard, you loon."

Hal didn't need to turn from his lists to see who'd come in.

The voice was enough.

"I heard, bird, you're seeking me."

Hal turned.

It was Farren Mariah.

"Could I ask your mean scheme, o my fearless leader?"

"You could," Hal said. "I'm proposing a jail break."

4

Hal took Farren to a waterfront dive, and, for the first time since discovering Khiri with her lover, allowed himself to have an unwatered brandy.

He hesitatingly told Mariah what had happened, still not wanting anybody's sympathy.

Mariah sat, silently for a time, thinking, then drained his glass and signaled for another.

"Your first lady, Saslic," he said, without a trace of his usual singsong cant, "may have been right when she said there wouldn't be any after-the-war for a dragon-flier.

"Like there hasn't been for you and your wife.

"And there didn't seem to be one for Chincha and myself, at any rate.

"She wanted to travel, I wanted to stay in Rozen. She thought we should start some kind of business, I wanted to try politicking."

"I remember you talked about becoming the gray father of your district," Hal said, grateful to be able to think of others' tribulations instead of his own. "What happened?"

"Aaarh," Farren said, slipping back into his street tongue, "I said truth and they thought I was lisping. Nobody wants what is straight from the bosom, cousin, and maybe it's not the truth anyway, and you ought to be doing a fancy dance in grays.

"That didn't go anywhere, especially when I realized I was being used as a front man for the district's business as usual.

"I fell in on their scheming, and things came to this and that and someone pulled a knife, and I got six months in the bokey-pokey and some people had scars, and Chincha had gone by the time I got out, leaving me with just a note saying 'Dear Farren. Screw it.'

"So I took up mopery around the streets. Did some spells, sometimes they worked, sometimes they didn't.

"And you know, Lord Hal, I found myself looking up every time a dragon flew overhead.

"I thought I was just being strange on the range, and actually found a flying club, for the love of somebody or other. I went to a meeting, listened to all their crapetydoo-dah about the glory of the clouds and the wind whistling through their ears, and decided what they thought was flying wasn't what I thought it was.

"And so back to diddling my doodling, and then your seeker found me, and you owes me, I thought he was a warder and I near had heart seizure for thinking I was going back inside for doing something I didn't remember."

"Sorry about that," Kailas said, not sure if he was apologizing for Manus the seeker or what had happened to Mariah since peace struck.

"So we're to be busting somebody out of the old dinga-donga-dungeon, eh? Who, if I can ask."

Hal told him.

Mariah laughed immoderately.

"I love this. We spend a whole frigging war trying to kill this Yasin bastard, think we've succeeded, and now that the Sagene are going to top the evil son of a bitch, we're going to try to stop them.

"Aaah, life, I loves, loves, loves you."

They would need eight dragons, plus two handlers per dragon.

Work on refitting the cavernous *Galgorm Adventurer* was proceeding apace.

It was a hideous ship, like most that are intended for one purpose only, and then made worse by changing the purpose.

The *Galgorm* had originally been intended to haul horses and, secondarily, men. It was a square-rigged three-master, with main and cargo decks. Both decks had stalls that had been later enlarged to accommodate dragons. Wide gangplanks had been installed on either side of the hull. Dragon "launching" and "landing" was done with a barge tied alongside, to the looward side. Dragons were led down one or another of these gangplanks to the open barge, and encouraged by their rider to take to the air. Since dragons never minded getting wet, a launch day could be fairly soggy for the fliers.

Since the *Galgorm* was now Hal's, he made certain changes, such as a proper-sized kitchen, and enlarging the cabins to be more than just man-containers. He might be playing the fool, but he wasn't going to be an uncomfortable one.

He and Farren then went shopping for monsters.

There were more than enough on the market.

Kailas preferred black ones, even though Storm was a conventional reddish with gold streaks.

He took only the best.

The dragons were at least sixty feet long, twenty feet of that spiked tail. He never ceased admiring their talent for death-dealing, from the dual-horned head with its lethal fangs and cruel neck-horn to the whip-spiked tail.

All of the beasts he chose had some domestication, if dragons could ever really be tamed, and so their carapaces had been painlessly drilled for rings to hold the rider's saddle and bags, just as the armored head had been fitted for reins.

It was great fun for Hal, until he noticed the expression, if expression it was, on one unchosen beast.

He swore it looked as forlorn as an unasked maiden at a village dance.

Thereafter, the pleasure was considerably diminished.

He wished he could free all these captive dragons.

But then what?

Many of them had been captured as kits, and had little if any ability to live in the wild.

Once again, he thought, man befouled what he did not destroy.

That put him a thoroughly bad mood, quite ready to deal with his next caller, Sir Thom Lowess.

He came into the office quietly, and sat down, without greeting Kailas.

Hal turned and looked at him, hard, for a moment.

"How long have you known?"

"Maybe . . . maybe a month."

"And you didn't tell me."

"No," Lowess said. "And it pained me. But I was friends

with Khiri, and you, and finding out about her . . . behavior put me in the middle."

"It did," Kailas agreed. His voice was harsh, flat.

"I came to apologize . . . but I realized that wouldn't be right."

Hal thought for a moment.

"No. No, it wouldn't."

"Lady Khiri desperately wants to talk to you."

"I've been instructed by my advocate to have no contact with her."

Lowess's jaw bulged. He was getting angry.

"Aren't you being a little sanctimonious, Lord Kailas?"

"Yes, I suppose I am."

Lowess nodded once, stood, started for the door.

"Wait a minute, Sir Thom."

Lowess stopped.

"Very well. I'll talk to Khiri. But in the presence of my advocate."

"That," Lowess said after a moment, "hardly sounds like you're interested in any sort of reconciliation."

"No, it doesn't, does it," Hal said. "But that's the way it will be."

Again, Sir Thom nodded.

"One thing," Hal said. "You've been a more than good friend to me. I do not want to lose that."

Lowess smiled tightly.

"Thank you for saying that. I feel the same. And I shall tell Lady Khiri what you have agreed to do."

They met at the office of Sir Jabish Attecoti. Lady Khiri looked very beautiful, Hal supposed. And he was a bit surprised that she came without her own advocate.

Khiri tried a smile, saw Hal's grim face, let it slip away. She looked at Sir Jabish.

"This hardly makes for an easy conversation, does it?"

Hal didn't answer.

"Would it help to say I'm sorry . . . that he was just a momentary impulse, and we'd been . . . well, together, for only a few days."

"Don't lie, Khiri," Hal said. "I know otherwise."

Khiri bobbed her head, shed a few tears.

"It was just . . . just that you've been so cold lately. I thought maybe there was someone else, and lost my temper, and oh hells!"

"There was never anyone else," Kailas said.

Khiri looked up at him, her face flushed.

"You sound like you're my commander, or something like that! Isn't there any room for forgiving me? Please?"

Hal just looked at her.

She took a handkerchief from her sleeve, wiped her eyes.

"I suppose . . . no. Never mind."

She snuffled once, got up and swept out.

Hal and Sir Jabish exchanged looks. Neither of them said anything.

It was a bright summer day, and the sunlight dappled the waves as two harbor boats warped the *Galgorm Explorer* out of Gart's dock, and swung its prow south, toward the open sea.

Sailors swarmed the yards, and a dragon honked in surprise as the first wave lifted the ship.

Hal looked back at the land, saw Gart waving, managed a smile, then looked ahead at the Straits of Carcaor.

There was nothing behind him any more to hold his mind.

5

Once, Frechin had sat on Sagene's coast. But ocean currents silted up the coastline, and, fifty years later, it was two leagues inland.

But the citizens of Frechin were canny, and built a winding, deep-water canal from the ocean to the city, and dug out a huge harbor.

The canal was guarded by twin fortified moles at its mouth, and the city itself by the great fortress-prison above the city, making it a safer harbor than before.

In midsummer, wherries brought the *Galgorm Adventurer* to a berth near the canal entrance.

Sagene citizens flocked to see the wallowing tub, and its load of dragons. Speculation ran rife as to what the Dragonmaster, famous even in a foreign country, was planning.

A few well-trained sailors, apparently in their cups, let on that Lord Kailas saw adventure and profit far to the south, on the almost unknown coast across the Southern Sea.

In the meantime, he was waiting for additional crew

members and soldiers, since the coast was reputedly rife with pirates and hostile tribes.

The *Adventurer*'s master said they expected to be tied up in Frechin for at least a month, and opened negotiations for food and drink to be brought to the ship.

Hal and the other dragon-fliers had spent every clear, calm day on the voyage south, down the Chicor Straits into the open sea, around Sagene's capes into the Southern Sea, flying and practising landing on the small barge that the *Adventurer* towed alongside as a landing stage.

It was good to make sure none of them had lost these skills, Hal said.

It might be very good. He hadn't seen Frechin's prison, but Hal had had an idea or two on how he might attempt to liberate Yasin even before they'd left Deraine.

With their story adequately established, he decided to visit Yasin in his death cell.

He was pleasantly surprised at the prison's warder.

Sir Mal Rospen was a long-mustached soldier, most dignified in his manner.

"I bid you welcome, Lord Kailas," he rumbled. "But I must advise you of something. *Ky* Yasin may be a convicted felon, and doomed to be hanged, unless his last appeal is successful, which, frankly, no one expects.

"But he did what he did in the conviction of rectitude, illegally purchasing supplies on the black market and flying them into Roche.

"In another time, in another country, he might be judged a hero.

"But the war savaged us all, and so he will hang.

"But he will hang as a gentleman, and I will tolerate no man mocking him."

"That," Hal said honestly, "is hardly my intention."

Rospen had a warder show him to a bare stone room, and Yasin was brought in.

At least they let him wear civilian clothes, rather than whatever monkey-garb Sagene prisons legislated.

He started, seeing Kailas, and then burst out laughing.

"This is proof that the gods have an evil sense of humor," he said. "The last time I saw you – other than when you shot me – I was the visitor and you were the prisoner.

"As I recall, I was full of pride, and just beginning to realize the war was turning against us, and I said some most intemperate things."

"You did," Hal said amiably.

"For which I was repaid by your first escaping, then returning and laying waste to Castle Mulde and liberating all of the prisoners we held.

"A fitting repayment for arrogance. I think . . . I hope . . . I have learned, if not to curb my haughtiness, to at least conceal it."

Hal indicated the other, rickety chair.

Yasin sat.

"So what brings you out of Deraine?"

"I have a question of my own first," Hal said. "I could have sworn I killed you, back over the realm of the demon outside Carcaor."

"You damned near did," Yasin said frankly. "I felt your crossbow bolt hit me, and a wave of pain, and then I was in the water.

"My dragon had crashed beside me, and was thrashing in its death agonies. All I wanted to do was join it.

"But I didn't.

"I think I swam away from the beast, and then I was on the surface, trying to breathe. Without much success.

"But somehow I managed to float downstream, flailing at the water. I guess I was afraid to die.

"Anyway, the current took me a mile or more away, where I washed up on a little beach.

"There was a scattering of huts. The people who lived there wanted nothing to do with cities or demons or fliers or war. But one of them was a passingly good witch and herbalist.

"She crouched by me, and I could feel I was fading, and she snarled, 'Breathe or die,' and that shocked me into wanting to live.

"I breathed, and then she lit a taper, and I was in a coma. Then came great pain, and I couldn't waken. The pain stopped, and I found out later they were pushing your crossbow bolt through me, until it came out between my ribs.

"They cut off the broadhead, pulled the shaft out, and packed the wound with herbs."

He made a wry face.

"And so I healed, while my country fell apart.

"But talking about wounds is like listening to old women natter about their ills, interesting only to them.

"I ask again, if I may, what brings you here?"

Hal tapped an ear, raised an eyebrow, and pointed around the room.

Yasin smiled. "You remember the skills of being a prisoner well. No. This cell is not listened to, unlike some. At least, I don't think so."

Hal had been lightly searched, but they hadn't found the tightly rolled linen in his boot. He pulled it out, unrolled it, revealing the letters of the alphabet.

"We have interests to the south," he said, his fingers touching letters.

W . . . E . . . W . . . I . . . L . . . L . . . T . . . R . . . Y . . .
T . . . O . . . R . . . E . . . S . . . C . . . U . . . E . . . Y . . . O . . . U.

Yasin's eyes widened.

"Well," he managed, "That sounds . . . interesting. I wish that I could accompany your expedition, but I seem to have other commitments."

"And you have let yourself fall out of shape," Hal said. "You're hardly fit enough for an adventurer."

"This is true," Yasin said. "I fear that our exercise time, which is only two hours a day, just at noon, has been uninteresting to me, since I don't know of any calisthenics that prepare you for walking on air."

"Still," Hal said. "You should get outside as much as you can. Your appeal hasn't been denied yet, and walking, *in the open air*, is good for you."

He wondered, if there were eavesdroppers, whether his words sounded as stilted as they did to him.

"You're right," Yasin said. "I should start immediately."

"In the meantime," Hal said, "while we're still anchored here, is there anything we could bring you?"

"A new trial," Yasin said. "Other than that, the warders here have been most gentle, and my mother has sent money, so I'm not living on prisoners' fare."

"Good," Hal said, and led the conversation into dragon-flying and the war for an hour or so, then took his leave.

Hal's dragons became a familiar sight over Frechin, soaring close to the heights, and waving at warders on the prison's walls.

Again, Kailas visited Yasin, with his linen roll.

T...W...O...D...A...Y...S...B...E...
R...E...A...D...Y.

Yasin's lips moved in and out, and Hal noticed that he had developed a twitch at the corner of his mouth.

Contrary to what some morons have said, the prospect of being hanged does not concentrate the mind, but rather shatters the ability to concentrate.

Hal wriggled in the predawn chill.

The *Adventurer* had pushed away from the dock before dawn, swung round, and, under a reefed mainsail, tacked clumsily down-canal toward the sea.

The story was that the ship was to be put out to sea for re-ballasting, since its master disliked the way it had tacked on the voyage south, and would return later in the day.

Now the sun was well up, and they were following Hal's simple plan exactly.

Just coming up were the two moles at the canal's mouth. The *Adventurer*'s master steered the ship around the jetty, and the bows lifted, meeting the first waves from the open sea.

The *Adventurer* sailed due south until it was out of sight of land, in case anyone on the moles might be watching.

It was good to be awake, to have hastily grabbed some cold cheese and ham on a roll, a glass of tea, and stumbled on deck to make sure Storm had been fed an hour earlier, and was ready to fly.

It was good . . . like in the war.

That was an odd, sudden thought.

Hal jolted, but there was no time for wondering about one's thoughts. He put it away for later, and led Storm down the ramp from the ship to the barge.

He climbed into the double saddle, and Storm quivered, then, at Kailas's rein-tap, staggered forward, wings at full stretch, and striking downward, and again, and the dragon was airborne.

Hal pulled up, and Storm reached for the skies.

Well, he thought, maybe Farren *was* missing something. There was a certain majesty to dragon-flight. Especially with action in the offing.

He glanced back.

The other dragons were on the *Adventurer*'s deck, and one was being led down to the barge.

The monsters would take off within the hour.

Storm climbed high, until the ship was a dot.

There was no need to hurry, for the dragon to strain.

It lacked an hour of midday when Hal turned Storm back toward land.

He thought, at this height, he might fly unnoticed, as perhaps a wild dragon.

He followed the canal's winding, saw Frechin below him, and, on the cliffs above the city, the fortress-prison.

He put Storm in a circling descent, orbiting down, just over the fortress.

Dots appeared, grew, became prisoners in the courtyard, just as on other days.

There were other dots, alert warders on the catwalks. Hal made a face. He'd hoped to find them dozing after the noon meal, should have known that someone like Rospen wouldn't tolerate slackers.

One of the warders glanced up, saw Storm, and yelped in surprise.

Hal could have shot him down, but he wanted the escape to be, if possible, without casualties. If a Sagene guard died, all of the rescuers might face the gallows if captured.

He scanned the prisoners in the yard. Most were running for shelter – Storm was only about fifty feet above them. One stood in the middle of the courtyard, holding his hands clasped above his head.

Yasin.

An arrow whispered past Kailas, but not close enough to worry about.

Storm flared his huge wings, and thudded down on the bricks of the yard. Yasin was running toward him, and two more arrows clacked near him.

Too close.

Yasin pulled himself up behind Hal, who gigged Storm into his staggering takeoff run.

Three other dragons swept down, flying close to the battlements, as Storm's wings flapped, and he was in the air.

The dragons dove and swooped around the fortress, like angry monstrous swallows, their heads darting at warders diving for cover, their tails lashing.

Hal thought of so many crows, savaging an owl.

Another couple of arrows clattered off the dragon's plating, and they were above the castle.

Hal grabbed the trumpet hung on a hook bolted to the dragon's carapace, blatted twice.

Then he turned west, in what was a transparent attempt to delude the Sagene that these four dragons had nothing to do with the four dragons seen above the Derainian ship that had just sailed.

The plan was that when they reached the *Galgorm*, they would sail on south, into the depths of the Southern Sea, before turning west. If they stayed well clear of land, they should be able to reach the great ocean, then turn north to Deraine without being caught.

There might be a stink from Sagene's Council of Barons later, but Hal knew King Asir would hardly turn his Dragonmaster over to them.

Of course, it would be some years, if ever, before Hal could use the apartment he and Khiri had bought during the war in Sagene's capital, Fovant.

But what of that? It had really been Khiri's from the first.

He turned his mind away from that, looked over his shoulder.

Yasin, a grin stapled on his face, clung to his back.

"I owe you a great debt," he said.

"Godsdamned right," Hal agreed.

"What next?"

"Next, we get back to my ship."

Hal brought Storm to a southerly heading, the line of the canal barely visible to the east; used it to find the ocean.

Bodrugan had replicated a spell his master, Limingo, had cast years ago, that acted as a sort of compass to find a ship.

Hal whispered the words, touching the dragon emblem he still wore around his neck:

> *"Beef of old*
> *Covered with mold*
> *We shun thee yet*
> *Your odor set*
> *We turn away*
> *Our stomachs at bay*

> *Protect us all*
> *From your horrid pall.*"

The spell had been cast around the salt beef all ships carried as a staple, and which most sailors and all landsmen detested.

Instantly, Hal felt a dislike for a certain direction. There would lie the *Adventurer* – and its barrels of beef.

The aversion was very strong. Hal frowned, then guessed it was his stomach, for he had not eaten any salt beef, thank the heavens, since the war had ended.

"It's nice to be in the air again," Yasin shouted. "Especially without a rope holding me up."

"Very funny," Hal said. "But you're repeating yourself. Now shut up and look for our ship."

"Which will be?"

"The only one around, I hope."

A few moments passed. Hal looked back, and made sure the other four were close behind him.

Yasin jabbed him in the ribs.

"Sail ho, or whatever sailors say," he said. Then, a little worriedly, "In fact, two sails ho."

Hal swung forward.

There were, indeed, two ships, dark dots, ahead. And they were fairly close together, certainly enough for them to have line of sight on the other.

"I guess one is yours," Yasin said. "But the other . . ." He broke off. "I don't have a glass," he said. "But I think the other is a Sagene patrol ship. We saw it often enough bringing supplies out of Frechin."

"Son of a bitch!" Hal swore.

This part of the rescue, after the actual lifting of Yasin

from the prison, had always been the weak link. He knew the thin story about re-ballasting wouldn't last beyond the sight of the dragons over the prison walls.

If the *Galgorm* was captured, Sagene's wrath might fall on the sailors, even though the main villains had escaped.

He'd made arrangements for bond money for both the ship and the crew with Sir Jabish Attecoti, and for Bodrugan and the captain to take charge of the vessel if Hal wasn't aboard.

He knew their problems would be worse if Yasin and the dragons were captured with them, and had told Bodrugan the dragon force would try to evade if they saw the *Galgorm* was in trouble. He had also ordered the magician to claim utter ignorance of his plans.

But he'd assumed the worst case would be capture after they'd had a chance to land and change to fresh dragons.

As it was . . .

Hal blew a warning note to the others behind him, pointed down at the two ships.

He turned Storm east, toward where he'd seen, on the ship's charts, small islands.

He reached in a pouch, took out a compass, thought quickly, and devised a heading.

"Look!" Yasin said, pointing again.

Smoke, no, fog was billowing up and around the *Adventurer*. It must be a spell, cast by Bodrugan. A second incantation, a standard confusion casting, drifted up to him.

The *Galgorm Adventurer* might have been a pig, far slower than the coastal patrol ship.

But perhaps magic could save it.

There was nothing Hal could do.

*

Just when Hal was starting to worry about missing the islands, and being forced to turn toward Sagene, and Storm was starting to tire, they saw them, a pair of dots ahead.

Hal brought his flight in over the islands, saw no sign of habitation, and landed on a rocky plateau.

All of the dragons were trained to a rein tie, and stamped about, panting hard, as their riders, grim and worried, came up to Hal.

"And so this is the ringy-dingy prize?" Farren said. "Doesn't look as if he's been starvin' from worry."

Yasin ignored him.

"I guess," Cabet said, "our best chance will be to wait, then use our spell to head back for the *Adventurer*, although I like that but little."

Calt, very definitely the junior man, said nothing.

"That's not a goer," Farren said. "M'beastie's sore tired, and needs watering and a rest."

Calt nodded.

Hal knew Storm could fly on, but he would be on his reserves.

"I don't think that's best," he said slowly. "I'm afraid we have to go back to Sagene, raid a village or a big farm, then figure what to do next."

"I know where we can go," Yasin said. "There's a big estate we used to resupply from not far from Frechin. That's the bastard who betrayed us.

"He could do with a bit of a lesson."

"Not from us," Hal said. "We're in enough trouble as it is."

Yasin nodded reluctantly.

"But we can *buy* supplies from him, perhaps. Or requisition them, at any rate," Hal went on. "And we'll be gone before the alarm can spread."

"To where?" Farren said. "We can't go a-raidin' hither and thither as we go northward, a song in our heart and a smile on our lips, and hope to get home or even to Paestum without attracting a scowl and a chase.

"I don't think we're the only dragons to be flying over Sagene, and we'll be pursued."

"You're not," Yasin said. "Their Council of Barons still maintains a border watch in the skies. I learned that the hard way."

"And we can't go looking for the *Adventurer*," Hal said. "We don't know if it escaped, or if it's in the hands of . . . of Sagene."

He'd almost said 'the enemy.'

"It seems quite obvious," Yasin said, an ironic smile on his lips. "The only safety we've got is to fly further east, into Roche."

6

They flew north-east, back toward Sagene, and made land-fall some distance away from Frechin. They flew about a mile inland and turned due east, Hal following Yasin's instructions.

They grounded where Yasin said to land, in the middle of the palatial estate that Yasin claimed he'd been betrayed at.

Hal and Cabet went to the main house. Yasin grumbled, and wanted to come with them, to wreak a bit of vengeance. Hal flatly said no, and he would have Mariah sit on him if he kept arguing.

The property's owner was supposedly in Fovant, they were told. But the rather nervous major-domo sold them beeves on the hoof, wine, bread, and preserved meats, after hearing the story that the dragons were part of a Sagene border sweep.

The four withdrew to a grove some distance from the estate houses, ate and relaxed. Being former soldiers, they could lie at ease, unworried, with unsheathed swords at their sides, as long as their enemies weren't in sight.

"Now what will we do?" Calt Beoyard wondered.

"As I said, push across the border," Yasin said. "Make for my lands. My family may not be as rich as we were before the war, but there'll always be food and shelter for men I owe my life to."

"Damned well better be," Mariah muttered somewhat darkly.

Yasin stared at him, and Hal saw the stocky man brace for a fight.

Farren Mariah thought about it, then shook his head.

"Naah," he said. "The Dragonmaster said we were to be friends, and that names it."

After an hour's rest, they flew on, toward Roche.

They passed over the ravaged border into Roche near dusk.

Hal thought, wryly, that if anyone had told him, three years before, he'd feel relief at being in Roche, he would have damned that person not only as a false prophet, but a total fool as well.

"Fly east by north-east," Yasin shouted.

Hal turned Storm in that direction.

Near dark, they approached a small town, little more than a village.

"That's Anderida. We can land there," Yasin shouted. "My family is well known."

Hal, not quite trusting Yasin, especially in Roche, made a few orbits before looking for a place to set down.

Anderida appeared quite untouched by the war, and by the civil disorders afterward.

Outside the town were armed horsemen, riding in pairs. One pointed to the sky, then galloped into the town center, where Hal lost sight of him.

Yasin told Kailas to land in the grassy square in the middle of town.

Hal chose an open field on the outskirts, and brought Storm in.

A crowd gathered.

Hal noticed some of them were armed, although they tried to keep their weapons hidden.

Kailas cocked his crossbow, letting a bolt drop down in the trough.

"You won't need that," Yasin said.

Hal didn't believe him. Nor did he disbelieve him.

He kept the crossbow hidden behind Storm's carapace.

The other fliers landed after Storm.

A rather fat man came into the meadow, holding up his empty hands.

"Greetings, strangers." He didn't sound very friendly.

"And greetings to you," Yasin said. "I am *Ky* Bayle Yasin."

There were shouts from the crowd, of welcome and cheers.

"I . . . I greet you, *Ky* Yasin," the fat man said. "But we heard you were in . . . well, desperate straits."

"I was," Yasin said. His command-trained voice, unraised, carried well. "These men . . . Derainians . . . rescued me from a Sagene death cell."

Now there were real cheers. The crowd got bigger, weapons forgotten.

"Then we greet and welcome them, as well," the fat man said. "I am the Town Leader, chosen after your last visit here, during the war, and am named Gavat. All that Anderida has is yours . . . and theirs."

Yasin turned back to Hal.

"You see? Now we own the city. As we shall own the whole of Roche."

Hal didn't know about the whole of Roche, but Anderida took the occasion to have a holiday.

They were given rooms at the best inn in town – there were only three – and payment was horrifiedly refused.

The dragons were put up in the stables behind the inn. The horses there were unceremoniously rousted.

Any time one of the dragon-riders peered out of the window, he was cheered.

They found that embarrassing.

They washed, and went to the taproom for a beer, and then were escorted into the dining room.

The fare was sumptuous.

It began with raw oysters, brought down the River Pettau, past the ruins of Lanzi. Someone said something about the problem they were having "up north" with barbarian raiders coming in from the east, and that if Lanzi still stood, patrols would have kept them away.

Hal, who'd been responsible for the total destruction of Lanzi, looked innocent. Mariah, who'd also been on the raids, as had Cabet, wasn't nearly so successful.

Yasin asked about Anderida's seeming peacefulness.

Gavat, who was serving as feast-master, nodded.

"Peaceful now, yes," he said. "But not before. There were landless men come on us, and . . . and there was an outrage. An old man was taken prisoner, and his feet held against his own stove, until he told them where his gold had been kept.

"The men fled, after killing their captive.

"But we have a witch, and she sought and found them.

"They were brought back here, and hanged on a gibbet in the square.

"After that, we had our young men – those who'd survived the war – ride guardian around the town's borders, as they ride now.

"Twice, lawless men tried to enter the town, and were driven off. We put their heads on stakes on the roads approaching the town, and since then have had no further problems.

"Not like what we hear from the cities. Merchants, who now travel in convoys, well-armed, have told us of the disaster Roche has fallen into since Carcaor was brought down in ruins and Queen Norcia set aside.

"Fortunately, we need little from the outside.

"But this is hardly a subject for a feasting's conversation," he said. "Try these pasties. But save room. The meal has scarce begun."

The pasties held caviar, also from the north, with soured cream atop them.

Small game birds, stuffed with an exotic fungus and goose liver, came next.

Coins of beef, with fungus atop them, in a rich wine sauce followed.

Hal was starting to founder.

He made it through the fruit soufflé, but caved in before the salad, the cheeses, and the dessert.

Some of his faltering came from the foaming dark wine that was served in profusion.

Some more of it came from his servitor.

Anderida banquet custom evidently dictated that each guest have his own attendant.

Hal's was named Brythnoth. She was nineteen, she had white-blonde hair that Hal thought might be real, a round face and slender body. She also had a soft contralto voice, and firm breasts exposed in an diaphanous loose blouse.

She seemed to think that he was the most fascinating man who'd ever lived, with the possible exception of Yasin, who'd been a family hero during the war, and whose portrait had hung next to the family gods, she said.

Hal wondered if she'd still be so friendly if he told her he'd done his best, through the war years, to kill Yasin at every chance he got.

Hal decided, feeling very comfortable, he'd rather not test those particular waters.

He was very full.

Too full, he thought uncomfortably.

He yawned.

"I am boring you," Brythnoth said, sounding as if she was about to cry.

"No, no," Hal said. "I just need some air."

"Perhaps you'd let me show you our square?"

That sounded like a good idea, Hal said. It also sounded, very vaguely, like a way of getting in trouble.

But he allowed Brythnoth to take his arm, and they left the others still eating, although Mariah gave him a surreptitious thumbs up.

Hal wondered what that was supposed to mean.

The square was quiet, deserted, in the summer dark.

Thank gods the claque had disappeared.

Fireflies flitted here and there, their glow reflected in a winding pool.

It felt quite right for him to put his arm around the girl as they walked.

Just as it felt right, when they stopped to watch a pair of ducks landing in the pond, for him to slip his arms around her waist from the rear.

He felt the warm curve of her buttocks, and his body reacted.

Somehow his hands slid up, cupped her breasts.

She turned in his embrace, and they kissed.

Hal had kissed a few other women since he'd met Khiri. But nothing more than a single, polite kiss before he stammered about his marriage vows.

He had been unbearably faithful.

And what had it gotten him in return, except, most likely, some women with hurt feelings?

So he kissed Brythnoth again, her tongue flickering in and out of his mouth.

He shouldn't be doing this, he thought.

Why not?

It wasn't like he was married any more.

He woke just at dawn.

His arm was asleep, Brythnoth's head pillowed on it.

He slid out of the covers, walked across the room, took a scrub from his saddlebag, and rubbed at his teeth.

He rinsed his mouth, went back to bed.

Brythnoth was half-covered with only a sheet.

Hal thought of the night before, expecting to feel guilt, indigestion, a hangover.

He felt none of these.

In fact, he felt perfectly damned wonderful.

He considered the sleeping Brythnoth.

She was, indeed, naturally white-blonde.

Thinking of that, he also thought it might be a good idea to kiss her.

She sort of woke, rolled on her back, kissed him back.

As he slid over her, he told his damned ascetic mind to remember what had happened, and stop being so gods-damned self-righteous all the time.

They took off a few hours later.

As Storm climbed, Hal looked back, beyond the town square, at the inn.

The dot that was Brythnoth stood outside, waving frantically.

He wondered if he'd ever see her again, decided it didn't matter, not for her, not for him.

They stopped twice at farmhouses, and, as Yasin had predicted, were the glory of the day.

On the fourth day, they flew over the Yasin grounds. They sprawled for miles, and mostly grew wheat, and table grapes, with the rest of the land given over to self-support.

"It sort of just grew," Yasin had explained, "over generations. Our real land is to the north, almost to the border, and it's said the only thing that can be raised there is sons to grow to be warriors.

"That's very noble, but my great-grandfather also liked to have a full belly, and so he started buying lands down here in the south.

"Little by little, we spent more and more time on these lands, instead of freezing our balls off, making manly poses as we did, up around the border.

"That land had been Roche for only a few generations, and there still were natives who felt they'd been robbed.

"Perhaps they had," he continued. "But we always wondered who they'd stolen the land from in the first place."

The war had cost the Yasin clan dearly.

Bayle's father had died in a duel, "defending Queen Norcia's honor."

Farren had made a wry face, and said, later, to Hal, "So the old man defends the honor, and then that duke, Yasin's brother, proceeds to take it as often as he can get away with."

That brother, Garcao, had been head of the Household Regiments, and rumored to be Norcia's lover. He had then led the group of barons that overthrew Norcia, blaming her for the way the war was going against Roche.

Garcao had died either in the final battle for Carcaor, the capital, or during the interregnum that followed.

Yasin was the only heir.

"Which means, of course," he'd said, "Mother wants me to marry – or, at any rate, breed – as soon as possible, and give up this damned dragon-flying."

Hal had noted that Mother was in capital letters.

He also noted, later, that Yasin never talked about his late brother. He couldn't decide whether Garcao and Bayle had been very close, or not at all.

In any event, Hal, an only child who, as a boy, had often yearned for a brother, thought it very odd.

They landed outside the main house, which was of dark brickwork. The thick walls had been built to withstand a siege, and there were fighting positions in the walls and along the roof.

Low towers dotted the land here and there, to keep off raiders or a full-scale attack.

"My kin, back when we were kids, playing war, would've peed green for something like that," Mariah said. "Instead, we had to make barricades from crates, and use greengrocers' pushcarts for our castles.

"There's no justice in the world."

"What," Cabet asked in astonishment, "ever made you think there was?"

"A man can dream, scheme, can't he?"

Bayle Yasin's mother was, indeed, fearsome. It could well have been her idea to refer to herself in capital letters. She was tall, rigid in her posture, and her gray hair was drawn back in a bun. It was very hard for Hal to imagine her enjoying the marital bed, except as a rather messy way to begin her dynasty.

She actually unbent a little to smile at Farren Mariah, of which he said, later, "Made my damned blood turn to icebergs, thinking she might be crawly jolly into my bedroom. Next time I need to think of somewhat to keep from coming, I'll be sure to let her creep into my mind."

"And lose that soggy erection you've been able to handwork up?" Cabet asked.

"You're forgetting the war too fast," Mariah said. "Keep to the rigid dignity of a flight commander . . . and in return, I'll not cast a wee spell that'll send the good Lady Yasin into *your* bed."

They were feasted and given their own cottages around the grounds.

Hal busied himself writing a very long letter to Advocate Jabish Attecoti.

He finished, sealed it, found the Yasins' amanuensis, and gave him money to have it sent, via the fastest courier, to Deraine.

Then there was nothing to do but wait.

Until he had word from Attecoti, and found out how much trouble he was in back in Deraine, there was no particular point in planning anything.

There were brick barracks on the estate, and workers trickled in.

It was almost the season for harvesting the wheat, and, before that, bringing in the grapes. Some went on wooden trays, to dry into raisins, but the better reds would be crushed and put in casks, mostly for trading, a little for the estate itself.

Some of the workers came from small local farms, but a lot of them arrived travel-battered, having made the long trek south from the northern lands.

Some, Yasin said, wanted to stay on here, and give up their homes in the north.

Hal, going past the workers' barracks one evening with Yasin, paused, and heard one worker talking.

He, and the rest of his village, had been clearing land for a new settlement. It had almost been a festival, living in tents, with the women and children preparing the meals, while the men cut and burnt the land.

Then the barbarians had struck them.

The worker said he'd hidden in a pile of brush, and they'd overlooked him.

The men had been killed, the children and young women taken off for slaves, and the other women . . . The story-teller hesitated, then said that they'd been taken in great cheering orgies by the barbarians.

There'd been half a dozen men who'd lived, all by hiding.

Twice that number of women survived, although three of them "kilt theyselves, outa the shame."

Hal had started to walk on, then noticed the look on Yasin's face.

There was a gleam, as if he'd just heard the call to arms.

That night, Yasin didn't join the other fliers after dinner, but was busy in one of the libraries, writing letters.

Three days later, he left for Carcaor.

A courier brought Hal a letter from Attecoti.

Ironically, it had been brought to Roche's capital, Carcaor, by a commercial dragon-rider, and from there by horse.

I'm sending this by the most rapid method I know of, since I can well understand your desire to be kept current on the events of the day.

First, the matter of your divorce — it is proceeding apace, and, thus far, Lady Carstares and her advocate have presented us with no surprises, or demands that might be deemed outrageous. As per your wishes, I am attempting to keep the entire matter sub rosa, so far with a marked success, although the taletellers have been importuning me for details on your marital dissolution.

I would estimate that the divorcement will be final by the end of this year.

On other matters:

First is the good news. I do not know, nor do I wish to know, the details of your adventure into Sagene. But the ship you purchased, the Galgorm Adventurer, has safely returned, with its entire crew, to Deraine.

I was told, and asked for no details, that the spell proved to be effective. There are some things an advocate should never inquire too fully into.

However, the Sagene ambassador has formally complained to the Royal Court about what he claims to be a wholly illegal act, in that you and some of your friends liberated a criminal, condemned to death, and he wishes all of you to be arrested and returned to Sagene for trial.

This matter I have been unable to keep from the taletellers and, frankly, it's become quite the sensation. I have repeatedly pled ignorance of the entire matter.

However, as I said, the reported involvement of the Dragonmaster in a rather scandalous affair has stayed in the broadsheets, if for no other reason than that there isn't a scandal quite as savory at present.

I have quietly inquired at Court, and been advised that our Royal Highness is not pleased at all. However, it seems that, if there are no further outrages, as he has termed them, the matter will be allowed to die, and it shall not prove necessary to make a response to Sagene.

Unfortunately, it will take some months for that to happen.

My suggestion, based on what I was told, is that you should, and I quote directly from a friend close to King Asir, "remain invisible" at least until the end of the year.

I am most sorry, Lord Kailas, since I assume you wish to return to your lands as soon as possible. But I would suggest the advice should be followed, unless your present situation is completely intolerable. If you must return home, you should be advised of the likelihood of being summoned before the king to answer in this matter, which I cannot recommend against too strongly.

I have taken the liberty of sending a letter of credit to a merchant banker in Carcaor, authorizing him to issue you any

specie you may need while in Roche, the sum to be paid by me,
from the profits of your estate.

Please stay in touch, and I shall do the same as circumstances
develop.

With best wishes,
Jabish Attecoti, Knight

Hal put the letter down thoughtfully. So he was stranded
here in Roche for the time being.

He shrugged.

If that was the price he had to pay, so be it.

At least Bodrugan and the men and women of the
Galgorm Adventurer were safe.

And at least he could now think about being able to
stop living off the kindness of strangers.

He guessed that Mariah and the others could return
home to Deraine if they wished.

He would be the only expatriate.

And what of that? He couldn't think of anywhere, in
Deraine, in Sagene, in Roche, that he regarded as home.

Hal guessed he'd consult that banker in Carcaor for help in
finding a place to live.

He'd already, wryly, composed an announcement:

WANTED
By fairly reputable nobleman, if currently somewhat
of a fugitive, a furnished apartment or town house.
Excellent credit and credentials.
Must have room for one companion:
A dragon.
Reply confidentially.

Yasin came back from Carcaor, beaming, as if someone had promised him the moon.

He asked Hal for a moment of his time.

"Lord Kailas," he began, most formally, "I would like to extend an invitation to you, that would involve risk, adventure, and a great deal of flying."

Hal's eyebrows perked.

"After hearing of the depredations the barbarians are making against our northern frontiers, I have spent some time with some friends, and with some of the barons who have holdings in the north.

"I proposed to them, and my plan was quickly approved, that I might be able to do some good in holding back these hordes from the sacred lands of Roche.

"In short, I am going to put together a dragon squadron.

"My idea met with quick approval, since, unknown to me before I met with my friends, several people in the capital had already proposed putting together a military incursion against these savages. As our peace treaty with Deraine forbids increasing the military beyond the paltry garrison units that already exist, this would be paid for and organized by civilians, although run on the strictest rules.

"We will fly north, base ourselves in the city of Trenganu, and provide this armed force with both scouting and fighting potential.

"Since you seem . . . meaning no offense, and considering how much my family and I owe you . . . at, well, a loose end, would you, and any of your friends who feel the same, care to join my enterprise?

"I'll add that, although I'll be commander, you can have my written guarantee that I shall never order or require you or any of your friends to do anything dishonorable."

Hal was jolted out of his own immediate concerns.

"I think," he said, "I could use a brandy to chew on while I mull your offer over."

Yasin hurried Hal to a library, found a decanter of very old brandy, and poured for them both.

Hal took two snifters while he thought, sipping them carefully.

Then he nodded.

"Why not?" he said. "Why the hell not?"

7

Hal told his men what he was going to do, said they were free to go, having more than fulfilled their agreement to break Yasin out, and added that he'd give them enough gold to get back to Deraine.

He told them he didn't think the law was after them, in fact most likely didn't even know who they were, but he thought it might be wise to stay out of Sagene for the immediate future.

"I bargained for an adventure," Farren Mariah said. "Plus mayhap a little madness. And chasing wild men about the great northern tundra sounds like both.

"I'll stick with you, Dragonmaster.

"'Sides, you'll need somebody to cover your wrinkly ass."

The other two made the same choice, although it took until the next day, and Hal thought Calt Beoyard seemed a little hesitant.

But when Hal took him aside, he said he'd made his mind up, and sounded much firmer about his decision.

Yasin was delighted to have them, and said that if Hal knew any other Derainians who might be interested, he'd be proud to add them to the company as well.

Hal thought about writing some letters, but, since he still hadn't heard from Manus, the inquiry agent, he decided not.

He was dimly aware that something was niggling at him, keeping from recruiting any of his ex-fliers, although he didn't think it was the idea of operating with the Roche.

Kailas set the matter aside.

He had more than enough to do, getting ready for another war.

The first step was moving to Carcaor, which Hal looked forward to. Yasin's estate might be luxurious, and his mother assured them they'd always have a home, but it was a bit too far out of the world.

Besides, Hal had to admit to himself that Yasin's mother made him almost as nervous as she did Mariah.

Summer was drawing to an end, and there was a gray drizzle coming down as they overflew Carcaor.

The great Roche capital was a near-total ruin. Here and there were the enormous craters caused by Kailas' and other dragon squadron leaders' sorcerous casting of pebbles that grew into boulders.

Large parts of the city were blackened, fired by either the dragon raids, the final battle, or the crowds rioting in the madness of defeat and despair.

Hal noticed the other fliers were looking at him, couldn't decipher their expressions, looked away.

Even though the remnants of Roche's army were not

involved with Yasin, still he'd managed to get permission to use their dragon barracks and handlers.

The terms of the surrender forbade the army to have more than two scouting squadrons of dragons, both deployed on the southern border, and a tiny fliers' school, so there was more than room enough in the half-ruined stables for Storm and the other three dragons.

That done, they set out to look for quarters.

It didn't take long, with Yasin's reputation as a hero.

One of Carcaor's main hotels, the huge Muab, although missing one wing, offered Yasin an entire floor for gratis.

They moved in that afternoon, each man getting a somewhat palatial suite.

The main restaurant maintained its grandeur, even though the city's water system was irregular, and sometimes ran brown.

But that certainly didn't bother any of the fliers, used as they were to privation.

The Roche loved heavy meals, and so it was at the Muab. That night, dinner was a river fish course, a wild boar in some sort of sauce, and a many-layered cake. Side dishes included various noodles and peppery sauces.

Sure that he was about to go under, especially after watching the bottomless pit of Farren Mariah gorge himself, Hal decided to go for a walk.

Yasin swore they were probably in no danger, even being Derainians, but all four carried their service daggers at their waists. Hal thought about carrying a sword as well, decided he was just as good at running as dueling.

Carcaor was even more of a ruin up close. Some of the streets were still blocked with rubble from the stonings, and many of the businesses not burnt out were boarded up.

The people were dressed shabbily, their eyes bare of hope.

A few streets still were lit, but not many.

"Damned good idea, this walky, and all," Mariah said to Hal. "As if I wasn't downcast frowncast enough already."

"I think we should be thinking about a drink," Hal said.

"Excellent thought, fearless leader," Mariah said, bowing toward an entrance.

They heard cheers, laughter as they entered, saw a low circular stage, surrounded by tables. The customers were well-dressed, fat, contented-looking, and their women were young and overdressed, or the age of their companions and laden with jewelry.

Yasin frowned, leaned closer to Hal.

"Black marketeers."

Hal had already recognized them for what they were. Deraine had the same sort of greedyguts.

It shouldn't bother him, here in Roche, once an enemy country. Black marketeers did almost as much to lose a war as a hostile army did to win it.

The entertainment was a rather threadbare magician.

They found seats, ordered drinks, jolted at the price of them.

"One and then we're for the cheapside," Calt Beoyard whispered.

Hal nodded.

The magician noted the four, most unlike the other customers.

"Ah," he said, "fresh blood, so a fresh trick."

He thought a minute, then waved his arms in an elaborate pattern, muttering a spell under his breath.

"Summer's almost gone," he said, more loudly. "And spring is just a memory. But something to think on, something to remember . . ."

He extended his hands, palms up.

There was a breath of a fresh wind in the club, blowing away the fumes of stale beer and musky perfume, growing a bit stronger, with the scent of fresh flowers.

It was as if the floor had become newly turned dirt, and flowers of many hues rose up around the tables. There was the chitter of birdsong, and flashes of bright color.

From nowhere, a butterfly appeared over their table, and darted to a safe landing on Yasin's nose.

There was laughter.

Yasin frowned, not finding this worthy of the dignity of a Roche officer, but kept trying to focus on the butterfly, which clung fast.

Mariah gasped with laughter at the cross-eyed Roche.

At last, Yasin's humor, little as it was, caught up with him, and he laughed more loudly than anyone.

Quite suddenly, the illusion vanished.

There was applause, and people cast money at the stage.

"I thank you," the magician said. "And that last took work, so I'll ask your help in what I am going to do next.

"I'm going to bring forth an animal. Your favorite animal.

"Think hard on its breed, its colors.

"The most powerful thought will carry the day."

"Uh-oh," Mariah said. "Don't anybody think of dragons."

The magician stepped off the stage, and waited.

The air shimmered.

And, quite predictably, especially with Farren Mariah's caution, a huge beast emerged on the stage, overfilling it.

The magician darted away, just as the dragon blatted, its tail sweeping across the club.

Hal ducked as the tail came at them, passed through them harmlessly, and the dragon, its breath quite authentic, screamed again.

"We're for the street!" Cabet shouted, and the four made for the exit.

The dragon-wraith looked after them, and honked in a lonely fashion.

They decided to stay with the street for a time.

Streetwalkers were out . . . more than Hal had ever seen before, even in the morally relaxed city of Fovant.

Some were clearly professionals, with a practised patter, and in various costumes, from farm girls to skin-tight black silk.

Others had clearly been driven to whoring by poverty. These women clung to the shadows, and timidly tried to smile when someone caught their eye.

Mariah was the first to notice that the costumed doxies seemed to flock to their own – a street all of milkmaids, another one with female soldiers, a third with garishly painted boys.

"Ah," he said. "The Roche love to be organized in their decadence, don't they?"

Yasin frowned at him.

"I don't understand."

"No," Mariah said. "A man with a butterfiggle on his nose wouldn't."

He started laughing, and Yasin was even more per-
plexed.

"Now, this should be harmless enough," Cabet said. "A
nice puppet theater."

Three schoolgirls went in before them, under the puppets
dangling from strings, and Hal wondered what sort of parents would let their daughters out this late, in this part of
town.

He quickly found out.

The puppets inside were large, almost lifesize, and their
manipulators were hidden behind a curtain.

And they were, for the most part, naked, and performing
as lewd a playlet as anything imaginable.

Hal was surprised that he was still capable of being
shocked.

His shock grew when he realized that there were many
"schoolgirls" sitting around the room, ranging from barely
pubescent to in their twenties, all costumed as if for the
schoolyard.

The male patrons of the room were mostly middle-aged,
many of them with women on their laps.

One girl got up, and sashayed toward the fliers, swinging
her hips.

She "accidentally" flipped her skirt up for an instant,
revealing that she wore nothing underneath.

"That's enow for me," Mariah said. "I think it's past my
bedtime," and he headed back out.

Hal, Cabet and Yasin started to follow him. Hal noticed
that Calt Beoyard was staring at the girl as if hypnotized.

"You . . . you go on," he managed. "I'll catch up to you
later."

Beoyard seemed to have entered another world. Hal shrugged and left.

Outside, Mariah was shaking his head.

"And I thought nothing could get to me," he said. "Those—"

He broke off, seeing an elderly man, wearing the worn uniform of a high-ranking Roche officer, beribboned and medalled, glowering at them, lips pursed, clearly aware of what the puppet show consisted.

"Disgusting," Mariah said, pretending utter shock. "No wonder they lost the war. There's naught in there but former generals."

Yasin didn't find that funny, but the other three did.

The old man flushed, and strode on as if he had a halberd up his ass.

They went back to their hotel, had a nightcap and went to bed.

After due thought the next day, Hal decided that Carcaor's night-time pleasures were a little rich for his blood, although Beoyard kept returning to the puppet show club night after night.

Hal spent most of his time at the stables, taking care of Storm.

Cabet and Mariah frequently joined him.

The hotel filled with recruits to Yasin's unit, some scarred and most experienced, others not much more than schoolboys who'd somehow learned to fly the monsters.

Eventually there were thirty beasts, and twenty fliers signed on, when Yasin decided they had enough to fight, and, without much ceremony, ordered his troops north.

"Autumn's here, and so, instead of heading south, we fly north," Farren said. "You can easy tell we're about sojering."

8

The long flight north was cold, and grew colder. They stopped at cities along the way, and were greeted with adulation.

Hal wondered if Yasin could be that much of a national hero, then found he'd sent riders north, weeks earlier, advising various city fathers of his route.

It seemed a little dishonest to Hal, but he decided that to feel like that was ludicrous. Didn't kings, after all, send criers in front when they visited the countryside?

Remembering what campaigning was and would be like, Kailas relaxed and enjoyed being made much of.

The Derainians, for some odd reason, seemed especially popular, even though they'd been Roche's enemies.

He didn't much like it, though, when some hero-worshippers, obviously in their cups, mumbled about Deraine finally learning what was right, by helping to keep the less-than-men from their borders.

But again, it really didn't matter.

All that did matter was that he retired at night, very full of choice cookery, to a warm, comfortable bed, and it was seldom empty.

What more could a field soldier want?

Yasin caught Farren Mariah casting a spell to predict the forthcoming weather, and thereafter treated Mariah most cautiously.

"He's even more spooky goosey than you are about wizardry," Farren chortled to Hal.

A week and a half after leaving Carcaor, they landed in Trenganu.

It was the rawest of frontier towns. The streets, such as they were, were unpaved, and turned to mudholes any time there was more than a heavy dew. There was one main street, with meandering alleys debouching from it.

Of course, there were no building restrictions, so a stable was next to a church next to an ironmongery.

They called it a city, but it was no more than a small town, with a population, including the expeditionary force, hunters and trappers, of about four thousand. There were no suburbs – Trenganu just stopped at a perimeter of farms, and then there was half-cut secondary timberland to untouched forest.

The close presence of the "natives," "barbarians," "barbs," here on "the edges of nothing," meant almost everyone went armed at all times.

It wasn't that much of an affectation – the natives were known for daring cross-border raids. Come in, hit hard, and pull back with slaves and loot.

Their warriors could run down a horse, especially one with an armored rider, gut the horse, then slit the rider's throat, and loot and strip him, before the animal stopped screaming.

Their magicians weren't much more than witches, but they had the advantage of numbers, of knowing the local herbs and power concentrations, and the Roche had very few magicians with them.

The natives showed no mercy to anyone. Women were ravaged, and the older ones killed, as were all men. Children of both sexes were made into slaves, the males after being hamstrung, to ensure they'd never be fighters if they were ransomed or freed.

The supposedly civilized Roche took their own slaves on the few occasions they could find a "barb" camp.

Yasin had already hired grooms, groundsmen, guards, servants, and the like, who had made the laborious journey north in clattering wagons, and they'd commandeered a drafty hall that had been a farmers' association for the unit headquarters.

The dragons were housed in sheds that had been intended for livestock shows.

The dragon-fliers themselves, though, were given quarters in inns appropriated by Yasin.

One man, a supply warrant, complained about fliers always having it soft, and Yasin hauled him up in front of the entire formation.

"Yes," he hissed, "the fliers are special. And they'll be treated the same as long as we're fighting.

"Because you'll notice that not only do they get all of the glory and all of the comfort, but they do all of the dying, as well."

He drove the lesson home by having the warrant stripped of his uniform, and literally kicked out of the city.

There were even uniforms for the squadron.

Someone – Hal hoped not Yasin – had found dark gray

uniforms that looked like they'd been intended for ushers. But they wouldn't stand out in the field, and that was more important than gilt and glitter, and better still, they were warm.

Trenganu crawled with uniforms, most of local design. But there were more than enough wearing Roche colors for Hal to realize that whatever military limitations the treaty with Sagene and Deraine had called for, the treaty provisions were dead letters.

Some of these men were volunteers, looking for adventure and blood. Others, particularly the more senior ones, were "observers," sent by the Roche government.

And some of the "volunteers" seemed very much part of assorted formations.

But officially, there was only one expeditionary force, led by a General Arbala.

Yasin said he was one of the better commanders from the war, known for leading from the front, yet without getting himself mired in the trivia of a skirmish and losing the battle.

He was young and scarred, and when Hal first saw him, and heard him speak, he reminded him of his late friend, Bab Cantabri.

The thought made him wonder what was going on with his divorce, and with life in general back in Deraine.

But there were more immediate matters to take care of.

Yasin broke the twenty fliers down into four flights of five, making sure there were at least two inexperienced fliers in each group.

"I know," he told Hal, "you flew in groups of three in the war. Too small to be effective if you got hit, too large to be unobtrusive."

Hal decided he disagreed, but didn't care one way or another. He was willing to try Yasin's tactics, so welcomed two novices to his "flight."

The next step was to figure out just exactly what the squadron's mission would be.

Yasin said the dragons would be used to provide intelligence, and not aerial fighting. There didn't seem to be any dragon-riding natives.

At least, not yet.

Cabet worried about whether the barbarians could also be hiring mercenary fliers – there were certainly enough out-of-work dragon-riders between Roche, Sagene and Deraine.

"Not to worry," Farren said. "The natives don't appear to have gold, and there's naught else to trade, except ox fur or hide or whatever they cover themselves with."

"Young slaves," Beoyard suggested.

"But who'd be the buyer?" Hal wondered. "I don't see anybody rolling in silver who's interested in crippled children around here."

No one had an answer, and so Kailas set out, with Yasin's blessing, to find out what Arbala's headquarters really knew about their enemy, the mysterious forest natives.

Almost nothing was the immediate answer. They were bold, big, and bad, which fit almost all enemies worth fighting.

As far as tactics, size of formation, leadership went . . . nothing seemed known. Yasin's unit was working utterly virgin territory.

Having heard stories about how the barbarians treated their prisoners, Kailas found a witch, had her make up doses of fast-acting poison, and found thin neck chains for them to hang on.

There weren't many takers among the fliers.

Most of them, including Hal himself, were self-assured enough to think that they'd never get taken prisoner, or, if they did, that they could somehow escape before they ended up in the torturers' hands.

He put his team aloft, well behind the "lines," such as they were, practising not the expected formation flying, but observation – learning to search the ground for possible ambush sites, small units of men, camouflaged positions, and the like.

Remembering his own first flights in combat, and how virginal he'd been, he took them east and north of Trenganu, into relatively safe territory, looking for barbarians.

The natives helped at first, by volleying arrows up at any dragons they saw carrying men, then learned they evidently meant no harm.

Little by little, his fliers, and the others being trained by Yasin similarly, got as good as they were able without having flown in a fighting war.

The ground formations having been brought into some kind of shape by General Arbala and his officers, the first operation was planned.

It wasn't very spectacular in design – the expeditionary force was ordered to march north-east, looking for natives.

They should have set off at dawn, but it was midmorning of a sunny autumnal day before they left Trenganu.

Yasin's dragon squadron was airborne, flying back and forth over the horsemen and infantrymen.

Hal took his own flight ahead of the forward skirmishers.

Yasin had briefed the fliers that Arbala's plan for this day was no more than a shaking-out of the troops. They would march a certain number of leagues, make camp, then return, via a different route, the next day.

While he'd been talking, he kept glancing, worriedly, at Hal, which Hal couldn't figure out.

Then he realized that Yasin was dreadfully worried that he would be angered – how dare Yasin tell anyone of Hal's rank what to do?

He was about to laugh, then realised that Yasin was putting himself in his place, and that if the situation were reversed, Yasin would be most irked. Then the matter became much less humorous.

But ignoring all the fripperies, it was nice to be in the air. Storm honked in pure glee, diving and darting to and fro, and several of the other dragons seemed equally sportive.

Kailas saw his two novices getting into the spirit of the day, and blasted a warning on his trumpet, pointing down, reminding them this wasn't a lark they were on.

The army was closing on a steep bluff. Hal swooped low over it, and saw, crouched behind boulders, at least twenty of the enemy, waiting in ambush.

He circled back, low over the nearest skirmishers, and blew a warning.

Evidently the riders hadn't been told of Hal's purpose, because the scattered formation didn't change, still keeping its flank to the bluff.

Hal cursed, pondered.

Then he swirled Storm down, and down, bringing him in for a landing just in front of the horsemen.

There was a young officer goggling at him.

"You, dammit!" Hal bellowed. "'Ware your front, sir! Archers in ambush!"

The officer gaped at the bluff, which appeared deserted. "But I've orders—"

"Damn your orders, sir!" Hal shouted, realizing he was sounding very much like Lord Cantabri, and the thought almost made him start laughing.

The officer clearly didn't know what to do.

The situation was resolved by one native, who arched an arrow high that clattered off Storm's armor.

Other bowmen followed suit, and that was enough for the skirmishers.

They rode directly toward the bluff, and three or four were cut down by arrows.

Then the horsemen overrode the archers, who ducked and fled, leaving a couple of bodies behind.

The man leading the skirmishers should have held his troops in place, and sent one man back to the main formation for reinforcements.

That would, should, have meant that no casualties would have been taken.

But the officer would learn that on his own – if he survived the next few encounters.

That evening, Hal was in the stables, burnishing and trimming Storm's talons, when Yasin sought him out.

He had half a smile.

"I have a complaint about you, Lord Kailas."

"From that young idiot."

Young idiot . . . Hal shook his head in amusement. Thinking someone was young, when he was but . . . what? Just turning thirty?

But how old in battle-knowledge?

"Yes," Yasin said. "That young idiot – who happens to be Duke someone's eldest son – went to General Arbala.

"The general told me about it, thinking the matter was a capital jest, and assigned the little duke to ride in the train for a few days to eat dust and learn."

Hal was mildly surprised.

He'd expected Yasin to take him to task, as he'd expected General Arbala to have torn strips off Yasin for letting one of his men dare, dare, to swear at nobility.

This expeditionary force wasn't behaving like a regular army.

Nor did it the next day.

Unfortunately.

Hal had been meandering about the skies, watching the troops move back toward Trenganu, when he saw something interesting.

It was a group of light infantrymen, chasing some barbarian men, killing one here, one there.

It looked, from Kailas's elevation, like men chasing children.

Hal shook his head at the lack of proper perspective, swung lower, and realized, with a sharp shock, that there was nothing wrong with his viewpoint.

The soldiers *were* chasing children, whooping every time they took one down, the attacker pausing to drive a sword into the youngster's back.

Hal should have minded his own business, if for no other reason than that he had certainly killed his share of women and children, stoning cities.

But he didn't, coming in for a skittered landing, and sliding off Storm in front of the pack.

"Halt, you!"

The lead soldier called an obscenity, lifted his sword.

Hal put a crossbow bolt between his feet, and the man slid to a stop.

"We don't kill babies in this army," he shouted.

The men looked at him sullenly.

"They killed Barthus!" one tried.

"Then Barthus must've deserved killing," Hal said. "For not being much of a soldier, letting a child attack him."

"They ain't proper kids, but demons," an older man said. "Learn killing from their mothers' milk."

There was a clamor of agreement.

Hal glanced over his shoulder, to see Farren Mariah orbiting just over his head.

There was no sign of the children.

They seemed to have vanished into a low, brush-covered hillside.

"Get back to the column," he ordered.

There was no point in arguing with a superior officer, who'd already spoiled the game.

Muttering, the men obeyed his order.

Hal, feeling very much the self-righteous do-gooder, climbed back aboard Storm, and prodded him into a take-off run.

They lifted away over that hillside.

As they did, a stone hurtled up, almost taking Hal in the leg.

That figured.

That evening, they came back to Trenganu.

Yasin gave the squadron the day off.

For the next day, Hal planned a critique of what had happened, which should sit well with a hangover, then time in the stables with the dragons.

But it didn't work out that way.

He was just coming out of the mess tent, trying not to think about the watery eggs, fried bread, and half-cured ham he'd eaten, remembering other, superior meals on the trip north, when he saw smoke rising beyond the city, to the south-west.

He wondered, decided to go see, and, even if it was unimportant, to make his flight aware that nothing in war could ever be planned.

Keeping track of how long it took, Hal ordered his men into the air.

The two new Roche did as best they could – Hal's Derainians were quite used to days that started like this, as were their dragons.

In ten minutes, they were in the air, the last storesman clattering crossbow bolts into the quivers tied to the dragons' carapaces as they waited to take off.

Hal had issued no orders other than to take the five-fingers formation on takeoff that Yasin preferred.

They were out of the pawky outskirts of Trenganu, and over partially cleared forest in minutes, homing on the smoke.

It came from a farming estate – a group of buildings clustered together for mutual protection, their fields spreading on all sides.

Beyond the houses were the barns, and two of these were burning.

There were bodies scattered in the central farmyard, and, even at this height, Hal heard women's screams. He saw half a dozen natives dragging farm women toward a hay rick, which they evidently intended for a bedroom.

Hal remembered that farm worker's story, back on Yasin's estates, and sharply tapped the back of Storm's head.

The dragon obediently went into a dive.

Hal blasted twice on his trumpet for the others to follow him.

He didn't know, didn't care, how many native raiders were down there.

He brought Storm out of the dive just above the ground, and came in over the farmyard.

Storm didn't need orders.

His talons reached out, took a pair of barbarians, and hurled them against the ground, as his fangs shredded another pair.

Hal brought him back in a sharp bank, as Storm's tail lashed across the ground not a dozen feet below.

From an outbuilding ran men, farmers, emboldened by the dragon strike, attacking the natives with flails, scythes, a sword here and there, pitchforks.

A bearded patriarch was grabbed from behind by a dagger-waving warrior.

Hal put a crossbow bolt neatly into the man's armpit. As he did so, he heard a warning shout, and Cabet, reins clenched in his teeth, crossbow aiming, almost ran into Storm.

The other Derainians had done this sort of thing before. They came in hard, and the battle swirled over the farm-yard.

Then the natives broke, running, and Storm went after them, gleefully tearing at them as they went.

It was certain death if they looked back, but they did, terrified of the pursuing horror.

Forest loomed, and Hal pulled Storm up. The dragon whined in protest at losing some of his prey.

They flew back to the farm, and this time, Hal brought Storm down.

Storm folded his wings, and Hal went looking for barbarians.

One broke out of a hut, and fired an arrow at the dragon, which bounced harmlessly off his carapace.

Storm took the man in his jaws, and neatly bit him in half, then spat him out.

A barbarian, wounded, stumbled out, dazed, eyes wide in terror, and one of the farmers spitted him on a pitchfork.

Another was trying to run, and a handful of women were on him, clawing, kicking. He went down, rolled, and a very fat woman dropped a small grinding stone on his head.

Then there was nobody left to kill, and nothing but the moans of the wounded Roche.

Mariah landed his dragon beside Storm, and slid out of the saddle, as one of the two new fliers did the same.

The new man was gazing at Hal with worshipful eyes.

Mariah shattered the mood.

"You're starting again, aren't you?" he said, angrily. "Playing hero . . . and you promised me."

Hal, breathing hard, was still looking for men to kill.

His breathing slowed, and he managed a smile.

"I'm sorry, Farren."

"I remember before," Mariah said. "Got me all speared and bloody and nasty.

"Don't be doing that any more, fearless leader. Or I'll put a spell of . . . of creepy spidgers in your drawers."

Kailas noted the shock on the young flier's face, and started laughing.

"Gods-damned glory-dog," Mariah growled.

9

The rescue of the farmers was made much of in Trenganu. There was talk of medals for Hal's flight.

He wanted none, having more than his share already.

"We could hold out for prize money," suggested Mariah, who also had his share of geegaws.

Hal didn't need any of that, and spent a morose hour wondering what, exactly, he did want.

Of course, the two Roche in the flight were ecstatic about the turn of events.

"Enjoy it now," Mariah said. "The only reason we're being lauded & 'plauded is first it's early in the war, which is always the best time to make your name fame, and second because nothing much is happening right now.

"In theory," he said, "there shouldn't be, either. We should be taking up winter quarters. But five against a goat we'll be parading out on a campaign any day now.

"Why'd you think General Arbarbabarbarala had us fartle out and then back?

"Just because we need a little exercise?

"Believe that, and I'll sell you valuababble real estate in Fovant."

Mariah was right.

Yasin was called in by the general, and told to make his squadron ready for a winter campaign, to march north along the coast, where there were reported barbarian villages to take and hold.

Yasin was passing enthusiastic to Hal.

"That'll push the barbs back to where they're supposed to be, and let our people come in and open up the wilderness."

"Why does Roche need any more land than what it's got?" Hal wondered. "Seems that the war left a lot of the land open, unworked."

"By next generation," Yasin said, "we'll have filled all that up, and be crying for new land for our people."

Hal almost asked if that wasn't the excuse the late Queen Norcia had used for starting the last war, but kept his mouth shut. If Roche decided they wanted all that tundra that lay to the north, let them take it, and contend with the oxen and the wild dragons.

He busied himself making sure that Yasin's supply section was buying winter coats, high boots, stable blankets for the dragons, all the things that generals didn't seem to think of until the first winter storm.

And seasons changed quickly this far to the north.

Which brought the first calamity.

The expeditionary force headquarters had been located in one of the city's few great houses. It was built of wood, and strangely styled after some of the stone mansions Hal had seen the ruins of in Carcaor.

Yasin had been kept late at a planning session, and was still preoccupied when he left, around midnight.

There'd been a rainstorm, turning into hail, and then cold winds.

The water on the wooden steps had frozen.

Yasin was pulling on his coat, a bit off-balance, when he came down the steps.

He slipped, tried to recover, and pinwheeled down the flight.

Soldiers came to help him up, but his scream made them stop.

He was barely conscious, and had Hal sent for.

By the time he arrived, Yasin had been given herbs and a spell, and was fighting to stay awake.

"What a bastardly thing," he growled, pointing at splints on his chest and legs. "They say I'll be wearing these for at least four months, and want me to go back south, for more expert care.

"Afraid I'll lose my leg, they are. Which I surely won't let them take."

Hal waited.

"So I'm out of any campaign until spring, gods-dammit!

"Lord Kailas, will you take over the squadron? You're about the only one I really trust. And I'll try to recruit more fliers and dragons for you."

There really wasn't any choice.

No doubt they could find another dragon-flier or, worse yet, put in some cavalry sort. Hal had seen what that produced.

Feeling very unhappy, he nodded.

"Yes. I'll take command."

And that was the last he saw of Yasin.

Later, Hal was very glad to have seen the back of him.

General Arbala was most concerned that Kailas could handle the job. Hal explained, trying not to sound superior, that he had handled squadrons of squadrons in the war, and doubted he'd have any troubles.

All that was necessary was to find the barbarians, and let the general and the forward elements of the expeditionary force know.

The natives hadn't any dragons of their own, and so far their magic wasn't very potent.

Arbala's strategy was quite simple, with no subtleties kept hidden from the common troops – march north-east along the coast, striking at every barbarian camp they encountered. Drive the savages back north, with tales of the valor of the Roche, so they'd never leave their damned wasteland again.

Hal came out of the meeting somewhat less than impressed with the general than before. He might have been a fighter, but he didn't seem much of a thinker.

And battles may be won by fighters.

But intelligence and cunning are what wins wars.

His opinion was reinforced when a light cavalry unit was sent out on a vague patrol to find out "what's out there," without a more concrete plan, or, worse, any troops detailed for their backup.

They encountered a native patrol who, seemingly, panicked at the sight of the brave Roche cavalrymen, and fled, conveniently into broken country.

The cavalry went in hot pursuit.

About four times their strength was lying in wait. The

cavalry, hit hard, retreated to the nearest hilltop, and sent a pair of riders for help.

Amazingly, one horseman made it back to Trenganu, and bleated for support.

But it was getting late, and no fool would move out of the city by night.

At first light, a handful of heavy cavalry went out, with banners and bugles.

Corpses need neither, and that was what met the relief expedition. All of the light horsemen were dead, creatively mutilated.

General Arbala swore, tears in his eyes, on his own sword, that the Roche would revenge the dead.

But that didn't seem to bring any of them back.

Fall brought rains and mud, seldom freezing, over the axles of some of the wagons.

The expeditionary force would have to wait until the first thorough freeze, when the weather would be better suited for modern war.

In the meantime, the scribes descended on Trenganu, entranced with the idea of a Derainian war hero fighting for Roche.

Hal managed to duck most of these awestruck fools.

But there was one he couldn't.

Aimard Quesney, dragon-flier and one-time war objector, showed up at the tiny room Hal used as an office, with a covering letter from Sir Thom Lowess saying Quesney was his representative.

His huge mustaches were larger than ever, and he seemed as morally sure of himself as when Hal had sat over him in a court-martial.

"I convinced Lowess to write that letter," Quesney said, "and I'll write something in the style I know he wants when I get back to Deraine.

"But all that's piffle, and hardly the reason I came east."

Hal waited.

"You did, as you told me at the time, save my life, although being adjudged insane may not be the prettiest way to do it.

"But I still owe you greatly.

"Your man, Manus, found me, just as I was about to enter the priesthood.

"At first, I had no intention of re-establishing contact with you . . . it's very clear our paths aren't meant to be coincidental.

"But I owe you, and, when I heard you'd taken service with Roche, I had to find you, and, perhaps, return a little of the favor.

"First, though, I approached your advocate, and was told your divorce is final, and your estates are doing very well."

"Thank you for taking the time," Hal said.

"I did it because I wasn't sure how I was going to say what I'm intending.

"But what the advocate told me wasn't of any particular help.

"Lord Kailas, have you gone completely off your head?"

Hal was taken aback. No one had talked to the Dragonmaster like that since . . . since, well, the last time he'd had a conversation with Farren Mariah.

The situation struck him as funny, and he started laughing.

He got up and went to the sideboard, poured a shot of

the raw spirits the people of Trenganu hopefully called brandy, and took it to Quesney.

"Unless you've gotten so pure you don't indulge in anything?"

Quesney took the glass.

"In Roche – and with this abysmal weather – I drink like a watering dragon."

He knocked the glass back, held it out for a refill as Hal filled one for himself.

"I didn't expect that reaction," Quesney said. "I thought you'd be too full of your rank ... sorry, your former rank ... and would have me tossed out of here on my ass."

Hal sat back down.

"All right," he said. "So I'm a fool.

"Explain."

"I think," Quesney said, "that you've gotten so in love with war, with fighting, that you'll take anything that promises excitement.

"That's a good way to get yourself killed, Kailas."

Hal nodded reluctantly.

"Breaking Yasin out of prison – yes, the street stories are very explicit – was bad enough.

"But helping these sorry excuses that call themselves Roche to grab real estate is pretty raw, you know. Hardly worthy of a great war hero and such."

Hal sat up, eyes wide.

"It was my understanding that the *barbarians* are the ones grabbing land."

"Which was theirs in the first place," Quesney said. "Before the war, the Roche were moving north toward the tundra, seizing land the natives had traditionally thought their own, even though it was kept open for hunting, not planted and plowed.

"The Roche stopped their land grab for the most part during the war, but now the old fever for living space has taken them once more."

"I had a letter from a man named Garadice who went north, looking for dragons," Hal said. "He told me the natives were moving south."

"Probably," Quesney agreed. "It gets cold up there, they tell me. And if the Roche are being their usual lovable selves and grabbing everything they can, why should the natives not try to get back some of the stolen land?

"Don't believe me," he said. "Ask around."

"I shall," Hal said. "Now that you've carried your message of woe and stupidity, would you like to hang around the squadron? It might remind you of the old days."

"It might," Quesney said, finishing his drink. "That's what I'm afraid of.

"No. I've done what I said I would, and given you a warning, not about getting yourself killed, but about losing your soul. I'll get the next fishing smack back west, toward Paestum, and then to Deraine."

"And your priesthood?"

Quesney nodded, started for the door.

"You know," he said, "I'm sort of sorry that I changed, or else that things did around us.

"I might have liked serving under you, on a squadron, at one time."

He shook his head.

"Thereby proving that the first loss you have as a dragon-flier is what little sense the gods gifted you with."

*

The army might have been waiting for the weather to change, but not Hal or his dragons. He took two flights out a day. Not at regular intervals, remembering the idiocy of a certain, now deceased, squadron commander, who used to send his dragons out like clockwork, so the enemy simply hid under a tree at the appointed hours, then continued on with their tasks.

The flights went out at roughly dawn and dusk.

Each of the new fliers was given a chance to lead a five finger flight – Hal kept Yasin's formations, since the squadron had begun by using them.

When they came back, each flier was mercilessly grilled about what he had seen, and what went unobserved.

Hal frequently sent one flight out after another, then gave the two formations a chance to compare notes.

And he regularly led not only his own flight, but each of the others, evaluating his men carefully.

He wondered why there weren't any women with the dragons, and decided that either the Roche men were stupid in ignoring potential talent, or, more likely, that Roche women had more sense than to want to tootle around on a monster's back when icicles hung from its carapace.

He always tried to approach the enemy in a direction they weren't expecting, such as a dogleg out to sea from Trenganu, turning north-east for a time, then circling back over the lines, such as they were.

He'd barely taken off one dawn when Cabet, who was flying point, blasted a signal at him and pointed down.

They were just over the beach, and the Northern Sea's waves crashed sullenly below.

Rolling in the surf were the bodies of three dragons.

Hal took Storm lower, flew slowly over the corpses.

They'd been dead for a time, and the seabirds had been at them.

Storm bleated unhappily.

Kailas supposed he didn't like being reminded of his mortality any more than a human did.

These dragons had been sorely wounded, torn and gouged, and the wounds looked to be some months old.

Hal remembered dragons, seen from the battlements of Khiri's castle, below on the water with their wings furled over their bodies, heads tucked out of sight, looking like so many paper boats, being carried from the unknown west by the currents.

Many of them were injured, or young, and behaved as if they were fleeing something.

He wondered again what monsters had sent them into flight, monsters worse than the ominous dragons themselves. Demons, perhaps.

But no one had ever offered a clue.

He pulled Storm up, and the flight went on with its mission.

Three days later, as snow stubbornly refused to fall, although it was freezing, and Hal was very glad he'd chivvied the supply sections for proper warm clothing, they saw something quite unbelievable.

He had led a deep penetration out, and was perhaps two days' flight above Trenganu, flying just a bit inland, over rolling scrub forest.

He was looking down, and caught, in the corner of his eye, movement below.

He looked more closely, saw nothing.

He signaled for his flight to fly in a single line, and took them low.

He was in front, Farren Mariah had the rear.

Four dragons passed over the area without incident, then someone below must have been driven to rashness, and three arrows came up, missing Mariah by yards.

Hal was ready to circle back to see exactly what enemy forces lay below, when he saw, on a hilltop, what looked like an encampment, tents of brown cloth, matching the landscape.

Closer, and he saw men, around smokeless fires.

He chanced going lower, and a javelin came up, touched Storm's forward leg, fell back.

Hal took his flight back up, in a circle, while he shouted orders.

Then they dove back down again, ignoring the arrows, counting the enemy.

"How many barbs did you see?" General Arbala's chief of staff asked.

"I'm not sure," Hal said. "I'd guess about a thousand, maybe two.

"And one hill back was another group of them, maybe a little larger.

"We tried a sweep due east, found three more clusters, tribes maybe."

Arbala looked skeptical.

"We've never heard of the natives grouping up like that," he said.

The chief of staff shook his head.

"Not at all."

One of Arbala's officers laughed. "If they are dumb

enough to knot up, they'll be all the easier to kill, now won't they?"

Arbala joined his laughter.

"Spoken like a true firebrand. And you're exactly right. And even if they are there, which I frankly doubt, how long, with the winter coming on, will they be able to hold?

"Savages are savages, and that's why we Roche rule the land!

"In less than a week we'll be ready to take them on . . . and if they want to stand around and wait, so much the better!"

Hal kept a frozen smile on his face, got out of Arbala's headquarters.

Back at the hall, he assembled the squadron.

"I want every man prepared to move within an hour's notice. That means packs ready, everything not in use in the wagons.

"Every flier is to keep an emergency pack, with rations, water, spare clothes, and a meal of dried meat for the dragons, at hand at all times."

Calt Beoyard came up to him.

"What are you expecting, sir?"

"Everything. Nothing," Hal answered honestly.

Hal feared that the natives might be laying huge ambushes, waiting for the expeditionary force to move out of Trenganu, and memorized what maps there were that showed what lay immediately beyond the town.

His strategic predictions were quite wrong.

Four days later, the barbarians moved first, and came out of the forests, wave after wave of them, with fire and the ax, intending to destroy Trenganu and everyone in it.

10

They came just at false dawn, having silently moved close to Trenganu in the night, in the rain. The sentries weren't expecting an attack, and it was far easier to crouch by a picket fire than walk the rounds.

The outposts and outer guards died to a man, and the natives pressed their attack.

The first Roche out of their barracks were cut down, and then the shouts of battle and men dying roused the town.

General Arbala's staff ran for their posts.

Which was just what the barbarians wanted.

No one ever knew how they figured out where the command center was: if it was magic, a spy among the "tame" natives, or careful reconnaissance.

But earlier that morning, a hand-picked team of barbarians had slipped through the lines, and hidden in one of Trenganu's abandoned shacks.

Seconds after the general arrived at the center, so did the natives.

They slashed their way through the still half-asleep sentries, killing as they went.

Arbala, his entire staff, and a good percentage of his commanders, as well as more than half of the observers from Roche's army, died in the first few minutes of the battle.

Hal rolled out of his bunk, his mind still asleep, but his well-trained body grabbing for a sword and his pants, wondering with part of his mind why men were so afraid of being naked.

He stuffed his feet into boots, and, bare-chested, ran out of his office, his first thought of the dragons.

They were doing very nicely.

Hal never knew if the natives who went for the dragon stables had been detailed, or were just attacking anything that moved.

It was a very bad mistake.

The barbarians had crashed in the doors of the sheds used for the animals.

Storm, more battle-experienced than most dragons, saw unfriendly men, with weapons.

His long neck snaked out, and he caught two of them in his jaws, and crushed them.

The natives stood frozen in panic at what they'd roused, and Storm's great tail lashed and took three more down.

The rest turned and ran, into the swords of the on-rushing fliers.

There was a brief skirmish, and one flier was down, as were five barbarians.

Somewhere in the mêlée, Hal lost two more fliers, but

then his men were strapping saddles on their mounts, and the dragons were thudding in their takeoff run through the door of the barn.

Storm was angry, wanting to stay on the ground, wanting more of these men who'd disturbed his sleep. Hal wouldn't let him, shouted him into the takeoff.

Hal saw running men, both barbarians in their brown, and men in uniform, and screaming women and children. A wedge of Roche broke through to the dragon sheds, just as Storm lifted into the air.

There were lit torches, and hayricks, and then houses on Trenganu's main street caught fire.

Smoke boiled, and Hal banked back, over the town.

There was chaos below, knots of men fighting, other men running, either toward or away from battle.

There were bodies scattered in the mucky streets, and more barbarians surging forward.

Hal saw a formation of natives, and, behind a barn, about a company of Roche, unaware of the natives, wavering, about to break.

He forced Storm down into a slithering landing in a mudwallow, and was off the dragon.

"You men," he bellowed, "where's your officer?"

"Dead, sir," somebody called back, and Hal noted there was still some discipline left if they could remember to use rank.

"Come on, then," he called, knowing that they wouldn't attack without a leader.

A burly sergeant moved toward him, then another, and then the men were dashing around the barn.

A native screamed when he saw the Roche formation, and then it was a free-for-all. There was a nocked arrow being pointed at Hal, then a spear grew out of the barbarian's chest, bloody point jutting forward.

Hal returned the compliment by blocking an axman aside, spitting him through the ribs, and kicking his sword free.

Another native came in, shouting incoherently, with a spiked club.

Hal knelt, came up as the club started down, and the man's guts spilled over his sword hand, blade buried to the hilt in his attacker's stomach.

He broke free, parried a man's spear thrust with his own spear, finished him off . . . and then there were no natives to kill.

Someone – Hal never remembered who – told him about Arbala's death.

It didn't mean anything. Hal was slipping into battle frenzy.

A woman, screaming, ran toward him, a child in her arms.

An arrowhead spitted her neck, and she splashed down into the mire.

"Let's go," Hal shouted. "Kill them! Kill them all!"

They ran toward the town's center, broke out into Trenganu's main street, saw a column of natives, and attacked.

The barbarians hesitated, volleyed arrows, and ran.

Hal went after them, caught up with one, and brained him with the pommel of his sword.

Other men were coming out of sidestreets, forming on Hal's men, without orders, and they pushed forward.

Hal heard a forlorn blatting, looked up, saw Storm overhead, then three other dragons came from nowhere, Mariah and the other Derainians.

Their dragons, better or more lethally trained than Yasin's, needed little guidance, and swooped low, talons reaching, tails whipping, into the back of the barbarian formation, and scythed through the natives.

This time they broke for good, and ran back toward the forest.

Panic took them, and the Roche were on their heels, killing as they went.

Hal had a moment of hope, thinking they'd driven them out of Trenganu for good, then another wave of natives, screaming defiance, came out of the brush toward them.

Hal, giving a needless order, shouted for his men to fall back, not to go in pursuit.

They were already moving back, back into Trenganu's center.

But, and Hal felt a moment of pride and hope, they weren't running, but retreating grimly, slowly, well-trained, experienced soldiers.

There were other men and women with weapons, or overturning carts to block the streets.

Hal wiped blood – not his own, thankfully – from his forehead, had a few seconds to take stock.

As far as anyone knew, he was the senior officer surviving. If any of the "observers" had greater rank, they knew better than to assume command of a disaster.

Kailas muttered an obscenity, then grinned as he thought of Aimard Quesney, who would probably be doubled up in hysterical laughter if he knew the plight Hal had gotten himself into.

The town around him was in flames, wooden buildings exploding, sending balks of timber spinning.

Across the square, he saw civilians, some wounded, some trying to treat the wounded.

There were others, standing, waiting, hopelessness large in their eyes.

At least, he thought, this godsdamned uniform is so drab nobody's running to me screaming for a solution.

So what are you going to do now, Kailas?

Hal spoke the only answer he knew half-aloud, looking up as a disconsolate Storm swooped overhead.

"All right. If we stay here, we'll die. We're going to fight our way out."

11

Kailas was waiting for the second wave of natives to overwhelm the surviving Roche in Trenganu, but they hesitated for a time, perhaps a little shocked at how many casualties they'd taken in the first assault.

Hal didn't care why. He seized the moment, grabbed armed men who looked like they weren't in the depths of panic, snapped orders.

Find ten men you trust, and go back through the town. Herd all the civilians into the square. Bring dry foodstuffs, blankets, warm clothes.

We'll march out at midday.

He chose other men to try to hold a perimeter against the natives when they attacked again.

Farren Mariah was there, and Hal put him in charge of the remaining fliers. Cabet in theory outranked him, but Hal utterly trusted Mariah, and in the madness he wasn't going to take time to give detailed orders. Besides, he had another mission for the ex-flight leader.

Mariah was to make sure the fliers had their emergency supplies, and the unit's wagons were ready to move.

Dump all supplies except weaponry and what was edible, and have the squadron's wagon-masters pick up the lame, wounded, halt, and elderly.

Other troops were ordered to collect anything on wheels, and anything from mules to oxen to horses to pull them.

He told Cabet to take a Roche flier as companion, take off and head east, toward the ruins of Lanzi, the nearest outpost of the Roche army, and get a rescue in motion.

Quite suddenly it was midday.

He put that burly sergeant, whose name was Aescendas, and that company he'd briefly led, in charge of the rear-guard, told him that if the men broke and ran he'd shove his sword up every one of their asses, and then think about serious punishment.

The sergeant started to laugh, saw the cold warrior look in Hal's eyes, nodded, and was gone.

An hour later, the survivors of Trenganu moved off, keeping as close to the coast as possible.

Behind them, the flames of the city rose high.

And then it started snowing.

The retreat on that first day was like wading through quicksand, with a nameless monster at your heels.

The barbarians eventually finished looting Trenganu, and started the pursuit.

The only good things that developed were that the rear-guard stood fast, not fleeing, but falling back slowly with the retreat; and the natives now had a superstitious fear of the dragons.

Each time Farren or another dragon-rider sent his mount diving on the barbarians, they scattered and fled.

But Hal knew that wouldn't last very long.

He wished he had a magician who could produce some sort of spell, like his pebble-to-boulder incantation that had ruined the Roche cities. Or firebottles.

But they had no bottles, and Farren said he hadn't the slightest idea how such a spell could be cast, and even if he knew how, he doubted he had powers enough to do any good.

So they marched on, as the light snowfall continued.

In late afternoon Hal ordered the wagons circled, and all able-bodied men, and the armed civilian women, to report to the perimeter.

He wanted to keep his fighters at full alertness, but knew better, and let half his troops sleep at a time.

The natives tried two half-hearted attacks during the night, both easily driven off.

Hal found himself crouched at a tiny warming fire hidden in a fold of the ground, next to an old man who'd armed himself with a native's bow, with a handful of arrows stuck in his belt.

"Y'know," the man said, trying to make some kind of conversation, "tomorrow, about midday, we should pass by my gran'sire's farm."

Hal made a polite noise, not caring.

"I remember growing up on it, right on the fringes of the frontier."

Interest came, as Kailas remembered what Quesney had told him.

"Then more settlers came, pushed past us, built Trenganu, and started letting daylight in the swamp, as they put it.

"And killing off barbs, every time they tried to claim woods back, after we'd rightfully took it with force of arms.

"That was the key marker on Gran's place – we had iron stakes in the ground, with the heads of any barb that we came across.

"Made sure they knew where their place was, and that they wouldn't *dare* mess with any Roche."

So much, Hal thought, for noble causes. The Roche *were* grabbing land, the natives fighting for what had been theirs.

Things like that didn't create heroic ballads, not without time passing and the villainous songwriters victorious, which didn't look like it would happen this time around.

The next dawn, as the column was forming up, Hal took Storm out, flying back the way they'd come.

It had stopped snowing during the night, so the bodies of those who'd fallen in the staggering march were still exposed, lying here and there.

Hal didn't get lower than he had to, not wanting to see how many of them were civilians, women, children.

He flew on, over the ruins of Trenganu.

There were still barbarians looking for something to claim in the smoldering city.

They shouted insults up at Hal, ran to cover when Storm swooped on them.

He flew back along the line of march. Not many people looked up as Storm screamed; they were too busy concentrating on the next step through the slush.

Hal put Storm in the air, unridden, and the dragon took charge of the three monsters whose fliers had been killed in Trenganu.

Hal moved back and forth in the column, chivvying someone here, encouraging an oldster there.

He passed a tiny cart, drawn by a pair of goats, with two children aboard, perhaps five and six.

Hal started to ask where their parents were, saw their tear-runneled cheeks, thought better of it, went on.

The natives dogged the line of march, swooping in now and again to take down a straggler who even Sergeant Aescendas couldn't keep on his or her feet.

They laid ambushes in front of the column, but these were spotted by the experienced settlers, or seen from the air.

Hal wondered, not without thanks, why the natives were suddenly behaving like raw recruits.

He guessed maybe their best war leaders had been killed in the initial assault on Trenganu.

"Naw," Sergeant Aescendas explained while the two were sharing a bowl of barley, crudely ground, cooked with a beefbone and some roadside herbs, "people fight best when they're on their own ground."

"But this used to be theirs," Hal said.

"Not for a generation or so," Aescendas said. "Time enough to forget.

"I've been fighting these bastards most of my life, and got no damned illusions about what they can and can't do.

"First time I went scouting with some of our peaceful barbs," he said, "we were camped on a hilltop, and I sent one of them out hunting.

"I watched him go out, zigging here, zagging there.

"He killed something or other that was potworthy, and I spotted him coming back.

"He was on the same damned track, ziggety-zaggety,

he'd gone out on, even though he could see our hill and could have come home directly.

"Barbs aren't the stealthy woodsmen city people think they are. They've just got a damned great memory for the terrain.

"And on this ground, they're as blind as we would have been if we'd gone out beyond Trenganu."

The wagons were full.

But the temperature dropped, and people on the wagons died.

Their bodies were unceremoniously cast into the ditch beside the narrow track, and there was room for more to ride.

They had jarred or dried rations, enough to let everyone feel hunger pangs, and hay and what could be grazed for the animals.

Some of those died too, and fed the dragons.

Hal tried to remember how many days they'd been on the march – four, five, more? – couldn't.

Each day started with his morning flight, as much for morale when the Trenganu survivors saw a dragon overhead and felt protected, as anything else.

Then he landed, and walked.

There'd be a rest stop somewhere around the middle of the day, and some sort of tasteless food, then they'd go on until almost dusk, make camp, eat, stand guard, sleep, wake, and march on.

The snow was almost continuous, and twice the column had to retrace its steps to find the narrow dirt road it was following.

Hal tried not to notice the bodies, frozen in the night, or killed by natives slipping close to the perimeter.

This nightmare, he lied to himself, couldn't last for ever.

Hal was treating himself to a whore's bath in a basin full of melted snow, while the column slowly moved past him. He was trying not to think how much he wanted a full-size bath, and then a day's uninterrupted sleep in a feather mattress piled high with down blankets, when a voice spoke beside him.

"Sir? We have a problem."

He turned, saw a small boy and a smaller girl.

"Yes," he said, trying to sound benevolent, and not snarl at having his daydream interrupted.

"One of our goats died," the girl said solemnly.

Then he remembered who they were.

The boy's face wrinkled, as if he was about to cry. He looked at the girl, put on a stiff upper lip, only slightly marred by a loud snuffle.

"We don't know what to do," the boy confessed.

"We tried to make him get up, but he wouldn't," the girl added.

"We've got to take the wagon with us," the boy said. "That's all that's left after our parents . . . went away."

This was absurd. There were perhaps five thousand civilians, and three or four thousand soldiers he'd taken responsibility for on this march.

He didn't have the time, or the energy, to worry about these two children, other than having someone find room for them on a wagon somewhere in the column.

But it suddenly became the most important thing in his world.

He poured the water out, toweled himself dry with his shirt that no longer made him wrinkle his nose at its filth, and went looking.

He found a pair of very bedraggled donkeys, and paid an absurd amount out of his own pocket for the beasts. The animals' owner swore this was costing him his dinner for the evening.

Hal almost took the beasts at swordpoint, but kept his self-control.

The donkeys were hitched to the wagon, the surviving goat tied to the back, and Hal handed the reins to the boy.

The girl looked at the angle the cart's deck now sat at, considered the donkeys, started to say something.

The boy shook his head.

"Thank you, sir," the girl said, instead of complaining.

"You are very welcome."

From then on, the boy and girl became a talisman for Hal. They had to live to reach the Roche positions.

And if they didn't?

He didn't know.

The column staggered into open country that had been cut, settled and planted.

But the farmhouses were burnt, the barns ruined, and the winter fields barren.

Men and women went out and scavenged the ruins, their need greater than the farmers who'd abandoned the holdings.

The sight of what had once been civilization sparked the column to a slightly faster pace, and for once, the natives didn't harry them.

Until late that afternoon, when they crested a rise.

Spread out in the small valley in front of them was rank after rank of the barbarians, waiting for the final battle to be joined.

Someone behind Hal screamed, and a harsh voice reproved her.

The response seemed perfectly reasonable to Hal.

He wished he were braver – if he were, he could just leap on Storm's back, gather the other three Derainians and leave these damned Roche exploiters to their doom.

But he couldn't.

And he wasn't exactly a general who might look at these serried ranks of barbarians, deduce a battle plan, and sweep the field.

The refugees took some kind of formation automatically, with fighters in the front and flanks, and the civilians in the middle.

Everyone was looking to Hal for an idea.

Then shouting came, and a man strode out of the native ranks across the valley. He was very big, very muscled, and wore his hair long, braided behind him.

Behind him came a man with a shield, and a very short, very stout barbarian wearing furry robes.

A wizard?

The big man shouted something.

A challenge.

Maybe.

The man waited for a short time, then shouted again.

It might have been a call to surrender.

The man waved a captured long two-handled sword, and laughed, sneeringly.

A definite challenge.

Or so Hal guessed.

He wished he could jump on Storm's back, take off, and murder the bastard.

But he'd probably dart back into the native ranks the minute he saw the dragon lumber forward.

Hal sighed, walked back to Storm, and took his crossbow and a magazine of bolts from where they were tied to the dragon's carapace.

Keeping the crossbow at his side, he walked out in front of the ragged formation of Roche, and drew his sword.

The great native warrior shouted something, laughed again.

Holding his sword in front of him, as a challenge, Hal walked forward.

"You need some backup?" It was Farren.

"No," Hal said, not turning. "Or, rather, yes. But you don't look like a division of the king's guards.

"Get ready to get the dragons in the air. You'll know when, and what to do."

Operating on the assumption that the man in furs was a magician, Hal advanced on the three natives, forcing his mind into thoughts of swordplay. Wizards couldn't read minds. Or so they claimed piously.

The warrior waiting for him was offered the shield, but disdained it, since Hal wasn't carrying one.

There was about forty feet between the two men.

Hal decided that was far enough.

Moving faster than he thought he ever had in his life, he tossed his sword aside, brought up the crossbow, slid the grip back then forward, dropped a bolt into the track and knelt.

This close, it was a sure shot.

Hal put the bolt into the throat of the magician, who screamed, spun and died.

The warrior shouted, most likely something about Hal's dishonesty, and ran forward, lifting his sword.

He'd never seen a repeating crossbow, and, when planning his great gesture, no doubt figured he'd have more than enough time to cut down any archer, any crossbow-man.

Hal slid the grip back, forward, put his second bolt into the warrior's stomach.

He half-turned, dropped to his knees, pulling uselessly at the bolt, which was buried to the fletching.

There was a great cry of outrage from the barbarian ranks.

Hal paid no attention as he reloaded, and shot the shield-bearer in the face.

Another bolt went into the warrior's chest, and he flopped back, dead.

Hal was running back toward his own ranks. He heard the shout of natives behind him, the crack of leathery wings ahead, and Farren Mariah and the other dragon-fliers rose from the knot of Roche and soared toward him, just off the ground.

Third back was Storm, and Farren was shouting at the dragon.

Storm flared his wings, touched down in the muck for an instant, and Hal swung up into the saddle.

Storm took off, and the flight of dragons attacked the natives head-on.

Crossbow bolts spat out, and the dragon claws were reaching.

Arrows came at them, bounced off the carapaces or the

dragons' armored faces, and then the beasts struck the barbarian formation, claws rending, tails lashing.

The surprise of their champion's death and the attack by the monsters was too much.

The center of the native formation crumbled, and men were running.

Hal brought Storm up and around, saw the Roche were attacking, and then, once more, the refugees were stumbling forward, a dirty, freezing, unstoppable mass.

The next day, they were in still-inhabited land, and armed farmers began joining them, and behind them came servants and women carrying an endless amount of food.

The refugees of the Trenganu massacre gobbled the food, poured home-brewed beer down their throats, and listened to the chatter of victory.

But few of them could smile, and no one loosened his tight grip on his weapon, nor did their eyes stop sweeping the woods around them for an ambush.

Hal sat on Storm, who lay contentedly in the middle of the swarming mass. The triumphant shouting was very dim in his ears.

A few yards away, a small boy, with an even smaller girl, in a cart being pulled by two ragged donkeys with a goat behind it looked at him, then solemnly, not smiling, lifted a fist, with its thumb pointed up.

12

There was a great banquet in Lanzi to celebrate the march west, as it was called, rather than a retreat, with capital letters only a taleteller or two away.

The survival of less than half of the residents of Trenganu, and a few more from the expeditionary force, was being regarded a some kind of victory.

But not by the soldiers or by the Dragonmaster.

One grizzled sergeant spat, "I claim we got our asses beaten like drums, and I don't like it."

The banquet's guest of honor was supposed to have been Lord Kailas of Kalabas, the Dragonmaster, for his brilliance serving a country not his own.

But he wasn't there for the party, nor were the other three Derainians. Those three, with whatever loot they'd been able to acquire, were flying west, planning to make a stop at Paestum, then across the Chicor Straits to home.

Except for Hal Kailas.

He, Storm beside him, sat on a low mountain to the south-east of Lanzi.

It was cold, clear, windy, and both moons were out.

Hal was considering what he should now do with his life.

He decided that not only would he not be flying for the Roche, with their still-grandiose dreams of conquest, but he had no interest in freelance military work.

It occurred to him that good causes – if, in fact, there were any – seldom came to mercenaries.

They were generally stuck with wars that were probably not that honorable, since there were always enough true believers around for the good battles.

He could, he thought for a short flash, possibly go back into the peacetime army of Deraine.

That brought a rather derisive laugh.

Storm stirred and honked what Hal thought might be an echo.

Being quite rich meant he could become a roué in Rozen. But that didn't sit well . . . he'd seen enough parties and partygoers on the flight north to Trenganu and, before that, in ruined Carcaor to make his liver tremble for years.

Hal ruefully realized he didn't make much of a decadent.

He considered.

At one time, his dream would have been to be a dragon-flier, with his own traveling spectacle.

But he doubted there'd be much interest these days, since most people associated dragons with war and death.

Besides, remembering the realities of a dragon show, the catering to stupid people with stupid questions, and giggling schoolgirls, that didn't draw him any more.

He thought, hardly for the first time, that the young wanderer caught up by the war was truly dead.

So the only option left, he thought, was to vegetate on his estates.

Perhaps he should think about drinking himself to death while boring everyone within a day's flight with war stories.

He remembered the words of his first great love: "There won't be any after-the-war for a dragon-flier."

It seemed that he was finding a new illustration of that truth, if not the one that Saslic had meant.

"Oh well," Hal said aloud. "At least I'll never starve."

Storm looked at him, and let go a long burble.

"My friend," Kailas said, "you're going to have to learn people-speak, since nobody's mastered dragon talk."

Storm made a noncommittal noise.

Hal realized the sky had clouded over, just as a spatter of rain hit him in the face.

Storm unfurled one wing, brought it like a tent over Hal.

"Well," Hal said, "at least I've got one friend in the world."

Somehow comforted, he got up, and climbed into the saddle. He pulled a slicker over his shoulders, and tapped Storm with his reins.

The dragon thudded down the slope, wings outspread, and took to the air.

Hal let Storm find his own altitude, then set a course of east-north-east as the storm broke about his shoulders.

Strangely, not at all unhappy, the lone rider flew on through the driving tempest.

13

A month later, Hal sat in one of the drawing rooms of his castle, staring out at the drifting snow.

Beyond that was the long, sloping beach that led to the sea, and which was dotted with small ice growlers.

It was a bleak winter, well suited to brooding hopelessly about the future.

Kailas had returned to Deraine, found nothing for him in the capital, as he'd expected, and flown on north to his lands.

There seemed to be nothing here either, but at least life was quiet, and there were no intrusions, other than the minor noblemen who discovered Lord Kailas was single once more, and threw parties to "get him out of his gloom."

Actually, of course, these parties were intended to introduce said noblemen's excessively eligible daughters.

At the moment, Hal wanted nothing emotional and no one in his life, such as it was, until he figured out what the hells he was going to do next.

At least he hadn't given in to either the joys of the bottle or, worse, falling into some sort of disastrous love affair.

Yet.

He ate, exercised, slept, rode Storm out over the ocean each day, and read many books – the castle's previous tenant had been much of a reader.

He'd sent to Rozen for more volumes, and read indiscriminately – romances, epic verse, history. The only thing he cared little about was writings about the war.

The storm had isolated the castle, which suited Hal quite well. He didn't want or need company, there were enough supplies to last for years, and there was nothing he felt terribly like doing.

About midday, when the weather had broken a bit, he grew bored with the book he was reading, pulled on boots and a heavy coat, and went for a walk down by the shore.

It was far too windy to take Storm out, but he stopped by the stables first, and fed a rather terrified lamb to the dragon.

Frozen sand crunched under his feet, and the wind wailed most attractively as he went.

A gust of wind sent particles of ice into his face, and he blinked them out, thinking he had spotted more bergy bits stranded on the beach.

He had not – the two bulky objects were dragons.

Wild dragons.

One was dead, being rolled by the waves, but the other still lived, and was able to pull himself further up, out of the water.

Hal tried approaching him, and the monster managed a feeble lash of his tail, and a burbling low screech.

The dragon was hurt – a foreleg looked broken, and there was a long tear along his side.

Hal wanted to do something, didn't know what.

A thought came.

He ran back to the castle, shouted up a servant, and told him to saddle a horse – no, two horses – and take a companion, for safety against the storm's rage, to the nearby village and bring back its witch.

"Tell him it's to deal with a dragon," Hal said. "Maybe that'll give him a clue as to what herbs to bring.

"He'll think I've gone mad, but remind him my gold isn't mad."

The man looked puzzled, then ran off.

Hal went to the stables, got Storm, and walked him down to the wounded, probably dying, dragon.

The two creatures exchanged angry hisses, then, proper civilities having been observed, the injured beast lay back down, full length.

Hal didn't approach him more closely.

Within the hour, the witch arrived, a rather rotund, cheerful man, bundled in homespun. Hal's two servants carried big wicker cases.

He spoke in the rather queer dialect native to the district Hal's lands lay in, and Hal had to puzzle his way through the man's words:

"'Tis sad to see any animal, even a monsker like a dragon, in pain, and aye, there's been many of them wash up on our shores this winter.

"Wonder if there's some sort of war going on, almost. Almost like they're as stupid as people with *their* wars.

"Always coming from the west, being washed a bit south to our beaches. Wager there's more on the western approaches."

Hal remembered the dragons that had sailed, wings

folded over their bodies, driven by the winds and the currents, past Cayre a Carstares, his ex-wife's citadel, and nodded understanding.

"I spent some time thinking, trying to bring up some spells, or some herbs or poultices that might help, tried 'em, almost got my head tore off for my troubles.

"But two, three, recovered good enough to swim back out and catch the current.

"Seldom saw one hurt as sore as this, but we'll do what we can."

The man cautiously approached the injured beast, who seemed to have lapsed into unconsciousness.

He muttered spells, and took packets of dried herbs from the baskets, packed the dragon's wounds, and loose-splinted his foreleg. He tried to tighten the splint, and the beast semi-woke, and struck at him with his fangs.

The man ducked away, and laughed.

"Better nor a bull in heat, you are. But I have your measure, I do."

But the witch was sweating in fear.

Hal had a sheep brought down, and killed in front of the dragon, but he showed no interest.

He brought Storm back to the beach, and Storm stared at the wild beast and began a high keening.

Then he picked up the sheep Hal had killed, carried it to the other animal and set it down in front of his nose.

The dragon's eyes opened, and he considered the meal, Storm, and Hal, the witch and several of Hal's curious staffers hovering nearby, then closed his eyes again.

Hal had his retainers pitch a sort of tent for himself, and set watch over the dragon as night closed in.

Storm curled nearby.

Hal didn't sleep that night, or so he thought.

But he dreamed.

Once before, during the war, he'd dreamed of being a dragon, Storm, and that dream had been so real he'd truly believed it.

So was this one, even though it was most strange, and lasted for only moments.

Again, he was a dragon, but one that knew not men.

The sun was warm on his back, and about a hundred feet below him was a savanna, its grasses just beginning to change with fall.

It was a land that Hal had never known, never seen.

He was just beginning to get hungry, scanning the ground below for prey.

Another part of him was watching the skies . . . for something.

An enemy?

He looked about, saw nothing except some scattering birds, went back to looking for his meal.

He thought of a full stomach, then quiet digestion atop a crag to the east, near the ocean, and was content.

He saw movement below, under a rocky escarpment, folded his wings and dove silently down toward what must be an antelope.

He was just below the rocks when two other dragons, big, red and black, dove at him.

The dragon felt fear, panic at the ambush, tried to dive out of it.

But the other two were clever, and forced him toward the ground.

He dove at one, struck with his tail, missed.

The other dragon was on him, lashing out.

The sound of his foreleg breaking was very loud, and he keened pain, rolled in midair to escape.

But both dragons were on him, ripping, tearing, and he felt the pain deep in his side. The ground was very close, and—

And Hal woke, sweating, hearing the nearby dragon moan and thrash.

Hal sat, helplessly, listening to the beast's last hours.

The dragon died without opening his eyes, just before dawn.

Hal felt pain greater than he'd known over the death of some men, and wondered at himself.

But at least he had an idea of what he might, perhaps should, do.

Hal left his castle on Storm that day, paying no heed to the dying tempest, and headed for Rozen.

14

Kailas's first stop was at the address that the dragonmaster Garadice had included with his letter.

Garadice's home was just outside Rozen, a large, sprawling, rather unkempt estate.

Hal found him in one of the outbuildings, staring at a large pile of tents, jarred rations, and heavy clothes.

"I'm not looking forward to going back north this spring," Garadice explained. "I hope you've brought something to distract me."

Hal explained his plan – he proposed to fund four or five teams, to be stationed along the west and north shores of Deraine. The teams would be composed of about six men, as many as possible with dragon-handling experience. One of the men would be a wizard, or, failing that, at least a competent witch.

Their job would be to help any wild dragons that beached themselves, first with medical treatment, until they healed enough to be able to fly, or, at the very least, return to the sea and let the currents carry them on.

Garadice made a face.

"Admirable, I suppose, Lord Kailas. But I sense something lacking. Once we – for I'll be delighted to aid you in any way I can – have our dragon all bandaged up, is there going to be any guarantee that it will simply take itself off our hands?

"Suppose the dragon *likes* being cosseted and hand-fed?"

Hal hadn't considered that.

"And the gods know we already have enough half-tame dragons on our hands from the war, with, as yet, no place to keep them or any task to keep them off the public rolls. We've seen how ungrateful the damned people are toward them already.

"Will there be any change in the way the populace feels?

"Remembering, of course, how quickly they've managed to forget the crippled soldiers who fought for them not so very long ago."

Hal was starting to get upset.

Garadice held up his hands.

"Don't get mad, Lord Kailas. You have me on your side, as you should know. I'm merely asking questions that I think we have to answer before riding off on what could be a fool's errand."

Hal, scowling, said he would think on the matter, and left.

After some pondering, he decided his campaign needed a popularizer.

There was none better than Sir Thom Lowess.

Lowess' mansion was, as usual, occupied by half a dozen young women, nobles of the outer provinces who were in the capital seeking excitement and, possibly, a lover or husband, preferably rich.

As far as anyone knew, Lowess merely liked these

women's company, and never took advantage of the various offers he'd had.

Lowess, unmarried, wasn't attracted to men, either.

As far as anyone could tell, he seemed perfectly sexless, although no one committed the social breach of asking.

The two men chatted for a while, Sir Thom carefully not bringing up the subject of Hal's ex-wife, then Hal explained what had brought him to the capital, and asked for Lowess' help in promoting his dragon teams.

"I am glad, I suppose," Lowess said, looking out the window, carefully not meeting Hal's eye, "that you consider me some sort of a superman.

"But that would be . . . will be . . . a very hard task.

"People are tired of the war, tired of reading about the war."

"But this isn't about the war," Hal protested.

"In most people's eyes," Sir Thom said, "anything to do with dragons – like anything to do with the Roche or soldiers – reflects back on the war.

"Look at it like this, Lord Hal. How long have dragons been among us?"

"What's that got to do with anything?"

"Perhaps everything. It's been what, a bit over two hundred years since they appeared from the west?

"You know, an awful lot of people had never seen or read about dragons before the war, in spite of the dragon shows and such.

"Dragons equal war equal death. Period."

"That's absurd," Hal said.

"It is," Sir Thom agreed. "But I'll give you an example: a young writer I know asked for help getting a collection of stories about dragons published . . . flying them, caring for them, nothing, other than a brief mention at the beginning, of their war service.

"I tried. I really tried. But all of the people I wrote to came back with about the same response: that no one wants to read about dragons, and for me to suggest to the young man that he find another field of interest. That went from broadsheet publishers, including my own, to those who deal in books.

"I'll give you another example, this one closer to home. The broadsheets wanted ink on your last adventure with the Roche . . . a few months back. Half of that interest, by the way, came from your divorce. Since neither you nor Khiri was willing to talk to the taletellers, there were incredible scandals floating about.

"But now, if I decided to write a piece on your latest crusade . . . I doubt if I'd find a ready market.

"You are, as the saying goes, yesterday's hero."

"Well, the hell with them," Hal said. "I'll go ahead with my teams anyway. I've more than enough money, and don't give a damn about having anything to hand on to the daughters and sons I don't have, don't particularly want, and seem unlikely to have anyway."

"Now, now," Sir Thom soothed. "Getting perturbed about something that does seem to be a fact won't do any good.

"Which brings up another point that just came to me.

"It's admirable – heroic, even – that you want to do something to help dragons.

"But is this it? Is this dragon team scheme the answer? And I'm not sure I know what I meant by that question."

"Answer?" Hal asked, honestly puzzled. "Answer to what?"

"I don't know that either," Sir Thom said. "Look. Let me think on it. There must be a way to do something for these pursued wild dragons.

"But do a stumble-witted man a favor. Think on what I just said."

Again, Hal dreamed he was that sore-wounded dragon. Now he was at sea, a great wind blowing over his tented wings, waves rocking him.

The current bore him steadily away from his homeland. Away from his homeland, but away from those red and black dragons who'd savaged him.

He longed for sleep, for death, but his body denied him.

He would heal, heal and find a new land for a home.

Hal sat in a taphouse, trying to feel sorry for himself, but mostly getting drunk.

Hells, he could have gotten this far staying at home . . . if those vast estates King Asir had granted him were really his home.

He realized he'd never thought of them as such, that in fact he'd really never *had* a home after running away from Caerly.

Kailas grinned, remembering an old sergeant, way the hells back when he was a young cavalryman, before the dragons, shouting, "From now on, th' *army* is your home."

Yes. Right. Of course, Sergeant.

What batshit.

He listened to the laughter and joking at the bar, had no desire to join the roisterers.

Hal realized that, way down deep, he probably didn't

like people very much. Noisy, scheming fools who seemed to do nothing but take.

So what, he thought.

That had nothing to do with anything, least of all dragons, which he'd decided would be his main concern for a while, until he thought of something else to do.

Another realization came: he'd probably be better off if he had to struggle for his meals and shelter, like most people.

Maybe there'd be more like him if everything came on golden platters.

Or maybe not.

This, he thought, wasn't getting him much of anywhere.

He glowered at an especially happy drunk, who lifted a glass in his direction, saw the expression on his face, and turned hastily away.

Hal felt a bit better for having ruined, if only for a moment, someone else's evening.

He looked for someone else to glare at.

Maybe it'd make him feel better if he got into a good, serious bar brawl on this night.

Although he'd probably lose, since it had been nearly for ever since he'd been in a fight with anything but killing weapons. He thought the warders of Rozen would hardly approve of him gutting some innocent lush with the dragon-flier's dagger he had at his belt.

His eye was caught by a placard on the wall:

!See!
Real Wild Dragons
!Marvel!
At their Rage
Against Us All

More than 10
Of the World's Most
Dangerous Dragons

There was the address of a local hippodrome.

Hal studied the placard.

After a while, he pushed his half-finished brandy away.

Now, *there* was something he could deal with.

Hal realized he was a deal drunker than he'd thought, navigating slowly and carefully through the snowy streets, having to stop and ask directions twice.

He carefully faced away from the people he questioned, not wanting to paralyze anyone with his breath.

He was in time for the last "show," such as it was.

It consisted of a gravel-voiced man talking about how dangerous the ten dragons were, and how brave their captors had been, without ever specifying exactly how the monsters were trapped.

The dragons themselves, paired, arbitrarily, in thick-barred cages, looked wilted and underfed, hardly a threat to anyone.

But the shill raked a length of steel across the bars, and the dragons obediently screamed, and spat at the man.

Hal paid little attention to the man's blather. He'd done better himself when he was a boy with the dragon-fliers' show. But he did force away his building stupor when the man talked about the hand-forged bars of the cage, and how only the system of locks kept the beasts from breaking free and ravaging Rozen.

After a time, Kailas decided there was nothing more to learn. He went out and found a closet in one of the halls, and crept inside, hoping there wouldn't be any broom-pushers after the "performance."

He either slept or passed out, but all was quiet and still in the arena when he awoke, except for the rather plaintive roars of the dragons.

Hal slipped out, head already starting to ache from the brandy. He thought he could hold on until he'd finished, then go back to his inn and collapse.

There was a brazier in the central auditorium, giving a bit of light.

Hal stumbled down the steps, looking for something. He found it still lying on the floor – the steel bar the barker had used to demonstrate the strength of the cages.

Hal picked it up, shook it, approved of its weight.

He braced himself, and swung the steel against the rather flimsy-looking lock of one of the cages.

The lock bent, the sound boomed around the arena, and the dozing dragons woke.

He swung again, and the lock sprung open.

Hal moved to the next cage, took a firm grip on the bar, and a voice came from behind him.

"Hi! You! What the blazes are you doing?"

Hal spun.

An old man, wearing what had once been a uniform, stood there.

"Are you out of your mind?" the man, a nightwatch-man, shouted.

Hal thought, decided to play the role.

He came out with what he hoped would sound like maniacal laughter, and advanced on the old man.

The man backed up.

Hal laughed again, and drew his dagger.

The old man yelped, found that his legs weren't as old as he'd thought, and fled back out of the arena.

He'll go for the watch, Hal thought.

But he didn't run.

Instead, he went back to the cages, and smashed the other locks.

Then he went to the arena's doors, and opened them wide.

Snowflakes and cold air blew in.

Hal went back to the dragons.

"All right," he shouted. "You're free! Get out! Go north, or . . . or wherever you want!"

None of the dragons moved toward their cage doors.

Instead, they huddled back at the rear of their pens.

Hal swore at them, without results.

He looked about, saw the brazier, had an idea. With his dagger, he ripped one of the stadium seats apart, wrapping the cloth seat back about its frame.

He fired the cloth in the brazier, then went behind the cages.

"Out! Out!" he cried, and waved his torch as it burst into flame.

One of the dragons whimpered, but, fearing fire more than the forgotten outer world, went out of the cage, and up the stairs toward the exit.

Two other dragons followed.

Hal chased the rest of them out of their cages, herding them toward the doors.

He kept the fire in front of his face, and while the dragons struck at him, it was half-hearted.

Only one lashed out with his tail, and Kailas ducked clumsily and drunkenly under the whiplash.

Then the dragons were outside, starting at the cold.

Hal stumbled about, waving his burning cloth.

The dragons broke, one, then two, stumbling forward, wings unfolding with a great cracking like a ship's sails in a high wind, and they were aloft, climbing out and away from the lights of Rozen.

Hal cheered at the top of his lungs, waving his torch as it burnt out.

"Go home! Screw mankind! Don't have anything to do with us!"

A voice came.

"Stand very damned still. You are under arrest."

Hal turned, saw a uniformed warder holding a halberd not a foot from his back.

He dropped the torch.

Behind the warder were a dozen other warders, all armed, some armored.

"I order you to obey my commands, in the name of the king."

15

Hal was unceremoniously tossed into what a warder called a "tank." He explained it was mainly for drunkards who'd also committed some minor felony that didn't hurt anyone.

That made Kailas feel enormously better, a fit compliment on his aptitude as a criminal, to go with his rapidly building hangover.

He took the not particularly clean blanket they handed him, ignored the dozen other wastrels in the cell, found a corner in the large room with its single-barred gate, and tried to get some sleep.

He woke late in the morning, with a raging thirst, and sat up.

Leaning against the wall next to him was a huge man, big in every dimension.

"Is there any water about?" Hal croaked, not particularly caring if the monster next to him was intent on robbing him.

"In th' bucket, over there."

Hal wobbled over to it, poured down evil-smelling liquid until his stomach promised it would be sending it all back if he didn't stop.

He went back to his corner and slumped down.

"You th' one they call Dragonmaster?"

"I am . . . I was."

"Before you started flying about and being a lord and all," the hulk said, "was you in the cavalry?"

"I was," Kailas admitted. "Third Light."

"My kid brother was with it, too. He was the good 'un in the family. Wrote letters home. And he was always going on about some Sergeant Kailas. Called him Lucky."

"What was his name?"

"Gachina. Finbo was his first name."

"I remember him," Hal said, telling the truth. "Guidon-bearer."

"That was him," the huge man said. "Got hisself killed in some damnfool battle. One of his mates I wrote to, askin' what happened, told me the godsdamned officers had made 'em ride out with no backup, and the godsdamned Roche heavy cavalry wiped them out."

Hal remembered that battlefield, and its corpses. He'd just been commissioned, been offered a chance to go to dragon school, had turned the offer down because of the responsibility he felt for his section.

After that battle, they were all corpses, and Hal's responsibility was over.

Hal hauled himself to his feet, stuck out his hand.

"Name's Hal," he said. "Your brother was a good man. I was on the field the day he got killed."

"Too godsdamned good for the godsdamned army," the man said, looking at Hal as if he expected a challenge.

"Most of us were," Hal agreed. The bigger man subsided a little.

"I'm Babil."

They touched palms.

"I'm a thief, normal," Babil said. "Now, since they didn't catch me slittin' any gullets, I'm waitin' trial.

"And I'm head man of this box." He raised his voice, looking about. No one disagreed.

"This is the Dragonmaster," he went on. "Nobody messes with him."

There was a scatter of agreements.

"Not that you've got much to worry about," Babil said. "These is all lightweights. The real felons go to Brightwater.

"Not to mention that you'll be out on bond within the day, even for doing something spectacular stupid like cuttin' those dragons free."

"How'd you know?"

"One of th' warders told.

"But like I say, you'll be bonded out quick. Not like th' rest of us, who'll gentle rot for a time 'til th' judges get off their arses and decide to see about us."

But Hal didn't get out on bond that day.

Or the next.

Or that week.

Babil asked one of the warders, who looked carefully about before telling him that someone, someone "up there," had put the word out that Hal wasn't to be freed.

No explanation.

"I figger," Babil said, "them dragons must've belonged to somebody muckety, or who had a friend who is."

Hal couldn't work out who that could be.

While he waited, he got to know the other felons in the tank, and others as they passed through.

One of them was a man without a name, a small, wizened character with canny eyes, who also happened to be quite mad.

He decided, for some utterly unknown reason, that he hated Hal, and was always muttering when he came within range.

Generally his mutters were something about how if he loved dragons so much, he oughta go live with them, oughta sleep with them, frigging bastardly lord bastard, and on and on.

He made Hal very nervous, even though Babil said there was no worry there.

One day, Babil came to Hal.

"You're either in good – or very bad – shape."

"Why?"

"I just heard, you're for the King's Justice."

"Huh?"

"A warder just told me. Guess that's 'cause you're a lord and all, hey?"

Hal shook his head, having little knowledge of Deraine's convoluted justice system beyond prewar experience of what they could do to a penniless wandering boy.

"Problem is," Babil went on, "King's Justice also means they can geek you if they wants."

Hal blanched.

"Can't understand what's going on," Babil muttered. "And I don't like not knowin'."

The next morning, they came for Hal.

*

Four warders, two with spears, two with crossbows, took Hal out of the tank.

He wanted to tell them that he was normally quite sober, that he had behaved like somewhat of a damned fool, although he really didn't regret freeing the dragons, but he didn't say anything.

A carriage took him to a public bathhouse, and the lead warder told him to wash the stink off, and put on the clothes he handed him.

He was busily soaping when it came to him.

Both Garadice and Lowess had been right.

He suddenly knew what he should be doing, and it was not running a bandage squad for dragons.

And it had come from the lips of a madman.

The only problem was getting himself free to implement the thought.

Hal had himself shaved by the barber in the bathhouse, and put on the gray striped tunic and breeches he'd been given.

A rather fat, imperious man came in and told Hal to follow him.

Hal thought he recognized the man, but told himself he had to be wrong. All the while his thumbs prickled.

Outside the bathhouse was a dark brown carriage, without windows.

Hal was told to get in, and the carriage started off.

He tried to tell where it was going by the turns, but since he wasn't sure where the prison was, he stayed lost.

It finally passed through two sets of gates – Hal could tell by the warders' self-important shouting of challenge and password – and came to an eventual halt.

Hal got out, and found his fears were quite valid: the carriage was in the royal palace grounds, behind the palace itself.

He had been right in thinking the fat man was one of the king's chamberlains.

King's Justice, indeed.

And what the hells could King Asir want with a common, or fairly common anyway, felon?

"Very good, Kailas," King Asir said in a sarcastic voice.

That was very bad. Hal was, in spite of his civilian wear, at the most rigid attention he'd stood at since . . . since dragon school, after having knelt hastily when the king made his entrance.

Also not good was the king not having used title, either nobility or Dragonmaster.

The king was dressed in dark linen, with short boots, and no crown, not even a circlet.

His face was more worn, and his eyes more tired than Hal remembered them from the war.

There were only the two of them in the tiny audience chamber.

"You know, you've annoyed me quite considerably of late," Asir said. He didn't seem to expect an apology, so Hal remained silent.

"First, you rescue that Roche killer from our ostensible allies in Sagene, which meant that I had to make up some covering story.

"That cost you points, right there.

"Then with this Yasin, you involve yourself in this border war with the northern barbarians, a war I'd as soon see them lose, and turn their attentions to fixing problems in their own homeland, rather than grabbing for more land they don't need.

"Then you take over the retreat when the grab goes sour, which makes all of the taletellers go goosey, and once again you're a hero, this time in a cause that is far less than admirable.

"I was of a mind to let you stew in your wilderness up north for another year, then call you to court and give you some sort of position that would keep you out of mischief.

"But mischief appears to be your goal, and so you get yourself plastered and become some sort of animal liberator.

"Forget everything except this last piece of nonsense, for which I really would like an explanation.

"Assuming you have one."

Hal waited, and the silence stretched.

"I think I do, sire," Hal said.

Asir stayed silent.

"Your Majesty, the way we've been treated since the end of the wars has flatly made me sick. Men, who can know why, is bad enough.

"But dragons . . . poor dumb beasts . . . are nothing but victims."

The king nodded reluctantly.

"It wasn't very wise of me . . . and I had been drinking, which I'm not offering as an excuse . . . but I did what I did, and honestly have few regrets, other than embarrassing you, when you've always been my benefactor."

"Well," the king allowed, "it seems you might have started something. A couple of soft-hearted and soft-headed barons have started an anti-cruelty league. Free the dragons and such.

"That does no harm.

"But I cannot have one of my heroes stumbling around as if he were a law unto himself, as if it were still wartime.

"No. That will not come to pass.

"I had my people inquire about what you were doing, and was told about your rescue groups, or whatever the blazes you were intending to call them."

"I hadn't gotten as far as a name, Your Majesty."

The king humphed.

"Not that it matters," Asir said. "The question is, how shall you be punished? I can't just ignore your depredations, even though all but one of them are technically within the law.

"I can't just throw you in prison for a year or so. The people will, no doubt, hear of your rescue groups, which will never happen if you're in jail, which in turn will hardly reflect well on me.

"I truly wish I was one of those kings of legend I read about when I was a boy, who had convenient islands to which they could dispatch an annoyance they weren't quite ready to behead."

"You do, sire," Hal said quickly.

The king gave him a puzzled look.

"Your Majesty . . . back during the war you once told me you regretted not being curious about the lands beyond, and that maybe that had helped bring on the war."

"I don't remember saying it, but I assume I did," Asir said. "It's certainly true enough."

Hal felt emboldened.

"Sire, I assume you know about the wild dragons that are carried from some unknown land east, to land on our shores, Black Island, or the northern tundra."

"Of course."

"An expert on dragons, a man named Garadice—"

"I know of him as well."

"He's theorized that these wild dragons are the ones that have settled this entire part of the world, since dragons have only been around for a few hundred years."

"You are trying my patience," Asir growled. "I didn't fall off the turnip boat, you know."

"I came up with the idea of dragon teams to help these poor wights that, wounded and exhausted, are carried east to us by the currents and the winds.

"I was ducking the issue.

"Sire, what I propose now is to journey west, using my own resources. I want to find who – or what – is at war with the dragons."

The king goggled.

"And, Your Majesty, if you grant me three or four of your ships, and some of your sailors, who are doing nothing now but sulking at the docks, or sailing up and down eating your rations and collecting your silver, looking for smugglers, I will attempt to end this war that someone is waging against the dragons.

"Or whatever it is," Hal finished, a bit limply.

"Hmm. Interesting." The king went to a sideboard, poured two brandies.

"You may lose that brace, Lord Kailas."

Hal obeyed, relaxing to a still-military, very formal at ease.

The king handed him a snifter.

He stared past Hal, out the window, at the snowy winter.

"Someone once said that if people have enough adventure, either done by themselves or in the vicarious manner, they'll not always be thinking of war, and killing their neighbor.

"I don't believe it, not at all.

"But I am of a mind to test the theory.

"Yes. I think I shall."

King Asir lifted his glass.

"Lord Kailas, it pleases me to set aside your crimes, and grant your request.

"Perhaps saving some dragons, or even trying, will wash our sins against them away.

"So let us drink to . . . to the Royal Exploration West."

16

That was well and good.

But . . .

Hal might have felt like trumpeting about his sudden rise from prisoner to explorer, save for one slight problem:

West was a hellishly general direction to go searching for something he wasn't quite sure of.

He found larger quarters, suitable for an expedition, and pondered the matter for some days.

Then he asked the king for a magician, a very good magician.

"You mean Limingo," Asir said.

"If possible, sire."

"It isn't the loaning for a day or so that I mind," Asir said. "It's the probability that that fey bastard will want to go with you, and good sorcerers are scarce, these days."

Nevertheless, he agreed.

Limingo, as tall, slender and elegant as ever, showed up, accompanied by a pair of curly-haired, elf-eared acolytes.

The magician had always been perfectly open about his sexual preferences, which didn't matter to Hal at all.

Limingo listened to Hal's problem.

"To tell you the truth, not only do I have no idea how to find out where you should seek, but I don't even have an idea on how to start looking.

"I'm sorry. But magic can only do so much."

"I had a thought," Hal said, almost timidly. Magic and magicians mostly terrified him.

"Ah?" Limingo said.

Hal explained about dreaming about being a dragon. Once it had been Storm, but this latest had been of being a foreign dragon, and being attacked by two others, over a strange land.

Limingo stroked his chin.

"I don't know, Lord Kailas—"

"Hal, if you would."

"Hal. I have no idea if that's a way in to our problem. Let me give it some thought."

It was two full days before Limingo returned to him.

"First, what we need is a dying, or very recently dead, wild dragon. Something that has recently tried to make the journey east.

"Do you know," Limingo added, "I almost said some-one. Odd, that."

Hal realized that he'd been thinking of dragons as "ones," not "things," for a very long time.

"The only problem," Limingo said, "is that the spell might involve some risk, and certainly some pain, for you."

Hal thought for an instant, then nodded.

"I'm game."

Hal borrowed scouts from the light cavalry, put them

out on the western and northern shores of Deraine, with silver as a reward for the first dragon reported.

And they waited.

It took three weeks, and the last of a dying winter's storms, before a dragon, just breathing its last, washed up.

It was far to the west, near the fishing town of Brouwer, which Hal had last seen at the party where he'd met Khiri Carstares, before the disastrous attack on the south of Roche where his first and greatest love, Saslic Dinapur, had died.

The magician and his assistants, plus two dogsbodies, set out immediately by road.

Hal was very grateful for Storm, overflying the mucky and slippery roads west.

They found lodgings in Brouwer, went to where the dragon's corpse lay.

The cavalryman who had found the dragon had been sent back, with three fellows, to guard the body.

It lay on a sandy beach in a cove just north of the long island that protected Brouwer, and was in perfect shape.

"Dunno if anybody uses dead dragons for anything, sir," he reported. "But I thought it well to take care.

"It only died two days ago. Made me uneasy, while it was thrashing about. Couldn't think of anything I – or anybody else – could do."

Hal made arrangements for the man to be rewarded for his forethought . . . and his concern.

Limingo had a tent in his wagon, and ordered the two men with him to pitch it, as close as possible to the green and white body that sprawled just above the high-tide line.

"Now for you, young man," Limingo said briskly, rubbing his hands together like a chirurgeon about to begin an amputation. "If you'll go in that tent, strip down, and rub yourself with this unguent . . . we'll take care of our portion of the ceremony."

Hal obeyed, shivering at the cold. There was nothing inside the tent except a camp cot.

He stuck his head back out, saw Limingo and his two assistants drawing convoluted symbols in the sand. The two laborers stood well back from the scene, near where the land sloped down to the beach.

Evidently Hal wasn't the only one who was a trifle goosey about magic.

The acolytes set up seven torches, on chest-high poles stuck into the sand, waved their hands over them, and they sprang into life. In spite of the onshore winds, the torches burnt steadily, never flickering.

The assistants took scrolls from their cloaks, began reading in unison.

Their chanting was a bit soothing.

Hal yawned.

"Now, you, back inside, and on the cot," Limingo said.

Hal obeyed.

"Now, I want you, as much as you can remember, to feel as you did when you had that dream, that vision."

Hal thought back, tried to obey.

Limingo took a small green leatherbound book from his cloak, started reading, in an unknown tongue.

Hal got sleepy.

Limingo kept reading, and it became a chant, and suddenly he switched to Derainian, or else Hal suddenly and magically understood the language he'd been speaking.

> "*Go in*
> *Go back*
> *Go in*
> *Go back*
> *Into the current*
> *Into the wind.*"

All at once, Hal was lying on the beach outside, feeling pain, the long pain that had carried him across the great waters, fading, ebbing, and he knew and welcomed death.

He realized he was now that dragon outside, dying, and he tried feebly to fight against death.

Somehow he knew he was moving backward, still the dragon.

Now he felt the waves wash over him, and whimpered as the pain came back.

Then he was in the surf, the waves crashing at him, at his brutally torn wing, his ripped-away tail, his battered carapace.

He was further out at sea, his wings, such as had been left him, wrapped around his head, a tent against the buffeting winds and waves.

He was alone, no land in sight, the current carrying him.

Part of him was this poor maimed dragon, being swept west by wind and waves, and part of him, a strange part, small, soft-fleshed, lay in some sort of cover on a far-distant beach.

A voice came:

> "*Let it take you*
> *Let it take you*

> *Watch the stars*
> *Watch the stars*
> *Let it take you*
> *Now come back*
> *Come out*
> *Slowly*
> *Just a bit."*

He peered out, into the storm's beginnings, up at the sky, as someone, something, had commanded him, saw the night sky, clouds whirling past.

It was day, and the pain was stronger, but so was his strength.

From the depths below rose a snake-headed monster, wide fanged jaws snapping at him, and he found strength, clawed talons striking out, and the surprised snake-head snapped back, hissed, went looking for weaker prey.

He was in the air, tumbling, spinning, crashing down, and for an instant the cold water felt good on his wounds, then it seared, as he came up.

There were strange things in the water, skeins, with fish leaping inside, the skeins being tended by odd, bulky things that were not fish.

He was in the air, floundering, and it was night, and again the voice came:

> *"Watch the sky*
> *Watch the sky*
> *Remember the sky."*

He obeyed once more, and then he was flying, barely flying, wing torn, fleeing from those three red and black monsters that had attacked his crag, tearing into his mate and their egg.

Something had told him to fly into the rising sun, and he obeyed, and he saw the sea below fade back, and then there was land—

And there was agony as the three monsters ripped at him, and his mate lay dying, and he fought back, without hope, uselessly—

And something cold dashed into his face, and a voice was shouting:

"Come out now! Come back! Or face the real death!" and it was Limingo, not chanting a spell, and Hal was back on the beach, remembered pain tearing at him, fading down and away as Limingo's spell receded.

He sat up, shaking, his body drenched in sweat.

He threw up suddenly.

Someone was kneeling beside him, holding a hot drink.

He managed to sip it, felt its warmth.

Then he was cold again, and someone draped a cloak over him.

He was one again, Hal Kailas, on a beach beside a dead wild dragon.

But he would never forget those moments of remembered dying agony, as he, the dragon, suddenly without a mate or kit, fled from his home across the ocean, currents and winds taking him west, hoping to see a peaceful land, finding nothing but death.

Hal Kailas remembered what Limingo had shouted, and he looked up at the sky, at the stars.

He shuddered, remembering quite exactly, knowing that he now knew where he must go.

17

!A GRAND ADVENTURE!
INTO THE UNKNOWN
WESTERN LANDS!
JOIN THE DRAGONMASTER
AS HE EXPLORES
LANDS OF MYSTERY
On His Majesty's
Service
HIGHEST PAY
AND SHARES OF ANY PLUNDER
BONUS FOR
THE EXPERIENCED:
Dragon-Fliers
And Handlers
Raiders
And
Officers & Seamen
ALL OF A GOOD HEART

AND BRAVE SOUL
CARRY THE FLAG OF DERAINE
INTO THE WILDS
Apply in person to . . .

18

Hal started putting the pieces of his expedition together.

The poster was nailed up around Deraine. Hal wondered what sort of recruits he'd find, but had other tasks at hand first.

But he did make a call on Sir Thom Lowess. The taleteller was somewhat nervous over not having told Hal about his former wife's peccadilloes, but Hal made no mention of that. Khiri, like many other things, was now in the dead past, and Hal mostly succeeded in not thinking about her.

Hal told Sir Thom that he wanted the maximum amount of publicity, to make sure he got the best in the land.

Lowess said he'd cooperate, but had a suggestion: the campaign was to wait for a bit, until Hal had something concrete to talk about. Also, he was to play utterly mysterious to the other taletellers.

"That'll bring 'em flocking around, sniffing like hounds. Then, later, I'll do my story. Since they'll have been dropping little tidbits until then, there'll be no way the other broadsheets can ignore your crusade, and so they'll go louder and bigger, like hounds baying after their better who's sniffed the prey."

Hal shrugged. He had less than no idea of how the taletellers worked, and even less curiosity.

Now came the ships. He already owned the *Galgorm Adventurer*.

The king gave him a basin to fit out in, and the *Galgorm* was taken into dry dock and given a far more thorough refit than she'd had before Hal set off for Sagene, including new yards, rigging, canvas, her bottom scraped and coppered, and a more seaworthy launching barge built, since they were to be testing the stormy Western Ocean. Also, both the galley and the cabins were made more luxurious. It might be a very wearisome cruise.

The *Galgorm*'s sister ship was given to Hal for a seedling rent, as were two light corvettes, the *Compass Rose* and the *Black Orchid*, as well as two fast dispatch boats.

That was adequate for Hal. He wasn't mounting a battle fleet. If trouble, big trouble, was encountered, the dispatch boats were to flee, and bring the word back to Deraine, while the other four would do what they could to escape.

There were more than enough shipwrights out of work to take care of the rebuilding of the six ships, so Hal turned his attention to the main concern: the dragons, their fliers, and their handlers.

He planned, since he had no idea how long the voyage would take, to take only sixteen dragons, plus replacements, which would give the monsters enough room to be comfortable.

He planned to divide his sixteen into two flights.

His first recruit was Garadice.

The old man came up the gangplank of the *Galgorm*, which Hal had made his headquarters, looked about and nodded approvingly.

"This is more likely a project than you forming groups of bandage experts," he said. "Of course, I'm along."

"Of course," Hal said, although privately wondering if the man would take to his command, since he'd been used to nearly complete independence during the war.

His old dragon doctor, Tupilco, appeared, explaining that no one seemed to need to medicate monsters these days, and signed the articles.

Next were the fliers.

Of course, Farren Mariah, the first he sought out, grumbled, glowered, and accepted the charge of being commander of the first flight.

The second flight went to the man who'd first commanded Hal, back at the start of the war, Lu Miletus. He didn't offer any explanations for why he wasn't content in peacetime Deraine, and Hal didn't ask, grateful for the man's proven ability.

Cabet showed up, which gave Hal an adjutant, and a known replacement as flight leader if there were casualties.

He asked Cabet casually about Calt Beoyard. Cabet grinned. "Remember that bordello in Carcaor? The one with the very young girls?"

Hal did . . . and he also remembered Beoyard's fascination with the dive.

"He's gone back into Roche, become the protector of the brothel, and swears he'll never get anywhere higher than a second-story bedroom, or demons can take him."

That was that.

Hal was trying not to lose his temper listening to a carpenter tell him how to reinforce the dragon pens on the *Galgorm* when a wiry man with amazing mustaches came aboard.

Aimard Quesney.

He and Hal stared at each other, then Quesney made a sort of salute.

"Are you coming aboard to tell me how I've found a new and interesting way to make a fool of myself?" Hal asked.

"I thought about it," Quesney said. "Especially after seeing your poster. Tsk. Plunder indeed."

"Unless I'm very mistaken," Hal said, "there'll be no plunder. We're sailing west to try to help the dragons . . . as you, and others, suggested. Or at least to find out what's driving them west, killing them when it can."

Quesney stared at Hal.

"I think I might owe you an apology," he said. "That is truly an honorable, if probably foolish, quest."

"I'm glad of your approval," Hal said sarcastically. "Might I ask what happened to your priesthood? Weren't they quite pure enough for you?"

Quesney flushed, then recovered, and stared out at the harbor.

"I deserve that, I suppose. I've not formally left. I came down to Rozen to see just what you were intending.

"Now I know.

"Is there room for another flier?"

"Are you willing to accept discipline?" Hal asked. "I don't need a doubter always behind me."

"If you'll have me, I'll serve faithfully."

Hal hesitated. Quesney was an extraordinary flier . . .

but he'd certainly been a pain in several areas, from his firm opinions to his dissidence.

And yet . . .

"I'll have you," Kailas said, making up his mind. "And don't make me regret it."

A trace of a smile came to Quesney's lips, and he rose, and saluted, a very crisp one this time.

"I won't," he said. "Sir."

The next step was putting Sir Thom Lowess into motion.

His fellow scribes had been frothing at the mouth, trying to get details on this royal expedition into the unknown. But nothing came from either the palace or from Hal.

Then the wave broke, with several long pieces by Sir Thom on the possible danger to the west that might threaten Deraine, the pogrom that was evidently being waged against the dragons. The best and the bravest would sail on a fact-finding mission, he wrote, "and if there's fighting about, there's no readier for it, or braver, than Lord Kailas, the Dragonmaster."

And so on and on.

Sir Thom's fellows had to catch up, with little facts beyond those Lowess had contrived.

Naturally, then, their stories were wilder and more heroic than his.

The second wave of applicants roared in, in person and, in spite of the poster's caution, by post and messenger.

It seemed everyone wanted to go with the Dragonmaster.

Sometimes this was good: there were more than enough applications from combat-experienced rangers, scouts, sailors, dragon-handlers, even clerks who'd spent time in the military.

Sometimes these included faces from the past:

Uluch, Hal's old and taciturn body servant, arrived, announced he wished his old tasks back. Hal asked him what had happened since he was discharged. Uluch said, briefly, "Went back to the greengrocer's. Didn't like it. The boss's wife didn't like me. That was that."

And that *was* that.

Another was Chook, the enormous and lethal cook from Lu Miletus's squadron, whose family had supposedly owned a great restaurant in Deraine.

"I went back, thinking I knew ten ways to steal from the owner. Found out other people, who hadn't bothered to waste time in the army, knew twenty.

"So I beat 'em all up, decided I wanted to lay low for a while, and heard about you."

Hal didn't give much of a hang about Chook's murderousness, remembered how good he was at making gourmet dishes out of ration salt beef, flour, and imagination, and signed him aboard instantly.

Sometimes things were heartbreaking:

No, Hal wouldn't sign someone on because his wife was unfaithful.

No, Hal wouldn't take the romantic student who'd avoided the war, regretted it, and wanted to prove himself.

No, Hal had no idea whether someone's missing wife had signed on under another name, and didn't have time to look.

No – and this was the worst – Hal couldn't accept the schoolboys who sometimes showed up at the docks, with improvised knapsacks, looking for adventure. He couldn't manage to be fatherly and order them back home, remembering himself as a young runaway. But he couldn't take them.

To see the hope in their eyes extinguished like a snuffed candle . . . this sat hard with him, and he took it out on the dockyard workers.

Sometimes it wasn't hard to turn down volunteers at all: men and women with strange, distant looks in their eyes, who wanted something from Hal he couldn't, didn't dare, offer them. Only a few of them were combat veterans, although several lied about their experience.

Sometimes, somebody he'd have liked to have aboard turned him down:

Sir Loren Damien, he of the gentle soul and deadly flying skills, arrived. He listened to Hal's spiel, then smiled.

"First, I'm not going with you. I'm perfectly happy on my farm, raising horses that don't try to tear my leg off, unlike dragons, and tenants who have no interest in anything beyond their plough, a bit of beef, and a pint in the local.

"I came down to test myself, which I suppose is unfair to you, but I wanted to know if I could be wooed by the thought of distant lands and deadly enemies.

"I find I'd rather read about it, later, when Sir Thom writes of your adventures."

He and Hal had a riotous night in the fleshpots, and Hal went back to his work much more cheery, even with an aching head.

Another who wouldn't go, because Hal didn't offer, was Sir Thom. Hal remembered the time the taleteller had gone into the field and found that the whisper of the ax and the whine of the arrow were not for him, except when they were told about at a distance.

Ex-fliers swarmed to him, including a few Sagene, who'd somehow heard of the expedition.

Hal was intrigued that a good percentage of them were women, wondered why, got no volunteered explanations.

He signed fourteen of the very best on, which gave him a few extra bodies to allow for sickness and loss.

He noted, and didn't like noting, a short, slender, Sagene brunette named Kimana Balf. She reminded him of the dead Saslic Dinapur entirely too much, and Hal had forced the past away and wanted nothing romantic in the present.

But she had a great deal more experience than her years and features suggested, and Hal took her on.

One of the last fliers to appear was Hachir. Hal had roughly recruited him at the beginning of the war as a crossbowman, to ride behind him and kill Roche fliers. Hachir had done well, then the ex-teacher had gone back to his infantry regiment.

Later, he'd shown up as a fledgling dragon-flier, explaining that he'd liked flying, and had applied and made it through school. But his return to Deraine had otherwise been a disaster, when he discovered his wife had found a lover.

Seldom smiling, Hachir had done yeoman's work in the final days of the war, managing to survive the vast aerial battles.

But now, he was still mournful-faced.

Farren asked if he was related to a beagle, or had hard times stayed with him after he got out of the military.

"No, the times weren't hard," Hachir said, trying a smile and failing. "I went back to teaching, but couldn't stand nattering little voices and the squeak of chalk."

Farren reported to Hal.

"Too well rehearsed a hoary story." He stopped, made a face. "I guess he's just one of the ones who should've died, maybe getting some kind of medal."

He was silent for a time, then said, very quietly, "Maybe there's more than one with us who that could be said about."

Hal bought Mariah a drink, added Hachir to the roster.

Garadice had found his dragons – mostly the big blacks that did so well, all of them with battle experience. These were in the peak of health, and as well trained as possible. Their riders would be responsible for the finishing touches, and making the beasts lose whatever bad habits their previous owners had given them.

Hal took Storm, even though he was neither huge nor a black, and a second dragon, one of the biggest blacks, which he wryly named Sweetie, after the dragon he'd once ridden that'd been named and raised by a little girl, and that had dumped him into captivity during the war.

Next to arrive were four magicians.

One, as King Asir had feared would happen, was the eminent Limingo. The second was his carefully schooled subordinate, Bodrugan. With them were two acolytes, of course chosen as much for their looks as their sorcerous talent.

"The king isn't going to like this," Hal said.

Limingo shrugged.

"Let him come up with more interesting needs for magic, then."

"What's he going to do, anyway?" Bodrugan asked. "Magicians, even clean-cut sorts such as ourselves, can wreak a terrible vengeance."

Hal nodded nervously, and had Mariah sign them aboard and give them the best staterooms on the *Galgorm*.

With over five hundred men and women, Hal was about ready to sail out.

He was on the deck of the *Galgorm* late one afternoon when he saw a rather large and shabbily dressed man come in the gate of the yard, looking about furtively.

Hal recognized him instantly – the cart-size thug, Babil Gachina, his cellmate.

Hal, half figuring what he wanted, went to the dock to greet him.

"Want to go with you," Gachina announced.

"How much trouble are you in?" Hal asked.

Babil looked surprised.

"How did you know?"

"You didn't exactly have the look of a good, honest working man about you coming through the yard."

"Mmmmh," Babil said. "Got to work on that. Maybe that's what give me away."

"You were doing what at the time?"

"A little robbin'," Gachina said. "Nothin' violent. But the man whose carriage I was rifling's got friends. Friends with other friends who're warders and such. Thought it might be best if I wasn't seen around the usual parts for a while."

Hal thought about what he was going to do and say, thought it would be the worst sort of romanticism.

"You know what happens to thieves aboard ship?" he asked.

Gachina shook his head.

"Sometimes they just get tipped overside," Hal said. "Or sometimes both hands get nailed to an beam, and the thief gets beaten, sometimes so he has trouble walking ever."

Gachina stared at him. Kailas, not flickering, stared back.

"My brother said you was a hard man."

Kailas didn't reply.

"Awright," the crook said. "I give you my family word, which I ain't never broken, that I'll do no harm to nobody or their property, and behave like a good an' proper citizen. At least until I advises you different.

"If you'll have me."

"I'll have you," Hal said. "We can always use a man of muscle. But break your word with me, and I guarantee there'll be no trial or beating.

"I'll deal with you myself."

Gachina looked at the deck, was silent.

Hal stuck out his hand.

"Now . . . welcome aboard."

A smile slowly spread across the big man's face, and he stuck out what had to be a hand, since it was at the end of his arm.

Finally, Hal could find nothing and no one more to require on the ships, and held a final conference for the baying broadsheet scribes, making a mildly revolting but no doubt sonorous speech about the expedition and the most honorable king who'd funded it.

Three days later, the six ships set out.

It appeared as if all of Rozen, and half of Deraine itself, lined the banks of the river leading down to the Chicor Straits, all waving flags and cheering.

King Asir's yacht sat in midstream as they sailed past, and the king was in the bows, holding his scepter, in ceremonial robes.

The adventurers bowed, then gave him a cheer.

Hal stood at the salute until they were past the yacht, then ordered sea watches set.

Everyone except Hal, Mariah, and the king thought the party was headed toward foreign shores.

It would be . . . after one stop.

There would be no room for mistakes beyond the Western Ocean.

19

The secret stop Hal ordered was off the fishing village of Brouwer, about as far west on Deraine as it was possible to be. He'd detached Cabet days earlier, and a detail of twenty men with wagon-loaded supplies.

The supplies were deliberately left in large piles on a dreary, rain-swept moor beyond the village.

Hal's ships were anchored off the port, and all hands brought ashore and marched to the moor.

The order was given to pitch camp, and stand by for further orders.

Everyone set to, after a few moments of surprise that the expedition wasn't well on its way to sea and foreign adventure.

Hal, Limingo and Farren Mariah worked as hard as anyone. Harder, for their eyes and ears were pitched for whiners or malingerers.

There were a few.

They were taken aside, and told they were discharged, effective immediately, from the expedition.

Most of them were astonished.

Hal brought them together, and made a short speech:

"Adventure starts in the shitter, most often. If you women and men can't handle putting up a few tents when it's soggy out, and still manage a laugh, how in the hells do you think you'll stand real hardship?"

They were sent back aboard one of the dispatch boats, which also carried letters to an equal number of the almost-qualified, telling them there were new openings with the Dragonmaster.

Most of the slackers eliminated, Hal called the survivors into a group, and made another short speech:

"You're soldiers, each of you. Now we'll train you to work together. An army, or an expedition, isn't just a group of wild-haired adventurers, in spite of what the taletellers blather."

Each man and woman was required not only to hone old skills and talents, but to learn another trade.

Hal anticipated casualties, with no replacements thousands of leagues from home.

So scouts learned how to clerk, farriers learned how to soldier, and, most importantly, everyone learned about dragons.

The training was, of course, hasty, and probably wouldn't hold together beyond the first encounter with an unknown foe, if there was to be one.

They even played war games, small-size battles.

These were remarkable because casualties were named in mid-problem. Suddenly a private would become a section leader, frequently with no idea of what the battle was about.

Officers and warrants were chosen, tried, and, sometimes, reduced to the ranks. This was no particular disgrace – the only privileges those in charge had were working harder, longer hours than their underlings, and wearing a dark strip of cloth around their right arm.

The dragons and their fliers were sweated as hard as anyone. Some of them, like the Sagene, didn't know the trumpet calls the Deraine warriors used, so they had to learn. Hal insisted on everyone knowing the signals for a few simple formations: line abreast, column, and a group of vees.

Each flier picked a wing mate, and trained with him or her, flying close company. If they didn't get along, or, more importantly, their dragons hated each other, they found another partner.

Garadice had done an excellent job of making sure the dragons were roughly trained and able to mostly get along with other beasts, so there weren't any major problems when the fliers applied their own finishing touches. There'd be more learning, for both dragon and people, when they finally set sail.

Hal was delighted at the smoothness and rapidity of the training, but gave little sign of his elation, consciously developing a reputation as a man for whom perfection was only passing.

He thought often of Lord Cantabri, and how much he would've liked to have been along, and how much Hal would have appreciated being just a dragon-flier under his command.

He paid little attention to his people's private lives, figuring that anyone who was willing to fight and die should be able to figure out who they wanted to bed or befriend. One rule was that any man lifting a hand against his fellow would be immediately discharged.

He let his men ruminate about what that would mean in practice when they were at sea, and beyond setting someone back on the road for Rozen.

After three weeks, he thought the force had learned as much as it could without stretching the training into months, and had a second shipment of wagons sent for.

When the wagons, filled with delicacies and luxuries, arrived, he told the force they were ready to sail, and would be off duty for two days.

He ordered that anyone found disturbing the peace in Brouwer might be tossed off the expedition, and at least would be given a set of lumps and kitchen detail for the voyage.

To make sure nobody got rowdy in the little fishing port, he detailed two sets of largeish people, including Chook and Babil Gachina, as peacekeepers.

Hal meant this as a final test of Gachina – if he misbehaved, or took advantage, he could walk back to Rozen while the expedition went on without him.

Kailas gave himself a day off as well – he paid for the exclusive use of Brouwer's best café, of the three available, and told them to do their best.

He intended to spend the evening there alone, thinking of anything but dragons, and then have a dreamless, peaceful sleep for at least eight hours.

Spring loomed, but there was still a bite to the air.

Hal left camp, and strolled through Brouwer. Only a few of his team were in the village – the villagers had been neither warm nor cold to the soldiers, something which Hal could have told them was typical of the north-western coast.

They'd already had their sendoff, anyway, back in Rozen, so almost all of the expedition members settled for the delicacies Hal had ordered and the simple joys of being back aboard ship, with a bed off the ground, and a roof overhead against the rain.

Kailas, an hour early for his dinner, went down by the jetty, and watched the fishing smacks tied to the docks for a time.

That was not a life he envied – hard, dangerous, and not terribly well paying. But those who loved it, loved it.

It was chill, a wind coming off the sea, and he pulled his cloak tightly about him, thinking of the warm brandy he'd be having in a few moments.

There was only one other person on the wharf, who was also staring to sea.

After a moment, Hal recognized her:

Kimana Balf, the Sagene dragon-flier.

He was walking toward her, intended to move behind her, without bothering whatever thoughts she was having, but instead wished her "Good morrow."

"And the same to you, sir," she replied.

"A bit chill out."

"I like the cold," she said. "Always have. When I was growing, that meant, unless it came too early, that we'd made it through another year."

Hal had expected some inconsequential reply, and then a good evening.

Instead:

"Why?" he asked. "What odd trade were you in? Fur coats, perhaps?"

Kimana laughed.

"No. I . . . or rather my father was . . . is . . . a vintner.

The first freeze, which should mark that all your grapes are off the vine and trampled into the vats, marks the first time you can relax, when the damned gods aren't be able to flood or bake or freeze your crop."

She shook her head.

"A hellish trade."

"I can think of a worse one," Hal said. "Two worse ones, really."

"Which are?"

"Scrabbling underground for coal, keeping one ear always cocked for the crack of a pit timber. Or," and he nodded his head at the docks, "going after fish in a little spitkit in the middle of a storm."

Kimana laughed. "I guess most jobs that you're not in, not part of, aren't attractive."

Hal decided her trace of an accent was delightful.

"True," he said. "I could never stand to be a clerk in a city, for instance."

They walked on, each trying to come up with a worse way to spend a life.

They came to the café that Hal had bought out for the evening, and suddenly the thought of another solitary meal became intolerable.

"Have you eaten yet?" he asked in Sagene.

Kimana shook her head, spoke in the same language. "I hope the mess cooks have saved something."

"A better idea," Hal said, and asked her to dine with him.

She looked surprised.

"We're both off duty," he said. "So tonight I'm just me."

"Which is, Lord Kailas?"

"Hal."

They went in, were greeted by the owner and his wife, and served dinner.

They ate smoked fish on bits of brown bread; oysters on the half-shell; crab on toast with a butter, dessert wine, cream, and spice sauce; great mushrooms, raw, with an oil, vinegar, and spice dressing.

"I didn't plan on drinking," Hal explained. "So I wanted a chilled herb tea."

"I'll have the same."

"And I don't want any dessert," he said. "Not much of a sweet tooth."

"Umm," she said, and so he sent the owner out for a trifle. He himself had cheeses, and was replete.

During the meal they talked of this and that, but never about the expedition, and Hal realized how very attractive the young woman was.

"I swore I wouldn't bring up anything resembling our work," he said, very apologetically, "but there is a question that's been working at me for some time."

"Ask," Kimana said. "You have only to face a silence if I can't answer."

"I've wondered why we had so many women volunteers," he said.

"May all your questions be so easily answered," she said. "That's easy: men."

"Pardon?"

"Most of us – certainly myself – grew up thinking that men were always in charge of everything, that they always knew best.

"Then the war came along, and they were looking for people who wanted to fly dragons, and almost nobody knew anything about that, particularly in Sagene.

"I'd gone for two flights when a dragon-flier came through, and loved it.

"My father forbade anything as bizarre as joining the army, let alone flying along on a great lizard.

"I was betrothed to the son of a nearby winemaker . . . had been since I was born, I guess. It was one of those things that everybody expected I'd do.

"Including me, I suppose.

"But then a recruiter came along. And to my complete astonishment, I found myself going with him. And I loved flying my own dragon more than being a damned passenger. I loved everything about it, including the fighting."

She made a wry face.

"And somehow I lived . . . I joined right at the end of the fighting, but saw a fair bit of action.

"Then it was over.

"I thought of going back, marrying Vahx, spending my life having babies and squishing grapes, and a cold chill went down my spine.

"So I ended up in Fovant, on a small allowance from my father. He was scandalized I wasn't coming home and doing the right thing . . . I can almost hear the capital letters . . . but figured I'd come to my senses, and so didn't disinherit me or anything drastic.

"The gods bless and keep him.

"I studied art, realized I didn't have an inkling, then just hung about.

"Instead of coming to my senses, I heard about your expedition . . . and that was that."

"Interesting," Hal said. "I guess that sort of thing's true for men, as well."

"I think you're missing my point, and where this whole

thing started," Kimana said. "You could have gotten out of the service . . . or maybe you did . . . and done whatever you wanted to. So could most of the other men.

"It's different for women. We would've had to go back to things just as they were.

"Mostly, that involved men and marriage."

Kimana shook her head.

"But that wasn't what a lot of us wanted."

"What *did* you want?" Hal asked. "I ask, because it doesn't seem that any of us men know."

Kimana looked forlorn.

"I still don't know. I wish I did."

"When you figure out," Kailas said, "be sure and tell us."

"Interesting," Kimana said. "I wonder why no man ever said that to me . . . or I to him. Godsdamn it, sooner or later men and women have to learn to talk."

Hal thought of telling her about his wonderings about why his marriage had collapsed, about Saslic Dinapur, and her "There won't be any after-the-war for a dragon-flier." But he didn't.

He also thought about taking her hand, and didn't do that, either.

They walked back to the camp without talking much, but were comfortable in each other's company and their own thoughts.

Hal slept well that night, and woke with a smile on his lips, although he couldn't remember what he'd dreamed.

He allowed a day for recovery from hangovers, final rearrangements of the cargoes, and a chance for last-minute hesitations and resignations.

To his surprise, there were none.

The following day, they set sail on the evening tide, just at twilight.

There was only one person, a small girl, probably a fisherman's daughter, frantically waving goodbye from the jetty.

20

It was very calm for the Western Ocean as they passed beyond the island sheltering Brouwer. But when the ships hit the first long, rolling swells, there were more than a few landsmen, and even sailors who'd been away from the sea for a time, whose stomachs came up.

Hal Kailas was one of them. He kept swallowing, but his guts kept trying to inspect his gums.

He thought he was doing all right; after all, he'd been at sea before, and this was just queasiness.

He put himself amidships, next to a mast . . . and a bucket . . . in case the old adage didn't work.

He was just congratulating himself on his victory when a grizzled sailor went past, loudly chewing a sandwich largely made up of greasy pork.

The bucket came into play then, but Hal felt better afterwards. He went to the scuttle, rinsed his mouth, and concentrated on the watch.

But he didn't go below when the meal was called.

The small fleet set its course west and south, following the directions divined by Hal's vision.

He had ordered the ships' captains to set not only the normal watch, but a second man with a glass at the mast-head, to look for anything in the air. That watch was mounted an hour before dawn, lasting, in two-hour shifts, until an hour after dark.

He'd also taken the precaution of having a very heavy crossbow, almost a catapult, mounted high in the rigging of the four larger ships.

He didn't think dragons could see in the dark. At least, none of his civilized monsters could. And since man couldn't, either, there was no point in cutting into the expedition's sleep.

There was little rest for either the innocent or the wicked. Warrants ran troops up and down ramps and ropes, regardless of whether they were expected to fight or forage, keeping them in shape.

Hal kept his fliers in the air for at least half a day, every day that weather permitted, slowly accustoming the drag-ons and men who hadn't spent time over water to the situation.

He had Limingo recast his spell to the ship's beef, so a lost flier merely had to touch an amulet, think of the salt beef in casks aboard the *Adventurer*s, and the spell would tell him in what direction he did *not* want to go. All the flier then had to do was ignore his stomach, and fly in that direction.

Outside of producing some gastric distress, particu-larly in Farren Mariah, the spell worked as well as it had earlier.

One thing Kailas did not do, and his officers were strictly

ordered to do the same, was waste his people's time with idiotic drills or details.

If you were off duty, you were off duty, and advised to get your head down, Kailas being a firm believer that sleep could and should be accumulated, as could fatigue.

If a soldier or sailor was caught larking about, then the kitchen called, with a loud and clarion voice.

And the passage wore on.

It might have gotten boring if all hands hadn't felt the unknown ahead, which is always a threat.

There were incidents to mark the days:

A huge whale, its back scarred by deep-sea battles with giant squid, passed through the middle of the formation one morning, its odorous spout guaranteeing attention.

Its wise and skeptical eyes considered what it could never have seen before, then it was beyond the expedition, and sounded.

Another time a school of dolphin frolicked around the bows of the ship, playing follow-my-leader, or tag, or who knew what.

Hal had been digesting a meal of the last of the eggs and fried ham and was contemplating feeding Storm and Sweetie, when the dolphin showed up.

They were leaping and cavorting, and Hal was miles away from the expedition, when a voice broke his contemplation:

"I don't believe in any sort of afterlife . . . but if there is, I think I might like to come back as one of them."

It was Kimana Balf.

Hal thought about it for an instant, nodded.

"There's worse," he said, and turned below to feed his monsters.

*

A storm struck, but one in the air. The sea was relatively calm, although the waves were whipped into froth, and the spray was a third element between air and water.

The ships had all sail struck, and kept a wide berth from their fellows.

Hal lay snug abed, listening to the clatter of the rigging, and the shouts of the seamen on watch.

Alone in his stateroom, he was almost asleep when the thought came that he wouldn't mind a bit of company.

That brought him fully awake, wondering just who his lecherous subconscious was thinking of.

It refused to tell him, and so he bundled back up in his blankets.

But he was not quite as content as he'd been before.

The seas grew warm, and warmer.

Men went on deck without gloves, or even a jacket.

Hal issued orders for any man taking off his jersey to be careful of sunburn, and promised that anyone who put himself in the lazaret for that cause could count on some nice healing saltwater baths to alleviate the pain.

Now a routine came:

Some men, those with little seagoing experience, spent time off watch staring at the horizons, hoping for sign of land, any land.

None came.

Experienced sailors remembered the past. Now, each man and woman had a space, self-assigned and created, only a few square feet. But when he was in it, he was alone, ignored by his neighbors on either side.

Similarly, officers could pace the quarterdeck quite precisely – so many steps toward the rail, turn, so many back, frequently with a fellow, dancing perfect attendance, pacing as he or she paced, turning when they turned. Others were doing the same, completely unaware of anyone else.

Hal felt the men and women could journey for years like that, with never a fight, seldom an argument.

Hal hurried with the others when someone shouted a flying fish was aboard.

He'd never seen such a creature, delicate fins, and light, multicolored body, its colors fading as it died on the wooden planks; had never sailed that far south.

Only the most experienced had, since Deraine was not a seafaring nation, and few of its ships had ever come into these unknown waters.

There was an argument starting about whether the fish flew, or just glided.

One sailor was pointing out, with inescapable logic, that it wouldn't be called a flying fish if it didn't really fly, when the shout came from the masthead.

High overhead, almost lost in the scattered clouds, were a pair of dragons.

Hal found a glass.

They were red and black, and even from this distance they looked huge.

Neither had riders, but they flew together in perfect formation.

Hal, remembering his dreams of murder and pain, felt cold fingers down his spine.

21

The dragons banked, then came down on the fleet as if they were no more than curious creatures who'd never seen man.

But they held to their close formation.

Hal watched, worrying.

Part of his mind reminded him that there were animals in his world that did the same – ducks, geese, the recently seen dolphins – without man's guidance.

Another part muttered, "Bullshit," and tried not to panic.

"All hands to alert," he shouted, and warrants' whistles shrilled.

Hal ran to the dragon stalls.

"I'll have Storm."

"Mine after," called Farren Mariah, checking his crossbow.

The wild dragons lifted from their dive about a thousand feet above the ships.

Storm, even though he was a domestically raised dragon, saw the red and blacks and started hissing like an angry teakettle as he came out of the stable deck, a groom hastily adjusting Hal's saddle.

"Shut up," Hal shouted, foot in a stirrup as he swung into the saddle. An armorer tossed him magazines of bolts, and his crossbow.

The dragon, still looking up at the red and blacks, and moving his head back and forth, thudded down the ramp to the launching barge in a timber-creaking run.

Storm's wings unfurled with a canvas-cracking snap. He took three more steps, was at the edge of the barge, and then he leapt up, and was in the air.

Hal snapped a magazine into place on the crossbow, brought the cocking piece back, then forward, and hung the ready weapon on its hook on Storm's carapace.

Behind him he saw Mariah's dragon climbing, wings slashing for altitude.

The foreign dragons pulled up sharply, and climbed, away from the ships.

They had speed and altitude on the two Derainian dragons, and, at about two thousand feet, converted height to more speed, diving down toward the water, and flying west-south-west.

Storm tried to catch them, but wasn't able.

Hal and Farren Mariah chased the two for a few miles, then broke off the pursuit, their ships still in sight, and turned back for safety, having no idea of what lay ahead.

The rest of the day passed without incident.

At nightfall, lookouts reported two more dragons dogging the fleet.

The dragons – or replacement scouts – were still there when the sun rose.

Hal didn't know what to do: the wild dragons weren't making any hostile moves, and all he knew about them was what he'd seen in his vision.

He didn't want to start a war or take sides in one yet, not knowing what caused the hatred between the red and blacks and other dragons.

But those two monsters endlessly circling overhead made everyone nervous.

The seas grew yet warmer, and the winds softer, but there was still no sight of land.

However, one of the dispatch boats saw something odd: a huge ring of floats, with nets hanging below them, but never a sight of any boats or men. It was torn, and appeared long abandoned.

Hal had Limingo cast a spell, to see if he could somehow sense the presence and form of the civilization that had made the nets, out there to the west.

Nothing came.

On the fourth day after the dragons had first been seen, lookouts shouted officers to the bridge.

There was nothing, at first, on the horizon.

A very sharp-eyed lookout in the bows, and one of the men at the masthead, were pointing due west.

Hal saw nothing, then slowly quartered the sea with his glass.

At first he thought it was a hair stuck to his lens. Then he saw another one.

There was nothing on his telescope.

He looked again out to sea.

The hair was larger than it had been, and was clearly closing on the fleet.

Hal waited.

In moments, it was clear:

It was some creature's neck, snakelike, sticking up about thirty feet above the water, leaving a purling wake behind it as it came.

"Ain't no seaweed-muncher," a lookout with a glass muttered.

Hal studied the creature. He could make out more of its features now. Atop the snaky neck was a flat, long head, with gaping jaws, and, even at this distance, sharp fangs.

No, it wasn't a vegetarian, not with teeth like that.

"Hands to alert," he called. "All dragon-fliers to their stations. Ready the beasts for takeoff."

Sailors hustled to obey.

The onrushing creature suddenly veered to the side, toward the *Bohol Adventurer*. A sailor was leaning on the rail, gaping at the beast. The beast's neck flashed out, jaws reaching, and Hal heard the scream across the water.

The sea monster had the man by the middle, jaws clenched.

It lifted the sailor clear of the ship. Hal saw his fists drum against the beast's head, to no avail. The creature turned on its side. Hal saw a thick body, fins fore and aft, and then the creature went under, carrying the sailor with it.

Another monster's head snaked out of the wake of the *Compass Rose*, reaching for the helmsman. But someone moved faster, and hurled a marlinspike into the beast's face.

It shrieked, rolled away, and then there was a forest of jaws coming out of the water beside one of the dispatch boats.

The creatures slammed into the side of the small ship, and rolled it hard, its rail almost going under.

The beasts tried again, and Hal realized they must have attacked ships before . . . or else they were far more intelligent than any sea creature he had heard of, other than a whale.

The dispatch boat rolled again, almost going over on its beam ends, and then there were dragons in the air.

One, flanked by his partner, dove at one of the monsters, and the rider sent a crossbow bolt into the beast's neck.

Correction . . . her partner, as Hal recognized the dragon as Kimana Balf's. Her partner, another Sagene, put his bolt into the beast's body, just at the base of the neck.

The monster screeched, rolled, snapping at itself, and went under.

Hal realized he had more important things to do than gape, and ran down from the bridge of the *Galgorm* to where Storm waited on the launching barge.

Farren Mariah was already orbiting above him, and Hal was airborne in seconds.

Dragons were pinwheeling, diving over the stricken dispatch boat, and Hal found a target, fired, hit the sea beast in its open mouth. It screeched, tucked its head underwater, and dove, Hal not knowing if it was wounded or killed.

He pulled Storm around, looking for another target as he worked the forehand of his crossbow back and forth, reloading it.

A pair of monsters were slamming against the dispatch boat's side, trying to overturn it.

Hal dove on them, and they saw him, and went under.

He looked for another target.

But the monsters had disappeared underwater, as if signaled by a leader.

The dragons patrolled around the ships as the fleet put on full sail.

But none of the sea creatures surfaced again.

After a time, Kailas blew the recall, and the dragons landed, one after the other, and were quickly led up the ramp to their pens.

Soldiers with spears and ready bows lined the rails of the ships.

But they weren't attacked again that day.

The dispatch boat's timbers were cracked, and the ship was leaking.

The crew wove lines through a spare sail, rove it overside as a patch. That would have to hold until they found secure land to careen the small ship and make more permanent repairs.

Hal thought of sending it, or the other dispatch craft, back to Deraine to report the incident.

But he decided there might be more important messages, and more information, to follow.

They sailed on.

Overhead, two more red and black dragons swung through the skies, watching.

22

They sailed on west, doggedly followed by alternating pairs of dragons.

"Clever enough by half," Farren Mariah observed. "Note, they change shift with the glass?"

Hal hadn't . . . it was worrisome enough that the dragons knew enough to replace one another. But now he kept track, and found Farren Mariah right.

Every now and again he ordered dragons into the air against them, but the bigger monsters, having altitude and speed, always avoided interception.

Then he gained another follower . . . or quite possibly more.

One of the snake-headed creatures appeared in their wake. When one of Hal's dragons swooped on it, it would submerge, then, stubbornly, reappear, never closing, never attacking.

Hal, assuming there were more underwater, posted a watch on the creature, and tried to put it out of his mind, without much luck.

He also noticed that the red and blacks liked these sea monsters as little as men did. One or another of them would occasionally, never with success, try to creep up on the snake-headed beasts, who'd always dive to safety in time.

Hal was starting to get nervous in this utterly unknown and foreign world.

None of the experienced seamen had seen either the red and black dragons or the snaky creatures before in their journeys . . . but then, none of them had been this far west.

The skies were clear and tropical, and temperatures grew still warmer.

But there was nothing on the horizon that suggested land.

Then, Limingo came to him one day and said he'd been having himself mesmerized, and, unconscious, let himself float west.

He'd sensed nothing, and had begun doubting the usefulness of this spell. Then one day, very vaguely, he'd sensed some sort of wizardry, "like a dull glow, before the sun rises, against the clouds," to the south-south-west.

He could nearly indicate the direction on the compass, and so Hal had the fleet's course changed in that direction.

Every day, he put up dragons in predawn darkness, hoping to ambush his followers.

But they figured out his plan, and now were almost on the horizon every dawn, only closing on the tiny fleet when the dragons came back aboard.

Hal gave that up, and put out paired dragons at dawn and dusk, directly on their course, and four more on ten-degree-divergent courses, sweeping ahead of the ships, hoping to see land, or at least whatever had sparked Limingo.

Four days later, they found land.

Of a sort.

The fliers returned to the *Adventurer*, had themselves boated across to the *Galgorm*, reported, in considerable perplexity.

Hal went out with Limingo behind him, flanked by three other dragons with Bodrugan and the two acolytes as passengers.

It *was* land, about two days' sail distant, and it was quite strange:

It was two islands, the larger about a third of a league in diameter, with reefs surrounded by a huge lagoon.

The main island appeared to be solidly wooded, with no sign of life.

The second island was lightly wooded, also with no signs of settlement.

But beyond the low reefs, which had waves breaking across them, were half a dozen of the net circles they'd seen earlier.

These ones were well-kept, and Hal, looking down on them, understood how cleverly they'd been built. They weren't free-floating, but fixed to stakes. Another net, on the inside of the circle, fastened to booms, extended from one side to the other.

A gate could be opened at either side of the circle, then closed, when fish were penned up.

Then the boom would be worked across, narrowing one of the semi-circles, making it easy to scoop the net's prey out.

But there was no sign of boats or men.

Hal took his dragons lower, but still saw nothing.

He swept over the island, and it looked even stranger –

as if it had been roofed, and then the roofing had sprouted branches and leaves.

That made no sense.

"There is magic down there," Limingo shouted over Kailas's shoulder. "Or there has been."

Hal nodded understanding, blew the recall, and they returned to the fleet.

He kept his crews on half-alert all that night and the next day, going to full alert as they closed on the island, even though they'd seen nothing but their constant followers overhead.

Limingo and Bodrugan cast and recast spells.

Nothing.

The snake thing had, thankfully, vanished. At least for the moment.

Hal took half a flight aloft as they approached.

The day before, the lagoon had been deserted, peaceful.

Now, it was a battlefield.

The snake things had swarmed the lagoon, and were tearing at the nets.

But they were not undefended.

Small creatures, smaller than a man, but thicker-bodied, were splashing about, doing their best to drive the snake-heads away.

They weren't animals – they were using sticks, some sharpened at the end, and clubs against the creatures.

But there were too many of the snake-heads.

Hal hesitated for an instant, remembered the old proverb that the "enemy of my enemy is my friend," and grinned to himself.

He blew a note on the trumpet, and Farren swooped close.

"Back to the ship," he ordered. "Bring the others. And spare magazines."

Farren, his reins hanging limply, made a "why are we doing this" gesture, laughed, and dove away.

Hal pointed down, and blew the single note:

"Attack."

And down they went, some on his heels, some hesitating a moment before gigging their dragons downward.

Hal noticed, and was oddly pleased, that Kimana Balf was one of the first to attack, her long dark hair sweeping back behind her.

But the disciplinarian in him made a note to chide her about the hair. It might have been beautiful, and most warrior-like to see, but Hal had known three fliers who had worn their hair long, and were somehow strangled by it, in battle.

He put such nonsense out of his head, loaded his crossbow, and looked for a target.

There were many of them.

He found one, aimed at its head, waited until Storm was very close, killed the beast.

Storm himself was hissing, snarling angry.

His tail lashed around, almost spinning him out of the skies, and caught one of the snake things and tore its head off.

He had another in his talons, tore its chest open as Hal killed his second beast.

Hal expected the snake things to break off, but they were determined to fight, swirling around the nets, striking up at the dragons.

The water creatures had a better chance now, as the snake things ignored them for the moment.

They drove their pathetic spears deep into the monsters' chests and necks, and when the creatures rolled, went for their underbellies.

Hal took Storm up, around, and back down in a dive, killing two more of the beasts.

He heard a scream, saw a dragon, caught by a snake thing by a wing, pulled down into the water. Its flier spun off, splashed down, and three snake things tore at him.

Hal kicked Storm around, killed one of the creatures. Then Cabet was coming in from another direction, killing a second.

But where the flier had splashed down, there was nothing but a froth of blood.

Hal brought his forehand grip back, forward, but there was no bolt in the trough.

He swore, pulled the empty magazine free, dropped it in the canvas bag beside him, clipped another magazine in place, and then Farren Mariah, at the head of six other dragons, dove into the fray, a whirlpool of screaming, killing dragons, and their prey.

The snake things seemed to realize then that they were being slaughtered, and broke away, swimming at their best for a gap in the reefs.

Hal's dragons harried them out, and then the monsters vanished into deep water.

Hal took Storm up and around again, and there, just outside the lagoon, was his fleet.

He wondered how the ships could have arrived so quickly, then realized the sun was low in the sky. It was almost dusk.

The barges were in position on the *Adventurer*s, and he signaled for the dragons to land.

He orbited overhead until everyone had landed, then brought Storm in, staggering with fatigue as he came out of the saddle.

He looked out, across the lagoon toward the island.

The water beings had swum to the edge of the reef, and bobbed in the water, only their heads in the air.

They reminded Hal of curious harbor seals.

One of the creatures eeled over the rocks into the open sea, and was swimming toward the *Galgorm*. He reached the landing barge as Storm was led up to the stable deck.

The being was covered with sleek fur, had a pug nose, and intelligent eyes.

It stared for a long time at Hal, as if evaluating him.

Then it lifted both paws – no, hands, with stubby but noticeable fingers – out of the water, palm up.

A sign of peace?

Hal didn't know, but he walked slowly forward, holding his own hands up, weaponless.

23

"Throw him a fish," someone shouted.

Hal glowered back in the direction of the voice. This was no time for japing.

"I'm not jesting," the voice came again, and Hal recognized it as Farren Mariah's. There came a wet-sounding *splot* on the barge deck.

The sea being still trod water close to the barge.

Hal, feeling very much the fool, picked up the fish, and, holding it in both hands, presented it to the creature.

He swore if he heard one laugh from behind him, that person would be sweeping dragon shit for the rest of the voyage.

No one laughed.

The creature lifted out of the water, took the fish, equally ceremoniously, looked up the ramp after the vanished Storm, then dove underwater.

And the watching sea beings disappeared as well.

Hal didn't know what to make of it.

"I s'pose," Farren Mariah said, "we'll now find out if that's a fish that meets their fancy. A fancy fish, as 'twere."

Hal grunted.

"We'll anchor out here," he said. "Put four dragons in the air, and a detail, with crossbows, on each ship to watch for those damned snakes. And man the crossbows at the mastheads."

Two turnings of the glass later, they found out, as sea creatures bobbed up, on the seaward side of the rocks this time, and, not waiting for an invitation, swarmed the ships.

Hal didn't know whether to sound the alarm, but found it was too late, as a wallow of sea creatures buried him.

One was on his lap, another was curiously nuzzling his neck, a third was seemingly fascinated by his smooth skin. All of the creatures were chattering incessantly and loudly, as if sure their listeners understood everything.

"Off me," he growled. "You're too fat to be cute."

But no one paid any attention, until they heard a sharp bark.

One creature – perhaps the one Hal had given the fish to – was splashing for attention about a dozen yards in front of the *Galgorm*. Another one motioned at Hal, chattered away, then pointed with a stubby finger at the creature in the water, who swam into the lagoon, turning and beckoning as he did.

Hal had an instant to think.

It would be better inside the lagoon, assuming there weren't any enemies there, than outside, with the snake monsters.

He ordered all six ships to up anchor, and, with a favoring breeze, to sail into the lagoon.

At least, he thought forlornly, we're making our own trap.

As the ships began moving, the creatures dove off them, and swam alongside.

The six anchored in beautifully clear, almost transparent water, and then the creatures came back aboard.

This time, they had fish of their own to present, and various kinds of exotic fruit from the island nearby.

Kailas guessed they'd made friends.

The sea creatures seemed fascinated by the least thing any man or woman did. They even tried to follow, flopping awkwardly on legs that were as much fins as anything, when someone went into the canvas-screened jakes in the ship's bows.

"Like dogs," one flier said.

"No," Quesney said. "Not like dogs at all. Something else. Something I can't put my mind to. But it's unsettling.

"I think."

Limingo was ready with his spell.

He'd taken a bit of fruit peel one of the sea people had cast aside, water from the lagoon, herbs from his chest, and put them into a cotton bag.

He'd dipped the bag in some noxious substance, and surreptitiously rubbed it against the furry back of one of the sea creatures.

He'd touched it to his lips, and then to Hal's, while murmuring foreign phrases, then:

> "*Speak tongue*
> *Ears listen*
> *From them*
> *To us*
> *Bring words*
> *Bring thoughts*
> *Carry them*
> *To us*
> *To our lips.*"

After that came a long chant, again in an unknown language.

Quite suddenly, the sea creatures' chatter came clear, many voices talking all at once:

"Big . . . so big . . . could use to pull nets . . . one like us . . . tall naked tree . . . sun higher . . . check nets . . . nets tight . . . new twine . . . fruit good . . . babe has hunger . . . foot scraped . . . watch for wolas . . . like Hnid . . . float well . . ."

"Great gods," Hal managed.

"Now we can talk to them," Limingo said.

"If we want to," he added wryly.

Naturally, once the sea creatures – who called themselves the Hnid – found out that two of the big ones could understand them, their nattering grew louder and quicker.

Hal had to listen to most of it, since Limingo was busy administering the spell to all officers, fliers, and anyone else interested.

"Pour me another brandy," Kailas said.

Limingo obeyed.

"I always thought primitive people – if the Hnid are people – had primitive languages.

"Hah. More fool me. Do you know, they have five different ways to describe how rotten a fish is."

"I'm not surprised," Limingo said. "And they *are* people, if not very advanced. Animals aren't that big a pain. Oh, by the way, those snakes are 'wolas', if you care."

"I'm not sure I do," Hal said. "Not to mention that I'm starting to doubt whether magic is always that useful."

"You and me both."

The dispatch boat the snake monsters had attacked was warped into shallow water near the smaller island, unloaded, then careened.

There was enough dry, seasoned wood in the holds of the ships to make repairs, and the seams were stuffed with oakum and the hull was tarred.

The sailors worked hard, no one taking more than a momentary break.

No one wanted to be stranded on this strange island if anything happened.

In two days, when the tide rose, the dispatch boat was righted with levers and rope pulleys taken from the ship's lines and yards, then bodily dragged when the tide was out into deeper water in the lagoon.

Fully afloat, its boats brought its cargo back aboard.

"Seamanlike, that," Farren approved. "Yo ho diddly ho, and have the cabin boy buggered by all hands as a prize reward."

So the sea people *were* on their side.

Except that "scent" of magic that Limingo had felt still needed explanation.

He, Bodrugan, and the two acolytes wanted to explore the islands. There was no objection to them landing on the smaller island and exploring it, which took minutes.

But when it came to the larger, wooded island, the Hnid began whimpering, almost trying physically to stop them.

Limingo halted his investigation for the moment.

It was the enormous brewer's wagon that was Babil Gachina who make the discovery.

The Hnid looked at him with awe, for his size. Chook the cook was similarly regarded.

Why Gachina swam ashore to the wooded island and began exploring was never explained. He claimed he was gathering fruit. Hal wondered if he was looking for something that might be worth looting, but held his tongue.

In any event, after a couple of hours, Gachina reappeared on the beach, looking shaken, and swam back to the *Galgorm*. He sought out Hal.

"There's . . . there's a frigging city under that wood!" he managed. "A frigging great city! With carvings everywhere!"

Hal quizzed a couple of the Hnid, got only the vague explanation of "dry home," "old home," and "home before," which gave him nothing.

But it was enough.

He collected Limingo, ten men of the expedition with raider experience, plus Gachina, Chook and Farren Mariah, armed them and went ashore. It might have been impolite, but they were too far from home to worry about proper etiquette.

There was more wordless complaining from the Hnid, but they made no move to stop Hal and the others.

"Here," Gachina said. "Here's the way I found to go in."

It looked like the entrance to a fox's burrow. The brush that had been cleverly arranged to hide an entrance hole had been shoved aside to make room for someone of Gachina's bulk.

Gachina went first, Hal behind him, holding back the desire to draw his sword.

He'd expected the burrow to close down, and pushed back his fear of closed spaces, but instead it widened out.

Hal was able to stand, and found himself in what might have been the hall of a forest king.

On either side were great squared stones, carefully trimmed to fit together without a gap.

Here and there were doors and windows, narrow, taller than a man, cut into the stone.

Overhead were the "woods." Hal puzzled, then realized that trees had been grown into saplings, then bent over and tied so they formed an arc over the stones and the streets between them, hiding the city.

He wondered why, thought about the red and black dragons, thought that might be an explanation.

"Here's your magic," Limingo said, almost whispering.

There was no threat, felt or seen, but Kailas felt as if he were in an eerie temple.

"I feel no sense of man's hand working these stones," Limingo said. "But the smell of magic is still very strong, if very old."

There was no point in just gaping.

The men spread out, as if they were on a combat patrol, and they moved through this deserted monolithic city.

It was not unoccupied – Hal saw a Hnid duck back into cover, saw a couple of pups on a higher landing.

But no one came to them, no one spoke to them, and there was none of the Hnid chittering to be heard.

The streets wound around, came back on themselves.

The city felt much larger than it was.

They came to a central square, and saw a ramped passageway leading down, high-ceilinged and wide.

Hal felt a vast reluctance to go down the ramp.

"Don't go down there." Limingo echoed his feeling.

"Why not?"

"I . . . I don't know. But it's not wise."

Hal waited for an explanation, but none came.

They found an avenue away from the entrance to whatever was underground.

The stones on either side, polished ebony, were carefully carved.

They began with beings like the Hnid, swimming in the sea, fishing, fighting battles with fabulous monsters, some of them snake things.

Then stones were shown being carved from a great, looming mountain, shaped, with no mason shown in the carvings, then somehow lifted out to sea and carefully stacked, and the city was born.

There were other islands pictured, other cities built.

Then there were great ships, little more than barges, with twin square sails, sailing away from the cities toward the land beyond.

After that . . . nothing.

There was empty space on the stones to continue the story.

But no one had.

No one knew what to make of it, and so they returned to their ships.

Hal, thinking of that eldritch passage underground, kept men on alert that night.

And, when he finally was able to sleep, he dreamed.

24

All there was, at first, was a soft, diffident voice, amid a roiling sea of gray. The words came haltingly, as if the dream was trying to find a common language with Hal:

I am Malvestin, of the Hnid.

I am but a simple recorder.

But I come from a generation of fisher-leaders, those we call kings, and it is my task to remember from the beginning, when we were but simple animals, living in the shallows, catching our brothers, the fish, with our fangs, as they did, then, later, as our bodies changed, with our fingers.

Hal was now in that street of carvings, of what was the Hnid's history. He saw the carvings, then they came to life, took on the colors of the real world, and moved past him as the voice continued:

That gave us power over our brothers, but we held it wisely, never taking from the sea more than we needed.

But then greed came on us, and we wanted more, and that may be our doom.

Strange creatures came from the depths, and we were their prey.

There had been stories before, about what could happen to those who ventured close to the depths that went down as canyons from our warm, comfortable shallows.

There were many kinds, some huge-winged yet still fish; some like the snakes of the sea that we avoided, but these were huge, and had gross bodies like whales; some were monstrous sharks; others jellyfish larger than any seen, with dangling tentacles that meant death to all who touched them.

We fought back as best we could, with our arms, then with sharpened sticks we found along the shore of the islands we lived near.

We grew more clever, and found our enemies' lairs, and destroyed their eggs, their sprats, just as they found our hatchlings.

Somehow, and this is an art that is now long lost, we learned to have thoughts with the tiny beings that make sea-rocks, and taught them to build in giant circles, around the islands that we chose to live near.

Now we were safer from our enemies, only the snake-headed creatures having sense enough to come in through the small openings in our reefs that we needed for entry and exit, and to work the nets in the outer waters that we had come to use instead of our fingers and spears.

All was good, all was far quieter, and we grew to love the power we had gained.

Now we struck back against the monsters, driving them from our shallow seas into the canyon depths.

Again, our power grew, and some of us learned to work spells, things that could reach for leagues and make changes, or make the fish come to us.

We grew bolder, and, leaning upon our magic as a weapon, we explored the seas, the islands, and found the great island to the west.

Emboldened, we left the water not just for hours, but for days, and our bodies changed, grew legs.

Land and sea were now ours, and we used our sorcery to reach inland.

We found a mountain, then others, who were as sounding boards to our magic, and whose boulders could be worked and transported by wizardry. We carved huge boulders out, and moved them through the water, and then, later, as our powers grew, through the air to our islands.

Fitting stone on stone, we built houses out of the water, then larger buildings we used for gathering places.

Our mother, the sea, was no longer trusted, and we took to the land more and more.

Our cities, our islands, were now outposts to warn against danger.

We built huge rafts, put wind-catchers on them, and sailed west, leaving only the best and bravest on our frontiers.

Now it was time to give up the sea.

We built, on the edges of the western lands, more cities, and, from these, we explored into the land.

There were huge beasts. Some we fought, others were no threat, in spite of their size.

The Hnid stood brave.

Now the world was ours.

Now the elements were ours to worship, but also to serve us.

There was nothing but good around us, and we were the world's masters.

But wise ones thought that we had come too far, too fast, and there was a nameless doom in store.

We laughed at them, but our mirth was hollow.

I wonder.

There was silence, and Hal's dream gave him no images, but in the background, very quietly, was the hiss of breaking waves.

Then another voice came:

Oh Malvestin, you spoke truth, for now is the tale of the downfall of the Hnid.

I am Quarsted, also a recorder, but of the people, not of those who called themselves kings, and ruled with no thought for the morrow and brought our people to grief.

We forsook the sea for the land, and our bodies changed, our lower limbs growing longer and with greater strength.

We settled the edges of the great land, pushed inland. Now our people sought things other than food and shelter.

Now the glitters that mountain streams held became precious, as did other baubles worn by our mates.

We, the Hnid, ruled the world.

Or so we thought.

And then it changed.

There had been dragons, winged snakes, in the skies when we found this new land, and at first we feared them greatly, for we saw them fight against the monsters of the land, and truly they were great warriors.

But they made only a few attempts against us, and so we forgot about them, since there were worse enemies closer at hand, the ferocious beasts of the forests and savannas.

And then it changed.

Our scouts reported a new sort of dragon in the skies. These were red and black, far larger than any we'd seen before.

We saw them attack the other dragons as if they were two different breeds, fighting wars to the death, and driving the older dragons out of the choicer roosting places.

And then they turned against us.

They acted as if they were at least as wise as we were, working in pairs, or trios, or greater forces against us.

They would attack our settlements, fighting from the air until they found an advantage, then landing, as if they were ground beings, and fighting with their deadly claws, fangs and tails.

We could not hold against them.

And so we fell back, from the mountains to the plains, using the rivers to move at night, very grateful that our bodies still held a bit of the scorned water-love.

We fell back and back, to our great towns along the coasts.

Even here these savage dragons attacked us, over and over, even by night.

We drew closer together, and fought as best we could. But that best was not enough, and now the land, and the cities we had built were no longer guardians, but traps for us.

Again, we retreated to the water, and, in time, gave up the mainland.

Our mother, the sea, welcomed us back, although she should have scorned us, and once again, our bodies changed, back to what they were before.

We did not need legs, we did not need deep thoughts, and so the sea took them from us as her price for safety.

Our minds grew torpid, dull, needing little more than the power to feed and shelter ourselves.

We Hnid retreated to our outpost islands, and the tall trees that had grown up on them were woven together to give our cities cover, for the huge dragons still attacked us without mercy.

No one knew why they struck against us, for we meant them no harm, could do little damage to these nightmares from the skies.

No one knew why they fought against what should have been their brothers, attacking without mercy. We saw dragons hard struck, wounded, fleeing to the east, and knew not what shelter they would find.

The snake beings returned from the depths to savage us.

Our mates saw little good in breeding, and so, as the years go past, there are fewer and fewer Hnid born, and fewer of those surviving to become adults.

Now we are as we began.

Woe is ours, woe unto the tenth generation.

All is ended for my people, I fear.

The gods or whatever greater beings there are, if there are any, help us, and those who come and hear our tale take warning for their own lives and the lives of their people.

25

Hal awoke, fighting back tears and rage for the people, the Hnid, of his dreams.

He splashed water on his face from a bucket, opened a port and let the warm dawn wind take away the memories of his dream.

If it was a dream.

He washed, cleaned his teeth, dressed and left his cabin for the deck.

He didn't want to speak to anyone until he'd recovered, but Kimana Balf was at the taffrail, staring down at the ship's wake, her face grim.

"And don't you look cheery," he managed.

"Don't rag me. Sir," she said. "I didn't sleep well."

Hal started to pass by, then stopped.

"You dreamed?"

"And never want to again," she said.

"Tell me about it," he said.

She pursed her lips, said nothing.

Hal took the lead, and told her of his dream, of Malvestin and Quarsted, and the rise and fall of the Hnid.

Balf jolted.

"I, too, dreamed of the Hnid. But my singers were female, and I don't recollect their names."

"I think," Hal said, after considering, "that we had best consult Limingo. This is most odd."

It grew more strange.

Limingo, Bodrugan, and their two assistants had also had the same visions, with small differences.

"Very strange indeed," Limingo said. "And, if it's a vision, the strangest thing is the way the Hnid change – or are changed – in a few generations."

"Not necessarily," Bodrugan said. "I've read of a lizard, in the far south, which can shed its legs and become a snake when it is dry, or grow flippers if the rains are heavy."

"Still ..." Limingo let his voice trail off while he thought. "It would seem, though, that the Hnid can hardly be considered men."

"I care little of that," Hal said. "But I think we ought to summon the officers of all four ships for a conference. And the fliers."

"I agree," Limingo said, and flags were hoisted, and boats rowed across to the *Galgorm*.

The officers assembled in the huge wardroom, and Hal told of the dream, and Limingo that he believed this was hardly a dream, but a true vision.

There were nervous stirs at that. No one said anything for a few moments, then Guapur Hagi, captain of the *Bohol Adventurer*, looked at Hal and cleared his throat nervously.

"I think . . . without meaning to sound like a poltroon . . . that this dream, assuming the wizards are right and it's the truth . . . means we should turn back to Deraine.

"For I, too, have dreamed this dream of sorrow and punishment of the gods."

There was muttered anger from a few, and agreement about having dreamed as well from others.

Hal held up his hand for silence, then asked, calmly, "Why?"

"Because, well, this sounds like these red and black dragons have some kind of state or something," Hagi said. "I think we might be being foolish, and continuing into what might be a trap.

"Or that we could be outnumbered.

"I think," he said, gaining confidence, "we should advise the king of what we've discovered so far, and see what he wants to do.

"Maybe try to make peace, or fit out some kind of expedition or something."

"We *are* the expedition," Hal said.

"I meant, like a fleet, with a lot more soldiers."

"As yet," Hal said, "we don't have enough information to do that."

"I think we ought to put it to a vote," Hagi said.

"No," Hal said, and his voice carried steel.

"This is not a village conclave. You people put yourselves under my command, which the king himself trusted me to hold.

"There is nothing that gives you the right to question me whenever you want, whenever things go awry. We came on this expedition because we wanted to experience and explore the unknown, and that is what we are facing.

"As you are my officers, I take what you say under advisement, just as I listen to the other men and women, and reach a decision from there.

"No more, no less.

"Now, if no one has anything to add," Hal finished, "this meeting is over. Return to your ships, and we sail on."

There were some mutters, but the officers behaved.

Farren Mariah caught Hal on deck.

"That, maybe, wasn't the brightest thing you've ever done, you know. You maybe should not have held this meeting, and let those dreams go unspoken and remain secret nightmares."

Hal made a face.

"I think you could be right."

"And I think Captain Hagi needs a bit of a watch over," Mariah said. "Or perhaps an anchor stone around his feet before he's given swimming lessons."

"Maybe."

But Hal made no order, and the ships raised their anchors, sailed out of the friendly lagoon, and went on, into the west.

Now land rose all around them, but not the solid mass of Hal's dreams.

It was as if they'd entered a river delta, except the water was salt. There were dozens, then hundreds, of tiny islets, growing into larger islands.

Some were swampy, little more than trees whose roots were submerged at high tide, and monstrous serpents, and legged fish that could leave the water inhabited the darkness between them.

Others were grassy hillocks, with tiny deer-like creatures bounding on them, and lithe cats to prey on the deer.

Some of the Hnid swam in the ships' wakes for a time, as if ordered to follow the expedition and report on its fate.

The passages were narrower, sometimes choked with vines, so the men had to kedge back out, and, cursing, find a new way.

Their progress zigged back and forth, and it was hard to hold to that westerly course.

The air was sweet, as the smell of dozens of spices hung around them, spices with no known equal.

"A woman could make a fortune here," Kimana Balf mused. "One cargo of these spices . . . whatever they are . . . brought back to Deraine, and you'd live in silk."

"True enough," Aimard Quesney said. "If the dragons let you."

The red and blacks were still up there, keeping their post, making no threat to the ships.

Yet.

Hal, a little worried they were off their course to the still-unseen mainland, took Storm up high.

The watching dragons paid little mind to the single monster and its rider, save to move somewhat west.

Hal went as high as he could, until Storm was panting, and he himself sucking for air, and looked west.

Dimly, on the horizon, the "delta" ended, and the seas opened once more.

Spices still hung close as they sailed on.

But now the islands were somewhat kempt, as if a gardener, albeit a careless one, was minding them.

They saw small huts along the water, but they were empty.

Then, one day, a seaman on watch saw the natives: they were like the monkeys men had brought back from the south, tailed, furry.

But they lived in the huts, and were seen with leaf packs.

What was in them was theorized to be spices.

But who, if anyone, they were gathering them for was never known.

Hal ordered boats launched, and tried to make peace with the apes, if apes they were.

But the animals would have nothing to do with men, and so the expedition went on.

Then the islands changed, and were wild and uninhabited once more.

Hal saw the reason: great lizards, almost the length of one of the dispatch boats, that hissed menace when they saw the ships.

Hal sounded an alert, and armed sailors lined the rails, their weapons ready.

But none of these earth-bound dragons did more than menace, and flash their foot-long fangs.

There had been no war so far between the expedition and the red and black dragons.

This changed.

As a pair of dragon-fliers were taking off, just after dawn, one of the wild dragons dove, talons extended.

There were shouts of warning from the ships, but the fliers evidently didn't hear.

The red and black caught one rider by the shoulders, plucked him from his saddle, and threw him into the ocean.

He didn't surface.

The two wild dragons climbed back to their heights, and continued circling.

After the shock subsided, Hal stood on the afterdeck of the *Galgorm Adventurer*, staring up.

Farren Mariah came to him.

"I think," he said grimly, "we ought to think about taking it to the enemy now, for enemy they've proven themselves, for unwarranted liberties."

"Yes," Hal agreed. "Time and time past."

26

The plan was mounted cunningly.

Long before dawn, Hal and Farren Mariah turned out, and moved silently to the *Galgorm*'s landing barge. Handlers brought out their dragons.

Although they wanted to protest, the two dragons were manhandled overside into the water, where they bobbed like cunningly carved corks in the light swells.

They decided they didn't mind the bath in these nice tropical seas as their riders clambered into their saddles.

The ships sailed on past them.

After a time, lights were turned on aboard the ships, almost on the horizon by this time, and sailors began preparing, quite loudly, for an early launch.

As they did, Hal and Mariah gigged their dragons into a splashing run that took them aloft.

Circling, they climbed for altitude, hoping the watching dragons' attention was fixed on what was going on around the fleet.

They climbed very high, gifting themselves with a private sunrise as they ascended.

Below them, in the lightening night, they could make out the dots that were the watching dragons, and below *them*, the ships.

There were trumpet blasts from the fleet below, and Miletus and Quesney, as arranged, made ready to take off.

Hal signaled to Farren Mariah, and the two dragons went into a steep dive.

On the *Bohol Adventurer*, Hachir and his partner also moved their dragons down to the takeoff barge.

The red and blacks were less than five hundred feet below.

Hal cocked his crossbow.

Miletus and Quesney's dragons thundered across their barge, and into the air.

Hal shot the first red and black from above, less than a hundred feet distant, aiming just between the shoulder blades.

The monster contorted, squealed in surprise, as Farren Mariah shot his partner in the wing.

Hal reloaded, fired into the neck of his targeted dragon as Storm dropped past then, on command, flared his wings and braked.

Farren Mariah sent his second bolt into the other wild dragon's throat as he dropped past it.

Below, the other dragons were airborne – but there was nothing for them to do but circle as the two red and blacks, still struggling, seconds apart, crashed into the ocean.

Neither of them came back to the surface.

Farren Mariah yodeled happily.

Hal did not. He swore he'd seen a flash of flame as one dragon hit the water, which made no sense.

It must have been a trick of the rising sun.

He forgot about it.

They'd taken the first step.

The second was soon to follow.

Half a day later, the second trap was set and sprung.

Hal and Farren Mariah had landed, and they and their dragons fed. They waited impatiently until a glass before the now-dead dragons should be relieved, then took off once more.

This time, both dragons carried packs with iron rations and drink for the men, and smoked lamb carcasses for themselves, in case this flight took too long.

There was a high haze, perfect for what Hal wanted.

He and Mariah again climbed high, and flew west and north, until the ships were mere dots almost on the horizon.

They flew in wide circles, waiting.

Hal kept watching the masthead of the *Galgorm Adventurer*. He'd ordered the officer of the deck to signal when his glass showed it was time for the dragon relief to appear.

The banner was finally run up the mast, and, on cue, a pair of red and black dragons appeared from the west.

Hal and Mariah were far above and north of them, mere dots in the sky, hopefully hidden in the haze. But Hal took his partner behind a cloud as the dragons looked for the watch they were to relieve, and saw nothing.

He heard, from below, squawks of what he assumed was

surprise, dismay, as the wild dragons saw no fellows awaiting relief.

He flew Storm to the wispy limits of the cloud, saw the dragons below turn back east. Clearly reporting the absence of their fellows was more important than keeping watch on the slow-sailing ships.

Holding altitude, trying to keep between the sun and the red and blacks below, Hal and Mariah followed the wild dragons.

Hal took compass readings as they flew, but the red and blacks held a straight course.

Very unusual – wild dragons, in Hal's experience, zigged across the landscape as they went, distracted by curiosity and appetite.

But not these two.

Ahead of them rose an unknown mass of land from the sea – jagged cliffs here and there, but mostly low coastline.

Unknown to Hal the man ... but not to his dream-dragon. There was the flashing thrill of home, seen once, never to be more than a reverie in the land between sleeping and waking.

Hal was trying to keep his mind on his mission, but he couldn't suppress a thrill, realizing that he was certainly the first Derainian, perhaps the first man, to see this unexplored land.

He forced that thought aside, concentrated on the job at hand.

The dragons made for one of the cliffs.

Hal took Storm in a wide orbit, to give distance.

The red and blacks flew over the breaker line, and a little inland, then dove sharply, and vanished.

Hal motioned Mariah to dive too, followed suit, and brought Storm out just yards above the low surf.

He had no idea what he was looking for in his pursuit of the red and black dragons, except to find their masters, their home city, and plan a strategy from there.

He knew dragons preferred cliffs and crags for their homes, since flying off was much easier from a height.

So he landed on a low cliff, dismounted, and used a glass to sweep the surrounding cliffs.

He saw no sign of dragons.

Nor did Farren Mariah.

Hal remounted, and they flew on, inland, over a great plain.

Finally, they spotted the dragons, far ahead, mere dots, flying steadily to the west.

Mountains rose from the plain, and the red and blacks flew into them.

Storm was getting tired, but Hal drove him on. Both his and Farren Mariah's beasts still had hours of endurance in them.

The dragons disappeared again into the ridges. Hal assumed the red and blacks couldn't keep in the air much longer than his own dragons. He flew to a high crag, landed, and glassed the rugged range, keeping away from the landward side.

Storm was increasingly nervous, which Hal decided meant he'd seen and scented the wild dragons, so they couldn't be far distant.

Hal soothed him before creeping to the edge of the crag and glassing the area again.

Still nothing.

He went back to Storm, and he and Farren flew on, this

time to the highest peak still on a westerly heading. There was a level spot, almost at the summit, and Hal landed, swept the landscape again.

This time, he found luck.

Of a sort.

In the distance, leagues away, was a fairly large plateau.

On it, he counted ten red and black dragons.

Hal made a face. He'd hoped to find some sort of city that would tell him who and what led the red and blacks.

But there was nothing here except rocks that the wild dragons were using for what could only be a temporary shelter.

That and, here and there, the remains of carcasses that the dragons had fed on.

There was no sign of a civilized building or even crude shelter.

Nor, though he looked for almost an hour, was there any sign of man, or any other being, except the ten dragons.

Hal thought about what he'd seen, then went to Mariah, who'd landed near Storm and was waiting.

He told his partner what he'd found, and not found.

He said he proposed to watch on, and for Farren Mariah to find a shelter, where overhead dragons couldn't spot him, and to return the next day.

Farren Mariah didn't like it, but obeyed.

He took off, and Kailas took his pack from Storm, slapped the dragon's butt, and pointed after Mariah.

The dragon whined, but obeyed.

Hal watched the two dragons disappear, feeling distinctly unhappy, not to mention slightly terrified.

He pulled on a jacket, and returned to his watch.

Two dragons took off, flew toward the sea. Hal guessed it was to resume the watch.

After a time, two others flew off.

It was growing late.

Without any signal that Hal could see, the rest of the dragons took off, and flew in different directions.

Hal tried to record the compass directions each took, but got only five.

He had no idea what they were doing.

But after a time, all returned.

Some bore prey – an antlered animal like a stag, smaller creatures like wild pigs, large birds.

The dragons piled the corpses in a pile, watched while two of them fed.

The two sated monsters left, and then the remaining six fed.

The feeding wasn't like the general chaos Hal was used to with wild dragons, but relatively sedate, with each dragon taking a body and devouring it, and the remaining bodies evenly divided.

Two carcasses were left untouched.

This, again, was new and strange – dragons normally ate everything in sight. But these red and blacks seemed to be saving a meal for the two watching the expedition.

Those returned at full dark, and ate.

Then the dragons curled up, and slept like obedient soldiers.

Hal allowed himself to drowse, woke somewhere in the middle of the night as the watch changed.

Then there was silence.

Before dawn, he heard the new guards going out.

At full light, six dragons took off, and formed a tight, arrowhead-shaped formation. They flew off, to the northwest.

Hal took a compass reading.

In about an hour, six other dragons, in the same sort of formation, appeared from the north-west.

It was as if the guard were changing.

Hal liked none of this.

If there were no handlers below, that could only mean that the dragons were ensorceled by a powerful magician or magicians, who could impel obedience either across a distance, or over a time.

Farren Mariah appeared, flying low.

Hal motioned him in, hurriedly mounted Storm, and set a course back toward the coast.

Once he reached it, he flew south along the shore, but didn't find what he was looking for. He turned north, and found, just out of the sight-line of red and black dragons returning to their base, what he'd been looking for: a deep bay that led inland, sheltered by ridges on either side.

He flew low over it, and it appeared as if the bay was more than deep enough for his ships. Also, there were easy tracks leading inland.

That would give the expedition a base.

He swung Storm back out to sea.

He'd circle around and approach the ships from the east, so the watching dragons wouldn't have a clue what he'd been about.

Then he'd assemble a stronger force, and follow that compass heading.

This time he would be after what appeared to be the *real* dragonmasters.

27

Hal wanted to follow the compass lead, which should take him to the lair of the sorcerers, with all his dragons, plus infantry riders for backup, and all four magicians for support.

But he knew better.

There was no way his tiny expedition could attack what could only be a great city.

The only option he could see was to find the wizards' headquarters, then return to the ships and sail back to Deraine, just as Guapur Hagi of the *Bohol* had wanted.

King Asir would have to take the next step of mounting an invasion force, trying to make peace with the sorcerers, or whatever.

Hal thought, were *he* king, he would try to form an alliance with Sagene and Roche, and then return to this new world, keeping all options open.

But he thought there would be only one option – to destroy or at least render impotent those who were controlling the red and black dragons.

Which would likely mean great magic, which, in spite of Limingo's presence, was far beyond Kailas's abilities. The spells to defeat that unknown city would have to be mounted by corps of wizards, since their magic would surely be stopped, and then a counterattack made.

Hal forced himself to the present.

If he were only to scout the enemy, he would want to be as little visible as possible.

That meant a minimal force of dragons and riders.

Of course his normal flying partner, Farren Mariah, would be one.

He caught himself, realized he'd best consult the man instead of assuming.

Hal found Mariah in his compartment and asked him on deck. He took him to the bow and told the lookout he was relieved for a time, and to go below and have a bite to eat.

"You asked me out here," Farren Mariah said, "in privacy. Assuming you aren't planning to proposition my young sitter, this bodes, modes, not well."

"Or not safety, at any mayhap."

"It's not," Hal said, and told him what he proposed.

"A better bitter way to die," Farren Mariah said. "And I'd be a damned fool to volunteer."

"I agree."

"But if you went bounding off, and got yourself dead, I'd be downcast as all hells," Mariah went on. "So I'm neatly trapped, aren't I?"

Hal didn't answer.

"Aaarh," Farren Mariah said. "All right. You've sprung your trap. Who else are you going to suck in?"

Hal considered.

"Two more fliers, I reckon."

"Who?" Mariah asked. "Every fool aboard'll be volunteering."

Hal grinned.

"Call 'em together, if you would. And have the others come over from the *Bohol*."

While Kailas waited, he went to Limingo, who of course said he would have felt slighted if not given the chance to volunteer, and probably would have cast a spell on the Dragonmaster that would have changed him into, say, a churchmouse.

"Can you do that?" Hal asked in surprise.

"Not at present," Limingo said. "But my wrath would have been such that I would have developed all kinds of new powers."

The dragon-fliers were on board the *Galgorm Adventurer* within an hour, and gathered in the wardroom.

Hal told them what he'd discovered, and what he proposed to do next.

As expected, the fliers all volunteered.

Hal was ready for that one.

He had torn up bits of paper, put them in a flier's hat, and bade everyone to draw one.

Hal barely noticed that Kimana Balf's hand lingered for an instant longer than necessary.

She was the first to announce she'd drawn one of the marked bits.

The second was Aimard Quesney.

That settled that.

Quesney insisted that everyone take adequate survival packs, to include dried rations, a waterproofed blanket, matches, and such.

"We'll not be needing those," Farren said.

"Suppose your dragon goes down?" Quesney asked.

"Then I'll be dead, won't I?"

But he obediently tied a pack to his dragon's carapace.

Hal would take Limingo with him; the others would carry the rations for the dragons and men.

His intentions were to fly to the plateau, which he thought was a way camp, then fly on for a day or two, following the compass bearing he'd taken from the dragons headed further inland, then go to ground and wait for the six dragons being relieved – or so he assumed was what was happening – and follow them to their home city.

"And how how howly will we keep from having those six dragons fly right up our arse?" Farren Mariah asked. "Not to mention if this great city of magicians happens to turn out to be only one day's flying away from where we start tracking the red and blacks, and we suddenly find ourselves shitting bricks and right over the main Palace of the Magicians."

"Then," Kimana said briskly, "we're truly screwed, and you can have my collection of manacles."

"You have a collection of manacles?" Limingo asked interestedly.

Kimana shook her head, didn't answer.

"Both your worries will be taken care of by our colleague's magic," Hal said.

Limingo raised an eyebrow.

"We'll leave an hour before dawn tomorrow," Hal said. "Anyone who wishes to pray has my permission."

But the dragon-fliers weren't a religious lot – not even Aimard Quesney. Which might have explained why he'd failed at attempting the priesthood.

Hal gave his final orders, including what was to be done

if there was contact with the red and blacks. If that happened, he said, there was no time for nobility. Any unengaged flier was to flee east, toward the ships, with whatever had been discovered.

He told his fliers to eat, get some sleep, and not think about the morrow, which he knew they would anyway.

Then he went to the captain of the *Galgorm Adventurer*, told him he was in charge of the expedition, and that all remaining would obey his orders.

Hal made a rough sketch of the land they were approaching, told the captain he was to anchor in a bay north of the dragons' flight-line, and wait for four weeks. If no one returned in that time, he was to sail for Deraine, and report everything they'd discovered to King Asir.

The officer told him that Guapur Hagi of the *Bohol* had signaled he wanted to come over to the flagship. It was very important.

Hal grimaced. He didn't have time for Hagi at the moment, told the *Galgorm*'s captain so.

The officer said, skeptically, that he didn't think ignoring Hagi was perhaps the wisest thing.

Kailas was starting to get a little angry. "I'll take care of him . . . and whatever frigging problems he has . . . when we get back. Tell him to put a knot in it for the moment."

Hal ate, slept well, dreaming of what a city of magicians and dragons might look like, and woke ready for action.

He'd reluctantly decided that he was depending too much on Storm, and decided to take his other black dragon, Sweetie.

The four monsters were led, one at a time, down to the barge, mounted, and their fliers took them off.

As the last of the four was airborne, other fliers on the

Bohol Adventurer started making a grand racket, sure to attract the red and blacks' attention overhead.

Or so Hal hoped.

He led his flight back east, then turned south and then west in a great loop.

He set his compass to bring them over land just south of the compass heading the dragons had taken from the fleet to their first base on the plateau.

When he saw land, he turned south for a dogleg, counted slowly to two hundred, then resumed his course east.

An estimated hour inland, he turned north, and corrected the dogleg, straightening on the old heading toward the plateau.

It was full light, and the fliers held their dragons to a moderate speed.

Below them were the mountains of the coastal range, slowly becoming foothills, and then the great plain spread before them.

Now Hal took time to observe what lay below him, since he was deliberately holding the formation to a far slower speed than he'd taken before, wanting a bit of warning before they came on something dangerous.

There were strange trees, and the land was torn by deep ravines.

It was hot, but not unbearably so at their altitude.

Hal thought this could be a simple training flight in peacetime, except for the unknown land below them.

It's so damned *big*, he thought.

The horizons seemed as distant as Deraine was to him, even larger than the sweep of the northern tundra he'd seen the fringes of.

There was a strong wind blowing the tall grass, Hal noted. Then he corrected himself with a chill.

The grass was moving in a streak.

There was something hidden under it making the plants move.

A snake?

But there couldn't be a snake that large. Hal estimated the creature's length to be well over thirty feet.

He saw Kimana looking down, then at him.

She made a face.

But nothing showed, and they flew on.

Limingo pointed down and to the left.

There was a huge herd – Hal guessed at more than three hundred head – herd of enormous buffalo, or some species of long-horned, shaggy cattle. Hal guessed they would be half as tall as a dragon.

They were huddled in a ring.

Hal saw the reason: there were four tawny predators stalking the herd. They were some species of cat, with mottled coats that made perfect camouflage. Their necks were long, and their heads sported great upswept fangs.

Then he saw something else:

A deep ravine ran beside the herd. In the ravine, creeping, if cattle could ever be said to creep, were a dozen bulls.

The cats hadn't seen them.

It was a case of the stalker being stalked.

Hal marveled at a land like this – cattle having the courage to attack beasts of prey.

Sweetie flew on, before the drama was resolved.

They landed under sheltering trees late that afternoon, not wanting to be in the air at night.

They didn't chance a fire, but ate their iron rations cold, after feeding the dragons.

"Ho for the life of adventure," Farren muttered, tearing at a chunk of hard-smoked and spiced beef. "I hope my godsdamned jaws hold up."

Hal was about to reply when a rustling in the grass outside the clearing made everyone dive for their crossbows.

After a moment, a creature waddled unhurriedly into sight. It was about half again the size of a domestic pig, and had long quills sticking out in all directions.

It went straight to Kimana, who'd dropped the fruit strip she'd been eating, picked it up in its jaws, turned around and trundled back the way it had come.

"So much," Kimana said, "for wild animals' instinctive fear of humans. I think I'll sleep in a tree."

The next morning, at dawn, they flew on, following the compass heading.

Far in the distance, purple mountains rose from the plain.

Just beyond would be that plateau that was the first dragon base.

Again, Kailas led his dragons on a dogleg north, then east, until he calculated he'd passed the plateau camp. He turned back, and started looking for a hiding place.

He spotted a grove of trees that would give them concealment, signaled to the others, and put Sweetie into a gentle dive.

At the last minute, he pulled the dragon up and climbed back for the heights.

The others needed no explanation.

They'd seen the danger.

There were three trees below them.

If they were trees at all.

For all three of them had tentacles instead of branches, tentacles that moved in anticipation of their prey above them.

There were bones scattered on the ground around the trees.

They flew on for a few miles, found another grove that was made up of real trees, landed and made their camp.

Limingo busied himself with spells after dinner, then came to Hal.

"I'm not sure," he said. "I'd know better if I had some kind of relic from the red and blacks. But my magic suggests there are dragons coming, from behind, probably heading toward that plateau."

"We'll wait for them to pass," Hal said. "Or at least until we know whether they're for real."

Limingo nodded, began gathering up his implements.

"You know," he said, without looking up at Hal, "I always wanted to be a soldier. Fun, travel, adventure.

"That sort of thing.

"But when I realized . . . what I am . . . soldiering didn't sound very inviting."

Hal knew what he was talking about.

Supposedly no one was supposed to discriminate in the army against people whose private life was different from the norm. And there were homosexuals in the military, but generally in branches such as medicine or clerking.

Hal had known all too many warriors, who evidently came from some village in a remote area or from one of the more repressive sects, who couldn't tolerate men who preferred other men, or women who liked their own.

He'd always thought those fools had some problem with themselves, some fear that they might be changed by contact with homosexuals, as if it were a communicable disease.

"Then I discovered I had a strong Gift," Limingo went on. "And that decided that."

He didn't seem to want any comment on what he had said, and so the others rolled in their blankets and tried to sleep.

They had to wait for a day, and then six red and blacks appeared, holding to the same northern course Hal had charted.

"Now," Hal said, "we follow them, and they lead us right to their home."

"Not too close," Aimard Quesney said. "I have an aversion to meeting dragons on their own ground."

"That's two votes," Farren Mariah said.

"Not to mention," Kimana said, "not being too quick to go home with them. They might object to uninvited house guests."

Hal made a face.

"You get more like Mariah every day."

"Proof," Farren Mariah said smugly, "that the woman has her wits about her."

They took off, and, keeping low to the ground, followed the red and blacks.

There were clouds in the sky from low to high altitudes, which made it easy to keep concealed as they flew.

The wild dragons began climbing as the mountains drew closer.

Hal held his formation close to the ground, only lifting when he had to.

Suddenly the six dragons ahead dove.

Hal was about to signal his flight to circle when, from a cave on a cliff face, some fifteen red and black dragons dove down at them.

They were well and truly ambushed.

28

Hal barely had time to shout a warning to Limingo to hold on as he turned his dragon into the red and blacks' attack.

They evidently weren't used to sudden aggression from foes they badly outnumbered, and the lead dragons in the attack balked, turning a bit aside.

That gave Hal a target, and he put a bolt into the base of the lead dragon's neck.

He shrilled, and went down, disappearing into the cloud cover.

Hal looked to see if there were riders on any of the beasts, saw none.

Aimard Quesney's dragon had spun, and had a red and black by the foreleg. The wild dragon shrieked in pain, and Quesney fired his crossbow into the monster's gaping jaws.

The dragon curled in agony, and rolled toward the mountainous landscape below.

Kimana Balf's dragon was locked in a face-to-face fight

with a red and black, but Hal had no time to watch as a pair of dragons attacked him.

Farren Mariah took one off his back, and Hal fired at the second, wounding it.

There was another wild dragon plunging in from the side, slashing at Hal.

Sweetie ripped at it with a wing claw, and it dove. But there was another red and black tearing at his tail.

Sweetie turned on himself, almost throwing Hal, as a second dragon came in.

Kailas barely sensed Limingo shouting something, then the wild dragon had his mount by the leg, tearing at him.

Limingo screamed, and fell free, spinning down and down to his death.

Kailas shot the second dragon between the shoulder blades, and he contorted and fell away. The first had a death grip on Sweetie, tearing at him.

Hal's dragon clawed at his opponent, paying no attention to his rider's shouts to 'ware his height.

It was too late.

Sweetie hit the ground hard, throwing Hal over his neck, into a thicket.

Hal didn't feel the prickers, but tore himself out of the brush, killed the first dragon, and worked his crossbow's slide.

But Sweetie was writhing in his death throes, ichor spraying, and guts bulging.

Kailas didn't notice. He was transfixed by the red and black's death ... if that was what it was. Again, as he'd seen once before, and thought it an illusion, the dragon flared into flame, and then there was nothing, not even smoke or ash.

Hal was gaping, then he heard a scream, and saw two red and blacks bearing down on him, exposed on the hillside.

He shot one, ducked behind a boulder as the other struck, almost crashed, but pulled up, turning for another run.

Kimana was there, her dragon striking at the wild dragon's neck, just behind the head. Hal heard the beast's neck snap, and then there was a pair of wild dragons on them.

One went for Kimana's dragon's throat, the second ripped at its wing.

The wing tore, and the dragon spun down.

The beast hit the ground, and Kimana sagged off the dying monster, lying against it, momentarily stunned.

Hal ran toward her, pulled her away from her dragon's body.

Four red and blacks were attacking the hillside.

Farren Mariah and Aimard Quesney came from nowhere, and the four wild dragons veered away.

Kimana was staggering up, recovering consciousness.

Hal pulled her pack from its ties on her dragon's carapace, and a quiver of bolts, threw them to the woman.

She took them numbly, then seemed to come to, saw her crossbow lying nearby, stumbled toward it.

Hal dashed to his own dragon's body, secured pack and quiver.

The red and blacks were coming back.

He sent a bolt in front of them.

These wild dragons evidently weren't used to bows, and climbed away.

Quesney was coming back, Mariah behind him, trying

for a pickup. But there wasn't time, wasn't room, and Kailas was shouting them away as other wild dragons bore down on him.

He shouldered into his pack, helped Kimana on with hers.

Aimard and Farren dove down, close along the mountain's cliff, too close for the red and blacks to get them, but Hal had no more time to worry about them.

He shoved Kimana toward the shelter of a nest of boulders. A dragon came in low, snapped at him, missed.

They were momentarily safe.

Hal saw a gap in the rocks ahead, went for it as the wild dragons screamed their rage, circling overhead, looking for the chance to attack.

Then the two fliers were in the open, running downslope toward a vertical face.

Kimana skidded to a halt at the edge, looked down, and shuddered.

Hal did the same, saw treetops forty or so feet below.

"Jump!" he shouted, as a dragon, claws extended, came at them.

She hesitated, obeyed, plummeting down.

Hal went after her.

They smashed into the trees below, crashed through, branches pulling at them.

Somehow neither of them was more than scratched, nor did they lose pack or weapons. They thudded to a halt no more than ten feet above the ground and clambered out of the saving trees, felt solid ground under their feet.

Hal couldn't see the wild dragons above him, through the tree cover, but heard them shrieking rage and hatred.

He pointed at a brushy draw that led on down toward a valley floor, and the pair ran for it.

Kailas was still breathing hard two hours later, as the sun fell.

He and Kimana had found shelter of a sort in a large grove of thorn trees.

The wild dragons had followed them almost to the end, finally losing them in a narrow ravine.

But they continued flying overhead, in ever-widening circles, until dusk.

Finally, Hal's breathing slowed.

Kimana didn't seem, other than her various scrapes, to be out of sorts at all.

"I think," she said drily, "we may have run into a different sort of dragon."

Hal managed a rather feeble smile.

"You noticed."

"I noticed. I always tried to keep track of where the Roche I killed fell. It kept my squadron commander quiet."

"Different sort," Hal said. "If they're even dragons."

"What else could they be?"

"I don't know," Kailas said. "Maybe magical apparitions, created by their masters?"

"Damned powerful magicians, if they can do that. What's for dinner?"

Without waiting for an answer, she moved her pack in front of her, dug into it.

"Naturally, not thinking I was ever going to need anything in this, and that we'd be back at the ships in a day or two, I didn't exactly pack delicacies.

"How about some nice dried vegetable soup?"

"How about," Hal said, "some jerked beef. I'd just as soon not light a fire."

Kimana considered.

"The bastards do fly at night," she said. "And they surely could see a fire, unless we found some sort of cave or something."

"I'm worried that they could sense a fire," Hal said. "Without seeing it."

"You're building these creatures up as something scary."

"They *are* scary," Hal said. "And the only reason I lived through the war was because I always took my enemy seriously."

He thought about his words, grinned wryly.

"I think that was as pompous as it sounded."

Kimana managed a smile, reached out, patted his cheek.

"That's all right. The Dragonmaster is permitted to sound toplofty."

Her hand stayed on his face for just an instant, then withdrew.

"By the way. I don't think I've thanked you for saving me."

"Or you for trying to save me," Hal said. "In spite of orders."

Kimana shrugged.

"I suspect I'm being punished. I never should have rigged the lottery in the first place."

"You did what?"

"Shuffled those bits of paper until I felt the inky one. I always was good with my fingers."

Hal goggled in surprise, couldn't find anything to say.

Kimana chewed jerky, swallowed. "Speaking of which, we'll have to hurry to make the coast before the ships leave. Twenty-four days is all we have left.

"I'm in no mood to play First Woman of the World around here."

Hal took a deep breath.

"Less than that, actually. Because I'm going to find that sorcerers' base first."

Kimana looked at him through the growing dark.

"You're mad."

"I'm mad," Kailas agreed. "But that's what we set out to do."

"*I* didn't," Balf said. "Those weren't my orders . . . and I never volunteer. Too easy a way to get killed."

"Which is why you've got a couple of choices," Kailas said. "We'll find you a cave, and you stay with most of the provisions. Give me three days, and if I'm not back, you strike for the coast.

"Or you can do that right now."

Kimana thought about it.

"I don't like the idea of sitting on my ass and waiting," she said. "And I surely don't like chancing those prairies by myself. Those pussycats didn't look friendly . . . and I don't even want to think about what whatever was shaking the bushes likes for breakfast."

She sighed.

"I always hated heroes," she said. "All the bastards were good for was getting themselves . . . and anybody around them . . . killed."

Hal saw her logic.

"But I can't just turn back. Not this close."

"No," Kimana said, and there was a hint of anger in her

voice. "You, being you, can't. And so you're going to get me killed, too."

Without waiting for an answer, she took a blanket from her pack, and wrapped herself in it.

"I guess we'd better get some sleep," she said. "We'll need an early start, and I don't see any point in keeping a watch. Everything we've seen so far could eat us without a fight.

"Goodnight."

She lay down, and gave every appearance of instantly going to sleep.

Hal tried to think of something to say, couldn't find anything logical, rolled in his own blanket.

The next day, they moved out, cautiously, heading toward the peak behind which the fliers had last seen the six dragons disappearing.

There were red and blacks about, snooping like dogs that had lost the scent but knew their prey was still near by.

But the pair weren't seen.

At midday, a gold-colored, unridden dragon flew toward them, keeping low, head snaking back and forth, watchful for enemies.

Its caution didn't do any good.

Three red and blacks came from behind a bluff, and savaged the other dragon out of the sky.

They kept walking

Kimana risked a bolt, and killed a rabbit-looking animal, skinning and dressing it as they moved.

They moved into a near-trot when the terrain let them, always thinking of the sands running, ever faster, through the glass.

Hal stopped before dusk, built a small fire from dry brush he'd collected. They cooked the rabbit hastily, ate it half-raw, went on.

That night, they found another thicket, crept into its midst, and slept, continuing their trek as soon as there was the slightest hint of light in the sky.

The next day, they reached the peak they'd targeted, and found a pass below it.

They started through, but there were dragons overhead, and the land was too open.

A huge bear headed their way, and they pulled aside, into a rocky niche, crossbows ready.

The bear, almost twice the size of any Hal had seen, even in the north of Roche, snuffled at them curiously, evidently didn't much like the way they smelt, went about his business.

There was a creek running downslope, with a pool. Hal saw what looked acceptably like crayfish, snagged a dozen, and they ate well, boiling them in a small pot they carried with them.

There was an overhang large enough to shelter them.

Hal took water from his canteen, scrubbed his teeth carefully, and kissed Kimana goodnight.

It seemed like a good idea.

She looked a bit surprised, then kissed him back.

That was the ninth day.

The next day brought one of the greatest surprises of Hal Kailas's life.

They found the city of magicians.

Hal hadn't been sure of what to expect. Certainly there

would be great buildings, standing impossibly high. They would be made of strange materials, and would glitter with gold and gems.

The streets would be thronged with their creations – slaves, bedmates, monsters.

The two had followed the pass around the peak, and, at its highest point, found concealment and looked down on the valley they'd seen the dragons drop into.

Neither of them believed what they saw.

Or, rather, didn't see.

There were dozens, perhaps a hundred, red and black dragons milling about.

But there was no city.

There were great slabs of rock, piled haphazardly to make shelters, not even monolithic construction.

No more.

Hal used the glass he had in his pack, and here and there saw the carcasses of animals, in various stages of decay.

It looked like a bigger version of the dragons' plateau camp.

Nothing that looked human, or like a magician.

"I don't believe it," he muttered inanely.

They watched on.

Perhaps this was just another way station, and their rulers' grand city lay further on, deeper in this continent.

But Hal saw no signs of dragons flying on east, or, indeed, making any flights other than short hops here and there, returning quickly.

They watched until almost dark, expecting something, finding nothing.

Then they went back the way they had come, to the overhang they'd slept under the night before.

"So where are the magicians?" Kimana wondered.

Hal could only shake his head.

"Maybe ... invisible?" he hazarded. "Or maybe the dragons are controlled by demons?"

"Or maybe," Kimana said, "they *are* the demons."

"Huh?"

"Normal dragons don't explode like a bottle of brandy thrown into a fire," she said.

"I still can't believe it," Hal said. "We'll have to go back tomorrow and make sure."

"And how are we going to do that?"

"I don't know."

They went back up the pass, and found hiding places just at dawn.

The dragons below were waking, stirring about, eating from the scattered carcasses.

About fifty of them were gathered in a circle in an open area.

In the center of the circle was a fire, a ball of flame, as big or bigger than any of the dragons below. But there was no fuel to be seen, and the fire burnt with a steady, high flame.

Then, from the fire's center, a second ball of flame appeared, rolled forward, and began changing.

The flame died, and where it had been was a full-size red and black dragon.

That was enough for Hal. He motioned Kimana back, and once again they went down the hill.

They stopped at their outcropping long enough to grab their packs, then kept going, back the way they'd come.

"What are they?" Kimana said, when they paused at a tiny spring.

"I still don't know. Demons, maybe, like you thought. That sounds good enough for me. Certainly they're not dragons. Maybe the demons came here from some other world, and thought dragons were the best form they could take to conquer, or at least survive.

"Maybe, maybe not.

"But we're headed back for the ships.

"If these things are to be fought, it will have to be with magic. And we don't have much of that with us."

They went down the pass as quickly as they could move.

They had to take shelter regularly.

Red and blacks were flying overhead, again as if they'd scented the man and woman.

The next two days were spent clearing the mountains, and then, on the afternoon of the thirteenth day, they came down to the plains again.

Each night, before they slept, it seemed appropriate for them to kiss.

Their kisses were hardly chaste, but Hal never went further.

He thought he smelt too badly to be acceptable in anyone's bed, barely into his own.

Kimana didn't seem to want him to pursue his romance, and Kailas wondered if she felt equally unwashed.

On the fourteenth day since they'd left the ships, they moved carefully across the plains, wary of encountering one of the great snakes, if that was what they were.

Twice they hid under a tree as red and black dragons passed overhead, but the creatures paid no attention to what was below.

Hal was startled once, seeing what looked like an enormous fat man waddling across the plains.

They hid, and the being approached.

It wasn't a man, although it was almost as large as one, but a furry being with a ringed tail. The fur was black and gray, with a mask-like configuration around its pointed snout.

The animal looked directly at the brush they were hiding in, sniffed, and kept on moving.

Kimana and Hal went on.

They came upon a stretch of burnt-over land, the ground bare, blackened, and still smoking.

Hal couldn't tell what had set the fire, decided it must have been lightning, although they'd seen no storm in their passage.

A confused antelope bumbled across their path, and Kimana shot it down.

Hal gutted it, and they carried the body until they found an idyllic place to camp – just at the edge of the fire zone, the ground hot, and trees a short distance away still smoldering.

Nearby was a bubbling spring, and next to it, a nest of rocks that appeared made for small furless creatures like themselves to hide in.

Hal skinned and butchered the antelope.

"Now, watch my woodsy lore," he told Kimana, and, clutching two haunches, trotted to the smoldering trees.

He used a great leaf to fan the fire to life, and cooked the meat until it was just done.

Hal came back to see no Kimana.

But he heard a splashing from the spring, and peered over a rock.

Kimana, naked, was splashing about in a pool surprisingly deep.

"Dinner," he announced, realizing his throat was a bit dry.

Kimana came out of the water, unashamed.

"I shall drip dry," she said. "Now, you have just enough time to scrape off the worst.

"Here. I found some soap in my pack."

She handed it to him.

"And I'll even wait for you."

Kailas hastily stripped off, and stepped into the cool water. He lathered, submerged, and used some of the soap on his filthy clothes, which were really beyond redemption.

He was about to wash again, when Kimana called:

"My civilized ways are fading. Get your behind out here."

Hal obeyed.

Not quite as brazen as Kimana, he pulled on his wet underbreeches, then went to where their packs lay.

"Sit," Kimana said, her mouth full. "Eat."

He obeyed, and thought no meal he'd eaten had ever tasted as good.

And Kimana, he realized as his stomach filled, was as lovely as any woman he'd ever seen.

She seemed, for the moment, oblivious of his eyes, and he forced himself to look away every time she turned her head toward him.

He was surprised to find his antelope haunch gnawed to the bone.

She had finished her meal, tossed the bone far out on to the plain.

He found a leaf, wiped his greasy, half-grown beard clean, wished he'd brought a razor.

Kimana was staring at him.

Hal had been married, had certainly been with his share of women, but still found himself blushing.

Kimana giggled, got up, went to the spring, and washed out her mouth.

She went back to her bed roll, which Hal realized had been laid out, with his next to it.

She lay back, one knee slightly raised.

Hal thought her the most lovely thing he'd ever seen.

His body agreed.

Kimana gurgled laughter.

"Come here, you silly . . . but clean . . . man."

He obeyed.

Both moons were high in the sky when sleep finally took them.

Hal would have liked to have lazed in Kimana's arms the next day, making love from time to time.

But he was a soldier. Of sorts, at least.

And so, muttering inaudibly, he spanked her awake, thinking of other pastimes that could arrive from such a beginning, and they broke camp.

They moved on, deeper into the plains lands.

They encountered scattered grazing buffalo, saw no sign of the cat-like predators.

The buffalo were even larger than they'd looked from the air, and they made sure not to come close to any of them, especially if they had calves.

The sky was overcast, muttering.

Hal's hair was on end, and then thunder crashed as ball lightning rolled across the sky toward them.

"For those trees," Hal shouted.

They broke into a trot for a distant grove.

Hal saw the buffalo starting to move.

They were walking, then running, massing up into a herd, and charging toward the two humans.

There was no way they could make the trees, even if the spindly things were strong enough to climb.

And Hal remembered what he'd learned about going to a high point, or a high tree, when lightning was about.

He also remembered something a herder boy had told him, forgotten years ago.

"Stop!" he called.

Kimana, just in front of him, obeyed, although she gave him a look as though she thought him utterly mad.

"What are you doing?"

"*We're* going to stand here."

"And get trampled?"

"Cattle won't run over you if you're standing still. They'll run right past us."

"Who told you that?"

Hal lied. "Common knowledge. And I used to herd cows, when I was a boy."

"I don't believe you," Kimana said. But she came close. She had her eyes closed.

Hal looked at the oncoming herd, their stretching horns, realized the herder hadn't said anything about what stampeding cattle did with their godsdamned horns.

He, too, closed his eyes.

The rush of hoofs became thunder, impossibly loud, louder than what was going on in the skies, and then they were buried by it, roaring on either side.

And then it was gone.

Hal opened his eyes in swirling dust and the overpowering smell of cowshit.

"I'll be dipped," he said, in considerable surprise.

Kimana looked at him.

"You *were* lying."

"Well . . ."

That was the fifteenth day.

It was about midday, and they were moving through tall grass, broken by copses of thorn trees, when Kimana saw movement ahead.

It was what they'd feared most – the grass moving like a long wave.

And it was headed in their direction.

Hal pointed back, toward the closest grove, and they ran hard for it.

He glanced over his shoulder, knowing better, knowing that slowed him down.

The grass was moving faster.

Hal didn't think he could run any harder than he was. He was wrong.

Whatever was chasing them was only a dozen yards behind as Kimana reached the first tree. Hal threw her up into it bodily and swarmed after her, ignoring the long thorns that ripped at him.

He reached the first crotch, less than a dozen feet above the ground. Kimana was above him.

She was staring past him, at the ground, and suddenly screamed.

Hal had his crossbow off his shoulder, and turned, almost falling, and triggered a bolt down.

He didn't see what he was shooting at, didn't want or need to. He worked the crossbow's action, sent two more bolts down, as Kimana fired too.

There was a hiss, more like a screech, and then the grass was moving away, zigging here, there, and gone.

"What was it?" Hal panted.

"It . . . it *was* a snake," Kimana managed. "I think. But it had stubby arms with claws."

They waited a few minutes, but the monster didn't come back. Kailas thought it might be more dangerous to stay where they were than to keep going.

They came down from the tree, feeling the pain of far more thorns than they'd felt going up.

For the rest of the day, they zigged from grove to grove, ready to flee if the beast, or his friends, came back.

But nothing happened.

They bolted the last of their iron rations just under the tallest tree they could spot, and then climbed as high as they could and wrapped themselves in their blankets, spending an uncomfortable, but safe, night.

The seventeenth day was a day of heartbreak.

They were moving fast, on mostly open ground, and saw a pair of dragons.

Hal glassed them, and saw they weren't the enemy, and, though they were at quite a distance, that both dragons looked to have riders.

They came out into the open, waved, even foolishly shouted.

But the dragons kept on flying away from them.

Hal, in desperation, dug in his pack, found his flint and steel.

He struck them desperately, but the sparks flew into still-live grass, and the fire didn't catch.

He didn't know if that would have turned the dragons in any event, but he sagged in defeat as the two monsters vanished into the afternoon haze.

That night they camped by a small river, and Hal shot a pair of large fish.

But neither of them had much appetite.

They made love in misery, in desperation, finally fell asleep.

The next day, they saw, rising in the distance, the coastal mountains, and allowed themselves a moment of hope.

Then Hal noticed billowing high clouds rolling in from the south, from the ocean. The rain came down in sheets, and they tried to push on through it. But the winds grew stronger, and the rain heavier, and they were forced to find shelter in a thick grove, afraid of what they might encounter in the near-total darkness.

They barely slept, and, still in the dark of the nineteenth day, went on, almost running.

But just after dawn, four pairs of the red and blacks appeared, and they had to hide.

The dragons, as if knowing the humans were somewhere below them, swept back and forth, only flying off in the late afternoon.

Kimana and Hal went on until well after nightfall, moving by moonlight, and were into the foothills when they collapsed from exhaustion.

The twentieth day took them into the mountains.

Hal found a pass leading due east that was smooth, and promised easy traveling.

Then, after two hours, the pass turned north, and ended in a blank wall.

They had to go back for an hour before they could find a scramble to the top of a ridge, and the ridge led on toward the blue glimmer of the ocean.

On the twenty-first day, the last day the ships were to still be waiting, they came down out of the mountains. Below them was the bay the expedition had hidden in, less than an hour's travel distant.

They could barely keep from running, and, well before twilight, crested the last low ridge, the bay fingering out below them.

There was only one ship, and its masts were canted at an angle.

As they grew closer, they recognized the *Compass Rose*, one of their fast corvettes, yards drooping and bowsprit smashed.

The ship was wrecked, dashed against rocky outcroppings at the water's edge.

The bay was otherwise empty, with not another ship to be seen.

They had been abandoned.

29

Illogically, but quite understandably, they ran to the water's edge, not knowing what they hoped to find – a message, a map, a clue, something.

But there was nothing, except marks where boats had been beached, then launched once more.

Further down the beach lay the wreck of the *Compass Rose*. It needed no seaman's eye to tell that it could never be repaired and refloated.

Hal's heart was completely empty, as was his mind.

Kimana raised her eyes, and they were hard, dry.

"The bastards left us here to rot," she said fiercely.

Then the shout came, and they both spun.

Coming out of thick brush up from the water were two men: Hachir, and Hal's longtime orderly, Uluch.

Hal could find nothing more intelligent to say than, "You didn't leave us."

"No," Hachir said. "*We* didn't. But some others did."

"None of us who want to fight ran away," Uluch said.

He was looking over his shoulder, up at the skies. "Come on, sir," he said. "Those devils are still about."

Hachir collected himself.

"Yes," he said. "We've only kept this watch out of . . . well, hope that you were still with us . . . and coming."

"What happened?" Hal asked.

Uluch didn't answer, but led them up the beach, taking care to drag his feet so the marks in the sand didn't look like footprints. He took them to solid ground, then, keeping close to brush, to a draw that sloped upward.

The draw widened, and in its center was a small camp, concealed by scrub brush and low trees. There were camouflaged canvas tents, a small, smokeless fire, and some fifteen men and half a dozen women.

Two men kept watch with crossbows.

Hal saw some of his best: Farren Mariah, Bodrugan, one of his acolytes, four of his fliers, including Hachir, others.

He counted the missing: Garadice, Quesney, Cabet, Miletus, among others.

"Bigods, bigobs," Mariah said. "Now you're here, and the show can begin."

"If someone will tell me what the hells happened . . ." Hal began.

There was a clamor.

The loudest came from Mariah:

"The bartarts went and mutinied on us."

Hal sat down heavily on a log.

"Shit," he said. "Guapur Hagi?"

"At the head," Mariah said. "Other fainthearts."

"I should've hung him before I left," Hal said grimly. "What're the details?"

Hagi had begun plotting even before Hal had left with the others on his long scout, finding sympathetic listeners among watch officers and soldiery.

He had presented his case skillfully – this was not so much a simple mutiny, as a protest against Hal's pigheadedness in not returning to Deraine at once, with the awful news of this land full of danger and the evil, almost sentient, dragons.

King Asir should be warned as soon as possible, so he had time to mount a proper expedition or . . . or whatever he wished to do.

Why Kailas chose to tarry on in this treacherous land was unknown.

Hagi's men passed harsh whispers about Hal's desire to save his own reputation, besmirched as it had been by his adventures with the Roche.

When Quesney and Mariah came back, with word of the ambush, the stories changed a little.

Of course Hal – and that woman with him – must be dead. If not by dragon, then by the horrid monsters of this unknown land.

And with Mariah's report of the dragons that weren't, bursting into flames like nightmare apparitions, that was almost enough.

The capper was the great storm. During the blow, the *Compass Rose* had dragged its anchor, and gone on the rocks. Its captain and half its crew were killed trying to save their ship.

"The muttoneers must've had their plans ready," Farren Mariah said. "Sheep-shaggers that they are."

The mutineers had moved at dawn, and before anyone could do anything, all five ships were in their hands.

Of the missing fliers, Mariah was sure that Cabet, Quesney, Miletus and Garadice must be unwilling prisoners.

That made Hal feel a tiny bit better, that he wasn't a complete fool at judging men.

Those who refused to follow Hagi had had but a single chance to flee into the undergrowth with what they could carry.

"It was only that monster Chook who made them set food, canvas and weapons out for us," Mariah said. "None of the fliers who wanted to stay were listened to.

"And we could hear from the shore Hagi refusing to let us have any of the dragons, the shitheel.

"We could hear our monsters howling, knowing something was wrong."

"So they sailed away, leaving us to die," he finished. "Which thus far, we haven't done, no credit to his worthless ass.

"And we've got what was aboard the *Compass Rose*," Hachir said. "Some dry foodstuffs, and a decent arsenal. Bows, some crossbows, enough spare quarrels for an army. No quartermaster supplies, which is why we're all looking a bit raggedy."

"Probably," one of the rangers said bitterly, "the king'll send somebody back in ten, twenty years, and find our skeletons, all dragon-chewed, and they'll put up a monument to us."

Hal tried not to look at the eager faces who were sure the Dragonmaster would come up with something clever that would save their lives and bring them back, in triumph, to Deraine.

He could think of nothing.

Go to ground and wait? With the creatures of this land stalking them?

Build rafts and sail to the Hnid, the sea people? And what then? Would they somehow help them build some kind of boat capable of the ocean passage? Maybe. That, so far, was the best impossible option.

And if they did build boats, what was to keep the red and blacks from attacking them when they were afloat?

Capture wild dragons and flee on them? The only man really skilled at taming dragons was Garadice, who was with the mutineers. Hal himself had only long-ago memories of taming half-wild creatures.

He could think of absolutely nothing that offered salvation.

30

With his worries, Hal thought he'd sleep hardly at all. But just knowing he was safe . . . or, at any rate safer than he'd been out on the plains, surrounded by armed, friendly warriors, instead of being with just Kimana in the wilderness, swept over him like a welcome comforter, and he slept dreamlessly until just after dawn.

Kimana was curled next to him, and woke when he did.

They wandered down toward the water.

There was a sentry there, watching for dragons.

They washed, came back.

Kimana took his hand. Hal felt a bit uncomfortable, but no one made any notice, other than Farren Mariah, who muttered, "'Bout damned time."

They ate well – some of the soldiers had unstrung clothing for the threads, and tied gill nets. Others had rocked the rabbit-like creatures and shot the small antelope.

Hal missed bread, thought himself a sybarite.

He thought more on what they could do to survive.

The first step was easy – get away from the water. The land was too open, and Kailas thought the red and black dragons would certainly spot them in time, no matter how careful their precautions.

And the wreck of the *Compass Rose* would draw the demons' attention even more strongly.

As far as escape went . . . nothing came.

Nor did he have any ideas about striking back.

So much, he was thinking, for Great, Inspired Leadership, when two of the sentries gave alarm.

Dragons, approaching from the east.

Everyone found weapons and cover.

There were four of them, three being ridden, two with double riders.

No need to keep guard – red and blacks had no riders.

The men and women burst into the open, shouting, waving, and the dragons circled for a landing.

Hal saw the empty-saddled monster in front, recognized him.

Storm.

Somehow . . . but explanations would be for later.

The dragon thudded down, and Hal had his arms around the reeking beast's neck, and it larruped him with its tongue.

Kailas couldn't speak for a moment, then recovered.

The men were Aimard Quesney, Cabet, Lu Miletus, Garadice, and Chook, the cook.

"Thought it was about time for us to come back," Quesney said, trying to be casual as he slid from the saddle.

"Godsdamned well escaped," shouted Chook. "Th' fools went and turned their back, and we were gone."

That, in fact, was just what had happened.

Sort of.

The guard aboard the *Galgorm Adventurer* had gotten careless, and Chook had his cleaver. Once before the massive cook had shown his talents, before Hal had known him, when some attacking Roche had made the mistake of invading his kitchen, and had died to a man.

Now Chook had been biding his time, and saw it.

The guard died, as did his watch mate. Chook bashed open the compartment the still-recalcitrant fliers had been locked in, and they found weapons, and seized the watch.

"There weren't enough of us to take the ship back," Quesney said.

"But we locked the watch below," Cabet added. "And set the dragons loose. Saddled four of them, even though your mount wouldn't let anybody on his back.

"We were trying to decide what to do next, when somebody on the *Bohol* sensed something wrong.

"They had the odds, and so we fled, after grabbing what gear we could."

"None of the other fliers – even those that'd gone along with Hagi – were bold enough to come after us," Lu Miletus said.

"And we thought it was time to see what you were about," Garadice added.

"Poorly," Farren Mariah said. "Poorly-roarly, until just now."

"And now what?" a soldier asked.

"Now," Hal said, "now we can fight back."

It had come to him in a flash, as all the pieces arrived.

At least, so he hoped.

All he needed now was the luck of the gods.

*

First, he took Garadice aside, asked him how long it would take to train a dragon.

"You mean a yearling, fresh-hatched, or an old, incorrigible sort?"

"Yearling. We don't have time for either a young one or an old fart."

Garadice considered.

"Rideable, unless it's the cantankerous sort, perhaps a month. Fightable . . . twice that. Capable of holding a formation—"

"We won't need that," Hal interrupted. "There's not enough of us to make a formation."

"Now," Garadice asked, "how are we to catch these dragons?"

"A mere piffance," Hal said, waving his hand with an airy manner he didn't feel at all.

Next was Bodrugan. Hal told him everything he knew or suspected about the red and blacks.

"If these dragons aren't dragons—"

"Which I agree with, from what you've said about them bursting into flame," the magician said.

"Then what are they? Demons?"

"I won't use the word demons," Bodrugan said, a bit pedantically. "For, after all, demons are only forces from beyond, from other realms, whom we haven't been able to master, as yet.

"I would choose to use the term elemental spirits, perhaps."

"Elemental?" Hal asked. "Like in earth, wind, water, fire?"

"Just so," Bodrugan said.

"That means they're very powerful?"

"They are that," the wizard agreed. "But also easy – or, rather, relatively easy – to force your will on, since any creature with that innate power will almost certainly be self-confident. Like people are.

"From the elements, back to the elements."

"So you can handle them?"

"I don't know about handling," the magician said cautiously.

"Kill them, then."

"Kill them . . . exploding them . . . is obviously possible. Wiping them completely out may be almost impossible. Perhaps bringing them under control can be attempted. Or sending them back to whatever realm they came from. Would that be acceptable?"

"If you could devise a spell that would do that . . . and keep the bastards from coming back again, hopefully ever, that would be more than enough," Hal said.

"I can attempt to devise such a spell," Bodrugan said. "I'm sure I can come up with something that might be helpful. But whether I can work great magic is another matter entirely."

He looked up at the sky.

"I *do* wish," he said, a bit wistfully, "Limingo hadn't gone and gotten himself killed."

It would take time to create a striking force, time that Hal certainly didn't have.

But he had no other options.

The first step, as he'd figured earlier, was to get away from the coast. There would be nothing to be gained by staying here.

Hagi and the other ships had been well toward the lands of the Hnid when the mutiny against the mutiny had taken place. It would be months before they reached Deraine, and the tale they would have rehearsed by then would certainly prevent another expedition from arriving within a year, if then.

The first stage was cautious scouting for a new base.

It was a pure joy for Hal to be aloft again, especially over land he'd struggled across so recently.

He sent scouts, including himself, to the south, with exact details on what to look for.

Farren Mariah found their new home, and Hal thought, after considering it critically, it was just about perfect.

It took little time to get ready to move. They would make packs of the *Compass Rose*'s supplies, cache what they couldn't carry, and the ground troops would march off toward the new camp.

The dragons would shuttle the men and women from the march to the base, since it was at least four days' journey distant.

There was one more to come.

He arrived in somewhat regal style.

The sentries reported a boat headed toward them.

It was a very small craft, a Hnid net carrier.

This boat carried one human:

Babil Gachina, the thief, Hal's one-time cellmate.

He stood, arms folded like a triumphant prince, in the prow of the tiny boat, very much aware of the impression he was making.

The boat was being towed by a dozen Hnid.

Hal was wondering what the hells had happened, recollected what awe the Hnid had for Gachina's size, when the boat touched bottom, pitching Gachina into the shallows in a most inglorious arrival.

Men helped him up, and he waded to shore, not forgetting to turn and bow to his servants, if servants they were.

He asked for fish, and men hurried to bring them to him.

The fish were pitched to the Hnid, who took them, and without ceremony swam back out to sea, towing the boat with them.

Hal told Gachina to tell his story, and it was quite a tale:

It had been two nights after the mutiny against the mutiny.

"All was quiet, all was still," Babil said, and Hal knew that, if Gachina survived the expedition, he'd never have to live as a thief again, but could make a most comfortable living as a tavern taleteller. "And they struck from nowhere, fiends from all the hells, screaming like damned souls . . ."

To cut through the bar room panoply, the mutineers' five ships had been becalmed, just beyond the skein of tiny islands before the Hnid's lands, when the dragons came out of the night.

Gachina had no idea what had summoned them, but there were "thousands" of them. He admitted to Hal, later, that he hadn't counted exactly, but there'd been at least fifty.

They attacked from out of the larger, waning moon, and there was only a yelp of warning from one sentry before the dragons were on them.

The large crossbows on the masts stupidly weren't manned, and so the dragons were able to swoop along the decks, tearing at men as they stumbled out of their quarters.

One dragon became entangled in the *Bohol*'s sails, and, accidentally, it seemed, brought the ship over on a hard list. Another lit on its foremast, which was standing at an angle, and the top-heavy ship capsized.

Drowning dragons and men screamed into the night, and then the *Galgorm* caught fire.

"Odd that," Gachina said, "because as it flamed up, the dragons seemed to veer away from it, as though flame was their greatest fear, and tore instead at the other ships."

Babil tried a tale of his heroism, but caught Hal's eye, and told what might have been close to the truth:

He came on deck on the *Bohol* just as it went over, ducked a dragon, saw Hagi ripped in half by a pair of the monsters, and dove overside.

The two frigates were being attacked by the dragons, "bit by bit, the wood ripped off, like peeling a fruit," and Babil stayed low in the water.

He heard more screams, then silence, and he kept down, and then there was silence for a long time.

The sun came up, and there was nothing living and no ships afloat. He was surrounded by bodies and debris, floating dragons and men.

"Then, after a time, the fish people found me, and took me to one of their islands, and gave me food, and then a boat, and brought me here."

Gachina's tale brought the satisfaction of just retribution for most, but Hal saw the expression on Kimana's face, and knew it matched his own:

Now there wasn't even the vaguest possibility of a rescue expedition for years.

He was even more shaken to realize that these demons, fifty or seventy or however many there were, could destroy five ships and several hundred men, and all but wipe out the expedition.

31

Four days' march to their new base equaled a day and a half's leisurely flight, as the dragons carried marchers as they went.

A few chose to stay afoot, Babil Gachina among them, and Hal, having things on his mind, didn't wonder about them.

The valley was, indeed, just about perfect. It jutted off to the west of a deep canyon, and its walls zigged so that it appeared to come to a blind end near its opening.

It was keyhole-shaped, half a league at its widest, two leagues long. The long base of the keyhole was sparsely covered with grass, spare enough that the revolutions of the dragons they hoped to capture and train wouldn't mark the land for overhead observers.

One side of the keyway was a nearly sheer cliff, pocked with caves both small and large, ideal for dragon shelters. The other side was thickly forested.

Hal planned to steal an idea from the Hnid, and have his

men bend the trees over, lash them to either their fellows or to the ground, and so roof the area.

All of his women and men were shuttled to the valley without being observed by any dragons, either the red and black spirits or the "real" beasts of the land.

Farren Mariah asked Garadice how they'd go about training the dragons. He grinned wickedly, and said, "I'd tell, but you won't like it, so I'd rather you lived in a bit of suspense."

"Suspense, harness, business," Mariah moaned. "Now I *know* I won't like it."

Hal was about to look for a cave for his quarters when Kimana announced she'd already found their living area.

It was a cave with a small entrance that broadened into three chambers:

"Conference room, living room, bedroom," she named them. "A bend between each of them, so we've a measure of privacy."

Hal could do little but agree.

A tropical storm raged that night, and Hal listened to the rain cascade down outside the cave. He thought of his palaces and mansions back in Deraine, decided he'd rather be here, then called himself a fool for thinking that.

He then considered that it was Kimana's presence that made the difference. Realizing he hadn't gone mad yet, he reached for her, across their bed of piled rushes with blankets atop and below.

Sated, Kimana fell asleep in his arms. Hal was just drifting off as well when a thought came, left him helplessly awake. The thought led to a question that he'd pushed away before, but now it loomed very large.

And better, or worse, he thought he might have a way to find an answer.

A dragon honked below them, and Hal wondered, before he, too, fell asleep, if Storm's presence had sparked his thoughts.

Never mind. He'd consider the matter the next day.

Kimana listened to his idea, which he presented without giving a complete explanation, then asked three cogent questions, which Hal was able to answer.

Then she made a face.

"Were we back in civilization, and were I the jealous sort, I'd think you were haring off to see a chippie.

"Why are you so insistent on going solo?"

"Because . . . well, because I don't especially like to be a fool in front of an audience," Hal said. He didn't add that there was a good chance of getting killed answering his question.

"Hmmph," Kimana said. "Playing the hero again."

Hal didn't answer.

"So when are you going to mount this grand expedition of yours?"

"The next big storm," Kailas said. "That blow last night gave me the idea."

"Hmmph again. Who'll command while you're gone?"

"Farren Mariah in charge, Cabet as number two to handle administration, Bodrugan in charge of magic and such."

He called the three together, told them he had a scout to make, refused volunteers and an explanation, told them to keep the expedition in the valley.

"And what about you . . . if you're gone overlong?"

Mariah demanded. "Look what happened the last time you saddled up and rode wildly off in all directions."

"That," Hal said smoothly, "is why, this time, I've chosen such obvious leaders as yourselves to keep things going smoothly."

It was three days before the next storm came in from the ocean, from the east.

Each of those nights Hal had slept, rolled in blankets, in the cave with Storm.

Kimana had started to make a joke, saw the haunted expression on Hal's face, decided not to.

For each night, as he'd hoped and dreaded, Hal had dreamed.

Once again, he was that wounded dragon attacked over his homeland by the dreaded red and blacks. Once again he fled east, across the great ocean, to a new land, where he found beings who were not especially friendly, sometimes his active enemies.

But he found a mate, bred, and his kits had spawn of their own.

Hal, waking, wondered if one of them was the dragon who would be named as Storm, realized he would never know.

Besides, this was not the direction his quest took him.

Rather, he tried to force his dreams back, back to the days before, when the dragon was young and adventurous.

Twice, his dreams obeyed him.

When the skies clouded over, and a warm but vicious wind whipped over the valley, Hal Kailas knew well which way he wanted to go.

He took off down-valley, gained height over the flat

lands, then turned, set his course into the storm, quartering north.

He didn't need a compass to set his bearing, but used one so that he would be able to give directions to his fliers.

Hopefully, if he survived.

He remembered a cozy hooded laprobe he'd had back in Deraine, and wished for it. The wind might have been tropical, but it still whipped at him, and the rain drenched him to the skin.

He flew on, all that day, then took Storm under the shelter of some great trees at the edge of the plains, where the mountains began their rise.

Over there . . . and he instinctively knew the direction . . . lay the home of the red and black dragons.

Hal's mission was to answer one question:

Was that home the only one the red and black monsters had? Was that the sole point where they could come into this world from their other?

He hoped it was, that his guess, seemingly so long ago, had been right, that there was only the one hellspot, so the ruins of his expedition weren't ridiculously outnumbered.

But he had to know for sure.

He curled up next to Storm again.

He thought, amusedly, that most people would be slightly put off by the dragon's smell.

But then, most people wouldn't be intrigued by his own odor, no matter how much his thorough drenching might have resembled a bath.

Dragonmasters of fable probably weren't supposed to smell like their mounts.

But then, he guessed that noble cavalrymen weren't

supposed to smell distinctly horsy either, and he surely remembered his days as a light cavalryman.

On that thought, he slept, smiling.

He woke before dawn, roused Storm, and fed him on two of the smoked "rabbits" he carried with him behind his saddle, ate dried meat from his own pack.

It was still raining, and he wanted a fire to heat water for tea and boil some eggs he carried so carefully, wrapped in a spare set of underbreeches.

But not this close to the red and blacks.

He was just morosely chewing the last bites when he heard the shrill screams from aloft, went to the edge of the grove, looked up.

Through the scudding clouds, he dimly saw a pair of the huge red and blacks pass over.

Had they somehow scented, or otherwise sensed, his and Storm's presence?

If they weren't real dragons, why did they need to call like them?

Were their cries supposed to flush real dragons into the open?

Deciding that was enough questions, he curried Storm, took him to pooled water, and saddled him.

Then he took off, this time flying due north.

To his west would be the red and blacks' sanctuary.

For half the day, he flew along the edge of the plain, then over rolling hills, studded with trees.

Here and there he saw grazing buffalo, once a stalking predator.

But never did he see another dragon.

This was as he expected.

He outran the storm, and it was windy, but clear.

The afternoon grew late, and shadows fell across the land.

The ground below him was familiar, as though it was something he'd passed over as a child, or seen old-time paintings of.

Here the land would climb, and there would be a miniature mountain range, actually a rough circle of peaks around a high, craggy plateau.

That was just what Hal saw now, in reality.

Storm made a noise when he saw the mountains.

Hal wasn't sure what it was, a whimper, a moan.

But the dragon turned, unbidden, toward them, his wings widespread as he reached for altitude.

They crossed between two peaks, and saw the barren valley of the tableland Hal had dreamed of twice.

Storm swerved, as if he had changed his mind, and didn't want to go there.

But Hal forced him to hold his course, and the dragon reluctantly lowered his feet as the land came up at them.

They landed, and Storm folded his wings.

There was silence, except for the whine of the wind, which Hal had thought would be ceaseless.

A few yards away were scattered bones.

Hal walked to them.

They were those of a dragon, long dead, the bones browning, scattered by small creatures.

He couldn't tell what had killed it, or if it had died naturally.

Storm made a strange keening noise.

The shadows were getting longer, and night was coming.

This was a high land that should be haunted.

Not by human ghosts, but by the shades of dragons who'd died long before.

Here, Hal knew, was the home of his dream dragon, his dream dragon and many more.

Then dragons had lived in closer-knit colonies than those they formed in their new world.

Why they'd changed, he had no idea.

He got back on Storm, gigged the dragon into its staggering takeoff, and flew low over the tableland.

There were many bones scattered about.

He spotted a small rocky outcropping, and a bubbling spring nearby, and landed.

He unsaddled Storm, watered and fed him, and found dry wood for a fire.

He didn't fear any red and black dragons in this place.

Storm was restive, curling up, then getting up and sitting, staring out across the plateau, before curling up again.

Hal didn't feel sleepy, but forced himself to roll in his blanket.

He slept, and he dreamed. But this time it wasn't dreams of a single dragon, but of this colony, years and centuries ago.

Four dragons had found the plateau, and made it home.

There was more than sufficient prey on the plains and hills nearby.

The dragons multiplied.

There were other tribes of the monsters, in other parts of the mountains, and they fought their wars of breeding and territory, mostly flash and bluff, although too often the bluff became real, and the great beasts tore at each other and dragons fell to their death before their rage cooled.

Then the red and blacks came into the world, and the wars with them were never bluff.

Every battle was to the death, and the dragons couldn't

seem to understand that they were being hunted down like vermin, the red and blacks always choosing their time and odds.

Kits were choice prey to the foreign beasts, as if the red and blacks were intent on exterminating the other dragons.

The dragons fought back, finding the red and blacks' sanctuary, attacking hard. But that single attempt failed to rid them of the red and blacks, and was driven off with many casualties.

Now the world belonged to the invaders.

Then there were far fewer dragons, and many of them flew away, to find other, safer cliffs for homes, or even to join other tribes.

Only half a dozen dragons were left, old creatures, set in their ways.

They were attacked one dawn by the red and blacks, and fought as hard as they could.

But there were too many of the enemy, and the last of the dragons were savaged from the skies.

The land was silent, except for the wind, and the triumphant screams of the red and blacks as they flew over the tableland, then away.

Then there was nothing but the wind, and the passage of empty years.

Hal awoke.

It was still dark, but the horizon was beginning to lighten.

He had the answer to his question, although he didn't know where he'd found it.

There was but the one home for the red and black dragons.

Now it was time to destroy them.

32

The return flight was uneventful, except for one incident: Hal had come out of the mountains, over rolling foothills, and saw another dragon in the distance.

Storm was quickly alert.

The other dragon appeared not to see him, and drew closer.

Hal was about to climb for cover in the high clouds when he saw it was not a red and black, nor one of his own.

Then the wild dragon saw him, and half-rolled in surprise.

It recovered, and, amazingly, neither attacked nor fled, but held its course.

Hal restrained Storm from his attack, and the two flew side by side, about a mile apart, for a few moments, then the other dragon turned away, as if its curiosity was satisfied.

Hal thought that very odd. In this part of the land, he would have thought all dragons felt they had no friends, whether red and black or any other shade.

But he forgot about it when he reached his valley.

His tiny unit was in an uproar.

The commotion had been caused by Garadice, who'd announced that, with Kailas's permission, he intended to make all of them dragon-fliers, from orderly to scout, unless they proved they suffered absolute fear of heights.

Hal was momentarily shocked, like the others, then thought about it.

Why not? After some consideration, he realized that the only thing that "made" a dragon-flier, in his estimation, was a love of being in the air.

Other than that, it was just a hazardous job.

And here, marooned in this alien land, what wasn't?

He announced, to moans, growls and, here and there, some eagerness, that he would go along with Garadice's decision, and that training would begin the next day.

The first stage, as in the famous rabbit-cooking recipe, was to capture their dragon.

Actually, the first step was *finding* a dragon. Or, rather, a cluster of dragons. Hal hoped that what he'd seen in his dreams or visions, that dragons in this land grouped together, still held true, and so he and his handful of fliers went looking.

A long day's flight away, they found a rocky outcropping on the coast that, as Mariah put it, was "friggin' *crawling* with monskers."

Hal refused to let the image grow in his mind, and took his four dragons, Quesney, Cabet, Miletus riding, plus Garadice, Mariah, Hachir and Kimana behind, to an isolated crag of their own, where they spent a day watching the wild dragons.

Garadice passed his time oiling a long, tough rope that had been part of the *Compass Rose*'s rigging.

The others picked two young wild ones, perhaps two or three years old, one male and one female. The next morning, before dawn, the hunters were in the air over the male's pinnacle.

Hal put Storm in a dive past it, and the young beast thought that was a challenge, and rolled out of his nest after him.

The beast didn't notice two other dragons diving on him, one either side, until they crowded close. The young dragon lashed out with his fangs, was pinioned around the neck by Miletus's beast, who didn't fancy having to perform in such a pacifistic manner and started protesting loudly. Garadice, sitting backwards on Miletus's mount, tossed the line around the youngster's neck.

The captive dragon was unceremoniously pulled away from its home rocks, kicking, wings flailing, for about a mile, then Miletus took it to ground.

Waiting men quickly staked the dragon down, helpless, then Garadice ran in, under the monster's tearing claws, and tied a weighted blanket behind its carapace.

It was left to shrill and stew, while the others went back to the crag and did the same to the female dragon.

This time Cabet got raked across his chest, and Garadice nearly had his leg bitten off, before the female was safely grounded a hillock away from its brother.

Next, the men went hunting game from the air, their targets on the ground below.

Four antelope were coursed down and killed.

One each went to the tethered dragons, who showed their gratitude by trying to murder their benefactors.

But, in spite of the rending howls of captivity that night, the next morning, both antelopes' bodies had vanished.

That was a good start.

That afternoon, a pair of the sheeplike grazers were caught, and half a dozen more of the rather stupid creatures driven into a draw and pinned there with brush to provide very fresh meat.

The dragons struck at their warders only half-heartedly when they were fed this time.

Two days later, they were baying for their meals in the afternoon, and paid little mind to the men bringing them.

"Good, good," Garadice said. "These appear to be smarter than the ones I've trained, especially those gods-damned black ones, who just want to kill people."

"Sensible sorts that they are," Mariah said. "Though I believe these are just waiting for their main chance to get us good."

The female almost proved him right, and nearly removed Mariah's ear at the next feeding.

Now the fliers moved their camp close to the dragons, giving them a chance to get used to humans night and day.

This was going very well, so well that Hal made another shuttle to their valley base, and brought back more fliers-to-be.

They captured, tied and mock-saddled two more dragons.

That cost them their first casualty – a scout got careless, taking a dragon his meal, and lost most of his lower arm.

The dragons were now well used to their "saddles," and the time had come to mount them. While they were half-asleep, real saddles replaced the blankets, and then heavy leather hacks, pulled into the beasts' jaws behind their fangs, were used. This last produced blind, lethal rage from the dragons, more than anything since their capture.

"I never thought," Garadice said, "I'd be missing things as basic as chains and bits.

"There's much to be said for civilization."

"You're telling me," a rather pale Farren Mariah, who was scheduled to be the first rider, said.

When the male dragon was familiar with his harness, he was taken aloft on a long lead handled by Garadice, who was sitting facing the rear on a dragon flown by Kimana.

Predictably, the dragon cavorted and twisted, but was too glad to be free of his earthly tethers to fight that much, and, sooner or later, swooped more or less under control at the end of the lead.

Then it got very dangerous.

A third dragon, Aimard Quesney in its saddle, flew close to the young wild dragon, Farren Mariah poised behind the flier.

The third beast veered close, and before the wild dragon could bank away, Mariah jumped, grabbed its carapace, pulled himself firmly into the saddle and hung on.

It was safer, trainers had learned, to make a first mount of a dragon in the air, for a dragon on the ground could roll, and use its great tail as a sweep to tear the rider off.

This one still tried, but the requirements of flying limited his options.

The beast twisted, turned, spun.

Hal, watching on the ground, felt himself pale a little. He'd never had to train a completely wild dragon, and was, at the moment, most grateful.

The question was, who would wear out first?

The wild dragon sagged, held a course, and then Quesney took his monster in close and Mariah leaped again, this time to safety.

"I'm very damned glad," Mariah said, once safely on the ground, "there's no spiritous liquors about, for I'd surely set a bad example.

"As 'tis, I'm grateful I'm wearing my brown breeches."

The next day, Mariah went up again.

The dragon knew what to expect, and so tried some new twisting maneuvers. But Mariah hung on.

This time, he was able to bring the dragon down for a landing, then jump off and run away while the others tied the beast down again.

In normal lands and times, that would've meant Mariah had his dragon, and would now train it.

But these weren't normal times.

Mariah, not having fallen off, would be used as first breaker on each of the wild dragons, to his wild objections.

But no one was listening – they were watching Kimana Balf in her first ride, a spectacular, sky-covering series of leaps by a most aerobatic dragon.

By that evening, there were two slightly saddle-tamed dragons.

Garadice and his team went out and managed to collect two more dragons, both females this time. They almost faced disaster when a third attacked Aimard Quesney, almost dumping Garadice from his perch.

But he hung on, and the two monsters were mock-saddled and pegged down.

"I'm starting to think—" Farren Mariah said.

"Glad of that," Hal interrupted. "About time, and all."

The two were up to their elbows in guts, butchering animals for Chook's ministrations.

"Sharrup," Mariah said. "Before I was so rudely crudely

interrupted, I was saying I'm starting to think there's good to be said for armies."

"Like how?" Kimana Balf asked. She was watching the slaughter from a few yards away.

"In armies, bigtime fliers like myself have underlings underlinged to take care of the slops ... like this one ... whilst they occupy themselves with sailing yither and hon among the clouds.

"The hells with this equal-opportunity adventuring."

"You want me to make it worse?" Hal asked. "Wait until all of the groundpounders are sailing in the clouds with you.

"Who'll then wash the pots and pans?"

"Quality will out, and all will be chosen for their true talent," Farren Mariah said, in an uncertain tone.

Kimana Balf and Farren Mariah turned their two semi-tamed dragons over to Hachir and Garadice for final training as their own mounts, while they moved on to breaking the second pair.

That went more easily than they'd expected – the two already-ridden monsters seemed to take an interest, and had a honking converse with the new dragons.

"I think they're being told to go along with the course of events," Balf said.

"More like," Farren Mariah said, "being told just when you gets careless and hangs your leg out for an easy nip-off."

Now it would get interesting.

Hal flew back to the valley, brought back more non-fliers, Bodrugan and, surprisingly, the eagerly volunteering orderly, Uluch.

He'd considered the bruiser Babil Gachina, gotten as far as putting him up behind Storm for the trip back to the pinnacles, then saw the look of complete terror of the air on the man's face, and his clenched eyes.

Another one who would have little of this flying nonsense was Chook, the cook.

Fairly sure of the answer, he thought, Hal asked the enormous man when he wanted to learn to fly.

The man set down the cleaver he'd taken with him on his escape, turned and considered Kailas, who, for an instant, thought of reaching for his dagger.

Or running.

But Chook said and did nothing but turn back to the roast he was preparing.

Garadice himself, strangely, wasn't the best flier Hal had. He seemed to lack confidence in himself, and was jerky with his rein commands, and sometimes too slow to react.

No, there would be some who wouldn't become fliers.

They'd taken enough dragons from one tribe, clan, or whatever it should be known as, Garadice decided, so they moved the forward camp further west, to a small mountain range, where there were more dragons.

Also, Hal thought the new fliers were skilled enough for them to start flying patrols, each paired with an experienced flier, and he rotated the pairs from the valley to the forward camp.

"I was just remembering something," Kimana Balf said lazily. She and Hal were in their rather crude tent, made of animal skins.

Outside, a low fog and drizzle kept them from flying.

The dragons were quiet, having been fed an animal apiece, and Hal had named the day a make-and-mend, with no one expected to do much.

"You were remembering what? One of your great victories in the war?" Hal asked.

"Don't be so godsdamned bloodthirsty. There is life beyond slaughter, you know."

"All right. I'm learning." Hal rolled over, put his head on her thigh.

"I remember, one time, after I brought down . . . never mind. Like I said, the point of the story isn't gore.

"Anyway, I did something that somebody of a great rank thought was impressive, and he told me to take a week's leave.

"The war was going slowly, and it was winter and there was not much going on in the air, so I wasn't shorting the war effort.

"I didn't have, as you know, much of a family, or anyway didn't feel like going back to the old winery for a visit, and there wasn't anybody special around that I was sweet on.

"So I convinced my squadron hostler he could spare a couple of horses, and saddled up and rode to Fovant."

"Nice city," Hal said, not mentioning that either he or his ex-wife owned a rather palatial flat there.

"It is, isn't it.

"Anyway," Kimana went on, "I knew of this old hotel, so traditional I don't think they admitted to anyone there was even a war going on.

"It was right in the center of the city.

"I had money, so I took a nice, quiet, huge room that fronted on the back garden, which was looking a little bit bare, since I guess all of the gardeners had been sucked up by the war.

"But I didn't care.

"There was a row of bookstores a block over, and I bought ten or twenty books. Some that I'd sworn I should read, others that didn't matter to anyone.

"Meaningless pliff, in other words.

"And I went to my room, built a fire in the grate and got into this big wooly nightie I'd found, and curled up under some wonderful flannel sheets and feather comforters.

"That was all I did, for the whole week.

"Read, and, every now and then, bathed and dressed and went to find a restaurant, where I kept a book open in front of me.

"Didn't talk to anybody, didn't go anywhere, didn't drink anything.

"Just read.

"And when I went back to my squadron, it was as if I'd been gone for a year or more. I felt like a brand-new person."

She was silent.

"Did you ever do anything like that?" she asked.

Hal thought.

"No. I don't guess I did."

No, he hadn't. He'd always been busy, with his wife, or with friends, or with the war or going somewhere or doing something.

He'd never just sat there and let things pass by.

Not unless he was worrying himself sick, or planning something.

"I wonder if I'd like doing that," he said, a little wistfully.

"Maybe we could try it. I'm sure the Council of Barons has forgotten they want your ass on toast by now."

"Maybe we could."

The training was going better than Hal had expected. But he knew he had only a limited amount of time before the red and black demons discovered him.

Every now and again one of the fliers saw one or two of them, arcing across the skies, as if patrolling their realm.

Sooner or later . . .

There was a great deal to what Farren Mariah had been complaining about – more than just who was to perform the scut details – regarding the virtues of belonging to an organization.

One was the small matter of clothes.

There was wear, there was tear, and there were only four or five needles in the group.

And no cloth, other than canvas that was originally meant to be sails for the *Compass Rose*.

Hal had a dream that they would be marooned in this strange land for years, and that when King Asir finally sent someone to find out what had happened, they'd encounter some stark-naked loons, with beards down to their belly-buttons.

They used animal hides for almost everything, scraping them in running water, then rubbing brains into the hides and stretching and tanning them. Canvas was cut and cursingly sewn into outer garments.

Their technique got better, but Hal still yearned for the feel of fine, clean linen against his skin.

*

A red and black swooped over the valley, and the men and women scurried for cover.

The dragon came back to take another look.

Hal wondered what it had seen. If anything. He thought he might have gotten careless at having the camouflage detail fine-tune their cover.

But the dragon flew on.

Seeing nothing.

Unless, of course, it planned to come back later.

Hal had no idea how demons thought.

Uluch seemed to have forgotten about his previous life as an orderly, or as anything else.

Now he was a companion to dragons.

When he was assigned his dragon, it was as if the beast, about four years old by Garadice's reckoning, was the only dragon that had ever existed.

As soon as he'd ridden it for the first time, he started spending his nights with the beast.

"Good thing Uluch's feeding him well," Kimana said. "Otherwise we'd come out one morning and find us one dragon-flier short, and that monster picking his teeth."

"Or worse," Farren Mariah said. "I suppose we should be glad Uluch's assigned to a male.

"Otherwise . . ."

He shook his head lasciviously.

"There's something worse," Kimana said. "Or more per-verted."

"Both of you can stop, right here, right now," Hal said.

Uluch didn't hear, and if he had, he probably wouldn't have cared about the canards.

Hal realized, to his considerable embarrassment, that he

knew nothing about the man, even though Uluch had spent years as his orderly.

It was a little late to be asking for a biography.

If it was possible to dote on a dragon, Uluch doted on his. He'd given it a name, but told no one what it was, for some unknown reason.

He brushed and washed it twice a day, wouldn't let it stale where it slept, flew it to water and bathed it at least every other day.

He'd personally drilled the saddle- and quiver-mounting holes in the dragon's carapace, wincing as he did, using the modified weapons they'd turned into tools.

It didn't hurt the dragon, Garadice swore, but it seemed to pain Uluch to the depths of his soul.

Uluch spent as much time in the air as he was allowed. Climbing high, he would push his mount through maneuvers he'd seen other, more experienced fliers do, and devised ones of his own, getting lower and lower until he ran out of altitude, when he would practise his low-flying skills.

Hal was watching him one day, as he sported with his mount in the open valley of their base.

The day was calm, peaceful. High overhead, Kimana and Quesney fought a mock duel.

Toward the coast, there were a pair of wild dragons. There'd been more of them seen around the valley lately, and Hal was starting to worry about someone not recognizing a red and black until it was too late, and exposing the secrecy of their base.

A pair of just-captured dragons were being taught shouted commands by Garadice and one of the new fliers.

Kailas could smell Chook's kitchen – the aroma of a

stew of various animals and wild plants. He thought wistfully of bread, fresh-baked, milk, a glass of charged wine, put those thoughts aside, and went back to watching Uluch.

It took a few minutes to figure what he was doing. He'd put handkerchiefs on the tops of grass stems, not a foot from the ground, and was diving low and having the dragon pluck them away with his talons or jaws.

Hal thought it incredibly dangerous, was deciding how he'd order Uluch to train more safely without sounding a complete fool, when the red and black dragons appeared.

Hal was on his feet, shouting a warning.

But there was no way Uluch could hear in time.

For an instant, Hal thought the red and blacks had mounted a clever ambush. But there would have been more of them if they'd discovered the valley . . . and then he noted their obvious surprise as the hostile dragons screeched, started to climb, then changed their mind and came in for the easy kill.

Uluch's dragon wasn't there for their fangs. Uluch had had an instant to realize he was being attacked, jerked his animal's bridle, and it had turned sharply into the attack, almost digging in a wingtip.

One red and black overshot Uluch, the other turned with him, striking for the beast's neck. Uluch's dragon reached with a talon, had the red and black's wing by the leading edge, and tore at it.

The dragon screamed in pain, ducked, but ran out of height.

He smashed into the ground, breast first, head and neck futilely lifting as he rolled, over and over, bones smashing.

There was the flash of flame, and then nothing.

The second red and black flew as fast as it could for the valley's mouth.

But Kimana and then Quesney had seen the flurry, and both were diving.

Kimana got there first, her dragon coming down just above the red and black, talons reaching for the monster's head, tearing at its eyes.

The red and black pulled, but was held firm, and Kimana's dragon had it by the neck, ripping upward.

Then it flared into fire, and was gone.

"We're half ready for them," Hal said to the somber group around him. "And I think that's about all we're going to get. We've pushed our luck as far as we can.

"We knew they'd find us, sooner or later. I don't know if they did, or if they just happened on us. I think it was coincidence, but we can't operate on that belief.

"I'm sending two dragons to the forward camp at dawn, and we'll regroup here, and start making battle plans.

"Tonight, I want four fliers on standby, two in the air, and two ready for takeoff. Change over every two hours.

"Fliers, sleep ready to fly, and the dragons will have to spend the night in harness.

"That's all."

It was getting dark.

Hal walked out of the ravine, checking the camouflage over it.

It looked all right.

Then he saw two things:

First were three dragon kits. He guessed them no more than months old, more cute than lethal-looking. They were really too young to have left the nest. Hal wondered if their parents had been killed by other dragons, or by red and black demons, and how and why they'd come to this valley.

They were crouched atop the valley wall, watching everything that happened below very intently.

Wild dragons should have fled, or never have approached the men.

Hal thought, for an instant, that these could be demons.

But they were green, deep orange, and a mottled dark purple, and Hal had never seen demon kits.

At least not yet.

Then he noted Bodrugan, in the middle of the valley, crouching about like he was collecting twigs.

He trotted to him.

The magician looked up.

"Did you see those dragonlets?" Hal pointed.

"I did," Bodrugan said. "I don't think they're hostile. I sense no threat, no danger. I wouldn't worry about them."

"What the hells are they doing?"

"Damned if I know," the wizard said. "Maybe Garadice would have an idea. Ah. Here we go."

Bodrugan knelt, carefully plucked blades of grass.

"Very well then, what are *you* doing?" Hal asked.

"This is where Uluch destroyed one of the dragons today," Bodrugan said. "I'm trying to collect any . . . residue. Perhaps I can develop some kind of spell with it that might help us."

Hal thought that was not a bad idea. Then he had one of his own.

"I want your assistant, Scothi," he said. "I want to put him, with one of my scouts, probably that thug Gorumna, in the mountains, as close as I can get them to the red and black base."

"Why?"

"I don't know, precisely," Kailas said. "I want them to watch those whatever-they-ares, and give me anything they can see.

"We're getting ready to fight them without a plan or a clue.

"And that sounds like guaranteed trouble."

"It does, doesn't it?" Bodrugan agreed, getting up.

"When do you want him?"

"Right now," Hal decided. "I'd like to put them in place tonight. Both moons are rising, and that'll give us enough light to fly by."

"I know two people who are about to become very unhappy," Bodrugan said. "And I suspect if Limingo hadn't gotten himself killed, I'd be one of them."

Hal inclined his head, didn't answer. "Let me know if you find anyone around these parts that *is* happy," he said.

Hal's idea might not have been elaborately planned, but it felt right.

Of course, he'd be one of the fliers who'd put the watchers in place.

He chose two other fliers to accompany him – Farren Mariah and Kimana.

The extra dragon was just in case there were any emergencies.

The two men for the watch, Bodrugan's assistant Scothi, and the former scout, Gorumna, carried heavy packs with food and their bed rolls.

As they were getting ready to take off, Bodrugan came

up with two small sticks. "I've ensorceled these two as one," he explained to Scothi. "When you reach your position, put yours on the ground, and don't disturb it. If you have anything to report . . . or if you're discovered . . . wiggle your twig, which my stick'll hopefully echo, and we'll do what we can to rescue you. If you have to run, keep the stick with you, and mine will be drawn to it.

"I wish we could figure some sort of voice-sending," he said.

The two men looked at each other, carefully keeping blank faces, kissed, and it was time to go.

Hal led the other two dragons north and east to the red and blacks' lair.

The mountains rose ahead of him, and he sent Storm low, just over the scrub trees.

The moons were very bright, and he could see almost as if it were daylight.

He brought Storm into a circle just short of the red and blacks' valley, and landed atop a mountain crest.

"The dragons are just over the next ridge," he told Scothi and Gorumna. "I'd suggest you get no closer than that mountaintop there, and find some sort of cover to watch from.

"Good luck."

There wasn't anything more to say.

The three dragons took off, went back the way they'd come.

Hal kept looking back, at the dark bulk of the mountains, hoping he'd been right in his plan, if it could be given that firm a name.

It was false dawn when they returned to their valley base.

The three dragon kits had gotten closer to the valley

floor. Two of them were curled in balls, sound asleep, while the other kept watch.

Hal wondered about them once more, then put the matter aside.

There were more important concerns.

33

For five days, about all the Dragonmaster had to do – all that he could manage, beyond the immediate demands of his body and his duty – was stare at Bodrugan's damned stick.

He noticed, but didn't pay much attention to, the fact that the dragon kits were now being fed, first by Chook and Uluch, then in self-appointed shifts by the others.

Uluch also piled dried grass into a mow, and the small monsters found that acceptable bedding.

That made Hal pay more attention, and he asked Garadice if he'd ever seen baby dragons behave like these.

Garadice said he hadn't, except when a dragon had been raised by humans almost from the egg.

Farren Mariah was listening.

He snickered.

"Like that wonderful nightmare you had, back during the war. Raised by an ickle pretty girl child from the bottle. What did you name it? Sugary?"

"I didn't name it," Hal snarled. "The little girl called it Sweetie."

Garadice looked for an explanation, didn't get one from either flier.

The original Sweetie was not one of Hal's favorite memories, since she'd neatly dumped him into enemy captivity, then vanished.

"Another thing I don't understand," Garadice said, "is why we've been having flyovers by wild dragons in the last few days. I'd like an explanation for that, too."

But no one had one.

Hal had the stick watched around the clock, and, just at dawn of the sixth day, it twitched. Before the flier assigned to it could call an alarm, it slowly started turning.

Hal was shouting for the fliers he'd named for the pickup.

He was taking a very heavy team of six dragons. He would lead three, with the other two fliers being Farren Mariah and Kimana. A second vee was led by Cabet, with Hachir and Aimard Quesney.

Bodrugan wanted to fly as well, but Hal told him no. He wanted the magician to ride behind him, with the stick.

The day was bright with promise, a crisp wind riffling the grasses of the prairies below.

In the distance, five wild dragons saw them, and turned to parallel their flight.

The plains ended, and climbed into foothills and mountains.

Bodrugan leaned over Hal's shoulder.

"The stick is moving . . . so are they. Which probably means they've been seen."

Hal thought for an instant, untied his trumpet, and blasted a note.

The other fliers looked.

He pointed up.

All of them pulled their dragons up into a climb.

If the men on the ground had been discovered, the red and blacks would be attacking them.

And there was no weapon as deadly for a dragon-flier as having height on his enemy.

Hal leaned back, shouted over his shoulder.

"Can you track them?"

"Yes," Bodrugan shouted. "Unless the demons have countermagic."

Hal took the other five fliers very high, until he would barely be able to make out the men on the ground, depending on the magician to spot the pair.

Now the foothills had grown into cliffs, and they were nearing the demons' base.

And they saw the red and black dragons.

There must have been a dozen of them, swarming around a tree-covered rise, smoke billowing from the ground.

Bodrugan jabbed him in the ribs.

"They're down there. Near the hilltop."

Hal could have guessed as much.

But he nodded thanks, and motioned down, not wanting now to give their presence away with his trumpet.

Two-to-one odds, he thought.

Oh well . . . there'd been worse than that in the war.

He tapped Storm on the neck with his reins.

The dragon didn't need any direction, but instantly ducked his head, and, hissing like a kettle, dove on the red and blacks.

Farren and Kimana were almost beside him, and, about twenty yards above and behind, Cabet and his two companions plunged into battle.

As they closed, a red and black dragon below suddenly rolled over on a wing, and hurtled toward the ground. It exploded into flames, vanished.

So the scouts were fighting back.

Hal heard the angry screams of the dragons below.

He cocked his crossbow, notched a quarrel, looked for a target.

He had no time for more than one.

Two, actually, as he noted Storm's talons reaching for the wing of a red and black. Kailas switched his aim to a second monster, fired, hit fair in the beast's neck. It must have died instantly, for it exploded in midair.

Storm had the second dragon by the wing, tore at it, ripped it almost away, then let go as they plummeted past, Hal pulling at the reins to bring his dragon out of its dive.

Storm came level bare yards from the ground, and, without bidding, climbed for altitude.

Hal chanced a shot at a red and black above him, missed cleanly, ducked as a demon flew close, its wings flailing.

He managed to reload, fired at that dragon, saw no sign of a hit, then there was a large red and black just above him. Storm had it by the throat, tore once, as a bird-killing dog does, and then they were in the middle of the swarming fight.

Hal found a target, and the red and black dove, trying for escape. It almost made it, clearing the ridge crest narrowly, going for the valley. But Hal had a steady shot, and hit it in the body, behind the carapace. The demon screamed, pinwheeled, and then blew up.

The sky was empty of red and blacks. Hal quickly counted his men, and came one short.

"I saw him taken," Bodrugan said from behind, in a shaken voice. Hal had quite forgotten about him. "It was Cabet, I think."

And so it was.

The veteran had been struck from below, torn from his mount, and the demon ripped at his corpse as it fell.

Cabet, Hal thought mournfully, as they landed on the ridge crest, and the acolyte and scout came running from cover. Poor bastard, after going through the war, not being able to find a life, and dying here, in this unknown land.

But then he cheered himself, thinking that everyone had to die, and Cabet, who seemed to have not much of a life beyond dragon flying, couldn't have found a better death.

Maybe.

They flew hard and low, back for their valley.

Hal pulled Storm up and around, in a high bank, making sure they hadn't been followed.

There were no red and blacks to be seen – nor any unridden dragon at all.

They landed.

The others in the expedition could count, and quickly realized who'd gone down.

Possibly the hardest hit was the young woman who'd been Cabet's dragon's handler.

He heard her say, in a very soft voice, "Whatever will I do now?" before starting to dissolve, noiselessly, in tears.

They mourned Cabet . . . but the story the scout and acolyte had to tell made most forget about the flier for the moment.

Besides, fliers and front-line soldiers had learned, in the war, to put their lost aside, or chance having their own souls die with the dead.

Perhaps Hal felt it a bit harder than most, since Cabet was yet another of the old guard who'd finally gone under.

"We moved away from the hill as soon as you'd taken off," Scothi began. "Gorumna took point, since he is the best at wildcraft."

The whole party was huddled around the scouts.

"We'd made it down into the valley by first light, and found shelter in a nest of rocks.

"There were red and black dragons overhead for most of the day, behaving as if they were suspicious of something, but not sure what.

"We didn't move until dusk, then went on, to the hill overlooking the dragons' nest . . . if that's what it's supposed to be called.

"We found a good hide – a rocky thicket. We cleared brush away from close to the ground, so we could watch the valley below.

"We laid out your stick, Bodrugan, like you'd told us, then we waited. I was too excited . . . scared, maybe . . . to sleep.

"At dawn, we could see the dragons, sprawled about, sleeping. They didn't seem to be keeping any watch.

"We counted at least fifty . . . they were piled atop each other, so it was hard to make an accurate count.

"When it was full light, four of them took off, and circled their valley a few times. We stayed still."

"Very still," Gorumna said. "Trying to think like rocks, not people."

"I thought about working up some sort of spell that might make them overlook us," Scothi continued. "But I was afraid of using magic.

"I could scent . . . well, not scent, but *feel* wizardry all around me, but didn't feel like there was any being cast. Maybe the remnants of magic? I'm not sure about this.

"At any rate, we watched on, saw nothing much in particular, except, Lord Kailas, as you thought, there were no more dragons arriving from any other places."

"It was eerie, watching them," Gorumna added. "When they ate, it wasn't with any kind of joy. Like they were just taking on fuel.

"They didn't sleep much, but when they did, they just stopped in their tracks, not trying to make any sort of bed, like real dragons do."

"The next day," Scothi said, "our third in the hide, was when we saw that ring of fire appear that you said you'd seen.

"Four dragons went through the ring, three came back out. Sorry. I meant, three came out. We couldn't tell whether they were the same ones or not.

"Then the ring closed. I didn't see any of the dragons making magic, or any signs of a spell being cast, so if there was one, I'd guess it'd be on the other side.

"The fourth day there was nothing, but the dragons seemed more suspicious, flying close around their home.

"But they didn't come any closer to our hill than they'd done before, so we didn't try to flee.

"Then, the fifth day, the ring appeared again.

"And something strange.

"Something came out of the ring, something that looked like a man."

Hal jerked closer.

"But a crude sort of man, like something a kid would make out of clay," Gorumna said.

"It walked around, stumbling, as if it wasn't used to walking, then went back through the ring, and the ring vanished again."

"We figured that was enough," Scothi said, "and it was time for us to leave."

"We'd no more than twitched the stick, and started backing out of our bush," Gorumna said, "than all of the bastards took off, as if they'd seen us. But there wasn't any way they could've.

"We ran hard, before they got height, figuring on trying for that hilltop you dropped us off on.

"But they were above us, and so we went on down, into a valley.

"They came down after us, flying close, trying to grab us, but we'd go flat when they came in, and warn the other when one of them was trying for us."

"Gorumna shot one down with his bow," Scothi said, "and that made them back off for a bit.

"I had an idea, and used my flint to spark a pile of dry brush into life, remembering how dragons, real dragons, don't seem to like fire much.

"It flared up like we'd thrown brandy on it, and two of the dragons who'd come in low got caught in the flare."

"They took fire like they were tinderwood," Gorumna said with satisfaction. "Smoke boiled up, and the dragons pulled up, and circled, a little cautious now."

"That gave us time to get to the next ridge," Scothi said. "And then you were coming, and . . . well, that was that.

"I hope we saw some things that'll be useful."

Both the scouts looked at Hal pleadingly.

"What was that thing that looked like a man?" Gorumna asked.

Hal considered, the flicker of an idea just surfacing.

"One of the demons?" Farren Mariah suggested. "Or the main demon himself?"

"No," Hal said, and it came to him.

"The demons that look like dragons came to this land not knowing anything," he said slowly. "Not who or what was the power here, or what form they should take to rule.

"The strongest thing was the dragons. So . . ."

"So that was the form they chose," Bodrugan said.

"Until we came along." Farren Mariah had also gotten it.

"Maybe so," Hal agreed. "I think so."

"So now," Hachir said, "we've seen a baby man. The more they're around us, the more they can learn from us, the more like men they'll look."

"Plus having whatever powers they've got of their own," Hal said.

"Which means we've got to stop them now. Before they get any stronger."

"Or," Farren Mariah said, "figure out some shape that's to man like man is to a dragon."

"All we have to do," Aimard Quesney said, "is work out how."

34

"A minor, minnyscule matter," Farren Mariah said.

"We know they don't like fire," Kimana said.

"I somehow don't think my dragon'll take kindly to my mounting up with a torch between my teeth," Mariah said. "Let alone how I'm to get close enough to the enemy beasties to apply it liberally to their heads and shoulders."

"Magic," a flier suggested, looking hopefully at Bodrugan.

"Magic how?" the wizard said.

"That's your department," Farren Mariah said breezily.

"At which I'm blank, so far. Sorry."

Hal happened to look up, and saw the three young dragons, huddled close together, about halfway down the rise, looking as solemn as young owls.

"This is getting us nowhere quickly," he said. "Let's eat, put our heads down, and be ready to hit them at dawn."

A chill wind was blowing off the ocean as the thirteen dragons flew north before dawn.

Hal wondered if the wind would blow their scent to the red and blacks, decided that was stupid – they were flying faster than any wind.

As the foothills rose, they turned slightly to the west, to come in on the demons' valley from out of the rising sun, and climbed.

Hal didn't want to take them too high, hoping to catch the red and blacks still asleep, and have the advantage of height.

He motioned as the first rays caught them, and the formation obediently closed up.

Hal was about to put Storm into a shallow dive when someone blatted on a trumpet.

It was Kimana, giving the alarm.

The red and blacks were already in the air, high above them and diving, coming in fast.

There was no time for tactics.

Hal kicked Storm into a sharp bank, tried climbing, and a red and black tore past him, talons reaching for Storm and missing.

A ridden dragon flopped past him.

Hal couldn't tell for an instant who the rider was . . . had been, for he was without a head.

Then he recognized the tatters of uniform on the body.

Miletus, his first squadron commander.

But there was no time for the dead.

Two dragons were on Storm's flanks, harrying at him. Storm thrashed his tail, and one dropped back.

Then Kimana was there, on the nearest, wings smashing at the red and black.

It screamed, rolled on its back, and Kimana's dragon ripped its stomach open.

The other dragon closed, and Hal put Storm into a tight turn. The red and black banked as well, and Hal kept his bank, pulling hard on Storm's reins, trying to turn inside the other dragon.

The bank was tight enough for Hal's vision to gray around the edges, and he could feel Storm losing altitude.

The other dragon was turning, turning, and now Storm was behind it, ducking the whisking tail.

The red and black held its turn, and Hal stayed behind it. He was able to force his hands up against the pull of gravity, aim his crossbow and fire a bolt. It hit the red and black near its left wing root, hardly a death blow, and again the turn tightened.

Hal caught a flash of green below him, to his right. They were very close to the ground. He yanked at Storm's reins, and the dragon rolled out of its bank as the red and black, still at a tight angle, scraped the ground with its wing, and bounced and rolled to its death and explosion.

Hal forgot about it, saw another dragon diving down, and cocked and fired. He hit it, he thought, and the demon hurtled on and slammed into a rocky outcropping.

Storm climbed back to the heights. The battle was still a roiling chaos – Hal guessed that all or most of the seventy red and blacks were in the air, and battering at his slender force.

He saw another of his dragons in a long dive, its rider lolling in the saddle. This one was a green and white one, freshly trained, he remembered, though he couldn't recall the rider for the moment.

A red and black was chasing it down, snarling at its rear legs, and Hal put a crossbow bolt through its neck.

The red and blacks were forcing Hal's dragons down toward the ground, and it was time to break free.

Which would have been a neat trick, if he could figure out how to do it.

Hal sent Storm down toward the ground, hoping he could find a defile they could fly into to escape the trap.

He saw something better – a field of waving dry grasses, and the idea struck him.

He drove Storm down, brought his head back to force the dragon to land.

Storm didn't want to, not with enemies in the air, but, whining, he obeyed.

Hal slid out of the saddle, reaching in his belt pouch, found fire-making materials.

Clumsy with haste and fear, not wanting to look up to see the demons diving on him, he struck steel against flint, saw sparks, did it again, and fire glowed in the dry grass. He blew on it, and it flared up, and he fed it more grass, ripping it up with his hands.

Then he had a proper fire, and Storm was screeching at him.

Another rider, Bodrugan, saw what he was doing, and landed clumsily, still not much more than a student.

His arms began waving in a spell, and the flames grew.

Kailas was back in the saddle, and whipping Storm with the reins. The dragon stumbled down the slight slope as the fire built, and they were in the air once again.

Now the battle was at low level, the red and blacks chasing the others around the contours of the hills.

The fire roared higher, and then there was a pillar of smoke.

Hal blew frantically on his trumpet, beckoned, and his

fliers saw him, understood, and flew toward the fire, through the smoke. Then they were through, and fleeing west, the fire a backstop, making the red and blacks climb over it.

But Hal's men and women were gone, dots against the plains, heading west until they saw nothing in the skies behind them, before turning for their valley.

One by one, they reached it, exhausted, barely able to stumble from their saddles as the few handlers tried to help.

Now Hal remembered who had ridden the green and white.

Hachir, the one-time teacher and archer, whose life had been shattered.

Three others, including Miletus, had died that day, almost a third of his fliers.

Hal was well and truly defeated.

The day went, handily, to the demons.

35

Hal didn't have much time to mourn his dead as the night closed on them.

The dragons were washed and fed, and then the men. The two low cooking fires permitted before dusk were guttering down as the shadows grew into each other. Hal sat at a distance from the others, staring at the embers.

He'd certainly been defeated before. But he couldn't remember a time when victory had been so important, although there'd been several wartime battles he'd thought vital.

Never before had he faced an enemy who, victorious, would not only dominate this land, but, if his thinking about the new homunculus was correct, might conquer all.

Looking at the dying fires, he chewed and swallowed his tasteless dinner, wondering why the gods hadn't given him a better mind.

He knew what might destroy the demons – the fire that had given them birth – but not how to use it.

And then, in the middle of his agonising, it came to him.

He called Bodrugan over.

The others, hearing the note in his voice, looked up, waiting.

Hal took only a few seconds to explain to the magician.

"It could work," Bodrugan said. "If my spell is as good as it was before."

During the war, Hal had had the idea of dropping boulders on the Roche. The only problem, of course, was that dragons weren't cargo-carrying beasts.

But Hal's idea had been to shatter a great boulder, and have a wizard cast a spell on the pieces, which potentially were the whole, so that when each pebble was thrown by a dragon-flier, it would become the size of its "father."

The spell worked perfectly, and Roche cities were knocked into shambles.

Bodrugan went to work, and in about two hours he had a spell.

"I'd like an assistant," he said.

"Farren," Hal said. "You've a bit of the talent. Help the man, if you would."

"I'm tired of being volunteered," Mariah growled, but obeyed.

Bodrugan had seen some red flowers in the valley, and men were sent to bring them in.

Flint and steel were positioned, and a stack of brushwood was built in front of them, the flowers in odd patterns around it.

Hal didn't like doing this, fearing there'd be red and black dragons about, but saw no other options.

Crossbow bolts were brought, and laid in circles, heads touching, around the brushwood.

Then the fire was touched off.

As it built, Bodrugan began chanting, while Mariah lifted the bolts, as if making an offertory, then set them down.

> *"Remember*
> *What took you*
> *Changed you*
> *Made you elemental*
> *Reaching out*
> *Finding*
> *Base power*
> *Feeling*
> *Building . . ."*

The fire was now roaring, reaching far into the night sky, beyond what the fuel could have given.

Hal looked beyond it. In the darkness, eyes gleamed; the three dragon kits had drawn close to the men and were watching.

> *"Growing*
> *Reaching far to*
> *Change*
> *What you touch*
> *What you hurt*
> *Blood*
> *Or what is used as*
> *Blood*
> *Blood to fire*
> *Blood to fire*
> *Blood to fire*

> *Reach*
> *Remember*
> *And slay."*

Very suddenly, the fire died to embers, and went out.

"Well?" Farren asked.

Bodrugan held out his hands.

"I don't know. The proof will be in the testing."

"And if it doesn't work . . . aarh. My grandfather's spells didn't always sing, either. Sing or singe," Mariah muttered.

But that was the best that could be done.

Hal said stand-to would be three hours before dawn, and gave his simple orders for the next day.

The fliers were told to put their heads down. Rest, if they couldn't sleep.

Hal didn't even try his usual pretense of sleeping soundly and easily, sure of victory on the morrow.

He checked the dragons, starting with Storm.

Babil Gachina found him.

"And what'll *we* do on the morrow, sir?"

"I don't know," Hal said. "Stand by and be ready when we come back . . . those of us who do."

Gachina shook his head.

"Not good enough."

Hal could have gotten angry, but instead was slightly amused.

"Considering your problems with flying, I don't see what you *can* do."

"I can wear a blindfold," Gachina said. "Long enough to put me where I can do some good. And others can do the same . . . or I'll deal with 'em.

"Put us on the ground, sir, in that valley where those damned dragons spawn, and we can surely kill any that come down to us."

Hal considered.

"Yes," he said. "That can be done."

"Good," Gachina growled. "I'll have the rest of my cowards up."

He vanished into the darkness silently.

Hal wandered the small camp, unable to sleep.

He found Uluch with the dragon kits. Two of them were curled, asleep, and the oldest was being crooned to by Hal's once-orderly.

He saw Hal, greeted him without embarrassment. Once he'd been almost servile in the way he talked to Hal. No more. Now it was as if he was an equal.

"They'll be ours, tomorrow."

"I hope so."

"No bare hope, sir. 'Tis a certainty."

Glad that at least one man was sure of himself, Hal went on.

Aimard Quesney was sitting, staring at the remains of the fire.

"You realize," he said, "that all of this is quite damned hopeless. They've got us outnumbered, what, ten to one?"

"Or more," Hal said cheerfully.

"Always good to be following a man who's confident," Quesney said, and stood up. "Oh well. I guess this land without a name's as good a place to die as any other."

He waited to see if Hal had any reply, heard none, so grunted goodnight, and went for his bed roll.

Hal decided that was a way to pass the few hours remaining until they were to fly off, and found his own blankets. Around him, Babil Gachina was rousing the non-fliers, and talking to them in low tones he couldn't make out.

Kimana Balf had her bed roll next to Hal, and was lying on her back, staring up. He saw her eyes were open.

"Well?" she whispered.

"Well what?"

"What of the morrow, fearless leader?"

"I'd rather not be there for it," Hal said. "I'd rather be safe at home, cowering under the bed."

"Would you? Really?"

Her voice was serious.

Hal looked for something else light to say, couldn't find anything.

"No," he said honestly. "No, I wouldn't be anywhere else."

"And that," she said, "is the idiot I've come to love."

She kissed him, and rolled on her side, away from him.

Love? Hal had never heard her use that word before.

He thought about it, and was, suddenly and surprisingly, asleep.

Someone was kicking Hal's foot. He rolled back an eyelid, saw the bulk of Chook standing above him. He was totally awake, sat up.

"There's tea," the cook said. "Anyway, herbs brewed up."

He didn't wait for a reply, but went on.

Hal got up, washed, and had some of the bitter brew Chook had made. There was also fried meat and tubers for those who wanted it. The thought of food roiled Hal's stomach.

Chook paid little attention to his duties, stropping his great cleaver, and stringing his crossbow.

Hal saddled Storm. The dragon was already awake, and seemed eager to go.

Around him the other fliers readied their mounts.

Some, the newly trained, tried to bite, or tail-lash their riders, but no one was struck, the dragons being as sleep-numbed as the men.

Babil Gachina waited nearby with the half a dozen men, non-fliers, who'd be part of his newly created ground force.

Chook joined them, looking somber, with his cleaver and a great butcher knife stuck in his waistband.

Hal tried to think of a noble speech, couldn't come up with one. So he looked at his tiny army, shadows in the darkness, and said, "Let's show them what we're made of," and walked toward Storm.

There was a pointless, ragged cheer, and his men and women followed.

As Hal pulled himself into the saddle, Babil Gachina clambered up behind and wordlessly extended a strip of thick cloth. Kailas bound it around the man's eyes. Gachina winced as if he'd been lashed, but remained silent.

Others of the ground force were already mounted on other dragons.

Hal forgot about his passenger, and gigged Storm into his stumbling takeoff run.

As the dragon cleared the ground, he suddenly screamed, a defiant challenge.

The scream was echoed from the ground, from the biggest of the dragon kits. Hal had an instant to wonder how a beast that small could make that great a noise, and then Storm was in the air, the other dragons following.

Half of Hal's force stayed low, following him toward the hills, the other half, led by Farren Mariah, climbed for the heights.

Hal had learned, in his thousand battles, that no plan survives the first sword-clash. Particularly if the plan is complicated and clever.

He kept his tactics simple:

He would deploy his ground fighters just short of the red and blacks' valley. Then he, and his fliers, would strike the demons at low level, before dawn, when they were still sleeping, or whatever demons did when they were lying down. He'd try to get as many of them on the ground or taking off as possible.

His second element would attack from on high, and wreak as much havoc as they could.

From there . . . from there it was strike where you could, when you could.

Flying low, Hal saw, on either side of him, at a great distance, wild dragons, flying north. He counted more than twenty in one group before he lost track.

He wondered what the hells they were doing about when it was still night.

Then they were in the mountains, climbing, and there wasn't time for anything but war.

Kailas brought Storm down on a hilltop, shrouded in pre-dawn blackness. He turned and pulled the blindfold off Babil Gachina. The hulking thug was pale-faced, and swallowing. But he slid off Storm without hesitating, and called for the others.

Since Hal had considered them skirmishers at the most, he didn't waste time, but kicked Storm into a takeoff.

He looked up as the dragon lurched into the air, and, far above him, saw a flood of dragons, high up, the rising sun just touching them.

There were too many for them to be Farren Mariah's element. He could only hope Mariah had climbed above them.

Hal cocked his crossbow, one of the enchanted quarrels dropping into the firing slot.

Storm was looking down, and saw still-motionless red and blacks below.

Hal kicked him in the ribs, and the dragon tucked his head and wings, and they went into a dive.

Kailas blatted on his trumpet, looked behind him, and saw his element was following.

But the ground was now very close. He pulled Storm up, less than fifty feet above the ground.

Below was a dragon, just rearing.

Hal whispered the fire-spell catchword, fired, spitted it through the neck, and the demon had an instant to scream before it exploded in greasy fire.

Another red and black died to the side from someone else's shot as Hal reloaded and found another target. He shot, missed, had time to recharge his crossbow and put his bolt, its tip just bursting into flame, into the dragon's chest.

He reloaded again, whispered, and killed another demon, and they were past the red and blacks' camp.

He brought Storm up, and back around, this time only a dozen feet above the ground.

There was a red and black fanged head level with his, and he shot at it and flew through the burst of flame.

Other red and blacks were dying, and then, almost beside him, one of his own was caught with a tail-lash, and smashed into the ground, its rider spinning away.

Unbidden, Storm pulled up, and Hal was about to shout a command when he saw the red and blacks that had been in the heights swarming down on them.

Storm hooked one of them with a wing claw, ripped down its neck with his talons, and Hal killed it with his crossbow.

A shadow loomed over him, and he ducked, just as Aimard Quesney's beast gutted the red and black, and it died, screaming.

Storm was climbing, and Hal saw two dragons on Kimana Balf. Storm drove at them, just as Balf brought her dragon in a tight circle, its fangs closing on a demon's throat, then letting go as the red and black screamed and went down.

He came in from the side on the second red and black, had time to shoot it twice before the monster blew up.

All was chaos then, and Hal had no sense of time as he and Storm, one being, one killing machine, tore in and out of the swirl. He almost shot a dragon, realized it was ridden, and swept past Farren Mariah, whose monster's jaws were slathered with a dark ichor.

Kailas saw men trot into the valley, taking time to kneel and shoot carefully into the demons. Babil Gachina and his handful were engaged.

Storm was turning hard, closing on a red and black, and Hal saw Garadice, his dragon with a wing torn away, caught in the jaws of a red and black, going down.

Storm flared his wings, a red and black missed him, and Hal killed it.

There was nothing in front of him, and Hal brought Storm back on the mêlée. There were smoke flares here and there on the ground, and dying, wounded dragons, with human bodies sprawled beside them.

A red and black dove on a standing man. It was Chook. The cook ducked a claw-strike, smashed with his cleaver, and the demon howled pain.

In the center of the slaughter-ground a circle of fire grew from nowhere, its flames gouting out, as if wind-blown.

Red and black dragons poured out of it, almost on top of each other.

Hal realized how few of his own monsters were still in the air, and how many demons were still attacking.

He had an instant to know defeat.

There were too many of them, and as he thought this, he saw Aimard Quesney caught at the waist in a red and black's jaws, and torn apart.

Storm, as if recognizing doom, screamed, that same great scream he'd unleashed when they took off.

Then he dove on a pair of red and blacks.

His scream was echoed, louder, from both sides, from the sky above, and then three wild dragons swooped in, and tore at the demons.

There were other dragons around them, paying no heed to any of Hal's ridden beasts, but driving into the red and blacks.

The scream was still echoing, as if taken by a hundred hundred other dragons, and the demons were swarmed by wild monsters, torn and butchered.

What had summoned them – Storm's screams, those odd dragon kits – Hal would never know.

The ring of fire flamed higher, and Hal saw, from a thousand feet above him, a ridden dragon diving on it.

It closed, and Hal had an instant to recognize Uluch, standing in his stirrups like a lancer, coolly sending bolt after fiery bolt into the circle.

He smashed into, through it, and the circle flashed into a huge ball of flame.

Then it, Uluch and his dragon were gone, as if they'd never been.

Hal brought Storm around, to see a single flash of flame as the last demon died.

There were no red and blacks in the sky.

There were dragons, wild dragons around him, more than he'd ever seen before, more than he could have imagined.

They swept back over the valley, making sure of the victory, then climbed, like wild geese heading for home, and were flying into the mountains.

That great scream died slowly into silence.

Then there was nothing in that blighted valley but the bodies of dragons and men.

There were fewer than half a dozen dragons still in the air, all with riders.

Storm screamed into the silence, and Hal felt it was a cry of sorrow.

Sorrow and triumph.

36

Storm bobbed happily near the shore of the Hnid's atoll.

Hal sat on the beach, watching him, wishing that men could forget the past as quickly as dragons did.

If that was true.

But at least they didn't show their grief, if they felt it.

Kimana Balf's dragon lifted above the roofed island, splashed in for a landing near the shore.

The last passenger on the shuttle waited dumbly until Kimana undid his blindfold, then Babil Gachina waded to shore, where Chook stood.

A pair of Hnid surfaced, and dove back and forth in happiness, seeing their . . . whatever they thought the giant Gachina was.

All was quiet, all was happiness on the island.

Hal wished he could feel the same, but with few more than a dozen survivors of his expedition, joy came hard.

The survivors of the final battle had returned to their camp, trying to celebrate their victory.

But they knew there was another struggle ahead – somehow reaching Deraine.

They'd begun one step at a time, shuttling supplies, men and women east in single-day hops.

They'd seen no more red and black dragons, and, to Hal, the land seemed cleansed.

Now it would be safe.

Safe for what?

For dragons?

For men to swarm west and colonize, making the creatures of this land their prey, their food, or their tools?

That didn't seem right to Kailas.

He wondered what he should, could do . . . and his rather bleak mood broke as Kimana Balf brought her dragon on to the beach, and a handler led it to where the other surviving monsters were being fed and watered.

"Are you brooding?" she said cheerily as she walked to him, and sat down.

"Nice, soft, warm sand," she said dreamily. "Not moving. I could lie here for a week."

"You'll not be allowed," Hal said. "As soon as Farren Mariah and his crew come back with whatever they've been able to scrounge off the wrecks, we'll all be at work."

"At least we won't be riding dragons," Kimana said. "Or fighting anybody."

"Maybe not," Hal said. "At least, not for a while."

"You really think we'll be able to build boats? Boats that'll make it all the way back home?"

"I don't know," Hal said. "At least some kind of big raft."

"Suddenly, riding the dragons sound like a better idea," she said.

Hal made a face.

That was the other part of his plan.

Those few surviving dragons would fly east as far as they were able. Then they'd land on the sea, and let the current carry them on, as dragons had left this world before.

But this time, they'd have their fliers sheltering on their backs, under their folded wings, as Hal had discovered dragons would do.

At least, the dragons they'd come with. Hal had decided to free the newly tamed creatures before they left.

That is, if they wanted freedom.

Most of them seemed fairly content in the company of man.

The others could join the wild dragons, three or four of whom had followed the remains of the expedition across the coastal waters.

Hal had hoped to see the three dragon kits, who'd vanished when the men had returned from the demons' valley, but without luck.

He wondered if they'd been real dragons, or spirits, and realized he'd never know. Bodrugan had chanced a spell, but found out nothing.

"After we get home," Kimana said confidently, "what do you want?"

"A hot bath," Hal said. "With real soap. A bottle of good wine. Bread. Dripping with butter. A meat pie.

"A nice warm bed, with a roof over it."

"That's all?" Kimana asked, disappointed.

"A bed with you in it."

"That's better." She scooped sand into a pile.

"Do you think we're ever going to come back here?" She caught herself. "Am I allowed to think of us as us?"

"Of course," Hal said, and realized the words came easily. "I mean to the us. As far as coming back here . . . right now, I think I've had enough adventuring.

"A nice quiet mansion, with servants doing all the work," he said.

"I've never had that," Kimana said.

"Past time you try being rich," Hal said, and kissed her.

Three thoughts, none of them spoken, came to him:

It was past time for Hal Kailas to stop being alone.

Maybe it was time to visit that hotel in Fovant with Kimana and a bunch of books.

And maybe it was time for the Dragonmaster to start learning how to master, or at least live with, people.

THE SEER KING
Book One of the Seer King Trilogy

Chris Bunch

A magnificent fantasy epic of empire, power and magic begins.

Numantia is a dying empire, the frontier ruled by outlaws, the provinces by rebels, the citizens by discontent. Ancient forces of dark magic grow everywhere, ignored by the Empire's rulers. For two people it is a time of immense possibility and infinite danger.

Hotheaded young cavalry officer Damastes and the wizard Tenedos were supposed to die in a mountain ambush. But their enemies underestimated the amazing powers of the seer and the bravery of the soldier. As they begin outwitting usurpers and necromancers, word spreads that theirs is a path of destiny. For Damastes, it will lead to glory and love. For Tenedos, it points to unimaginable heights of ambition. And for Numantia, it shows the way to a renaissance . . . in service to the Goddess of Death.

WIT'CH FIRE

Book One of the Banned and the Banished

James Clemens

Long ago, the Mages of Alasea, beset by a dark and
implacable evil, made a last desperate stand to
preserve some remnant of their once-beautiful land.
Knowing their own destruction to be inevitable, the
Mages gathered the last of their magic and stored it
away against the need and peril of a distant time. In
doing so the Mages gave the people of Alasea a future
and a hope – and damned themselves forever . . .

Now, five centuries after their destruction, the power
of the Mages is about to be unleashed.